D0090239

STRANGE GODS

ALSO BY ANNAMARIA ALFIERI

Blood Tango
Invisible Country
City of Silver

Annamaria Alfieri

STRANGE GODS

MINOTAUR BOOKS
A THOMAS DUNNE BOOK
NEW YORK

This is a work of fiction. All of the characters, organizations, and events portrayed in this novel are either products of the author's imagination or are used fictitiously.

A THOMAS DUNNE BOOK FOR MINOTAUR BOOKS.
An imprint of St. Martin's Publishing Group.

www.thomasdunnebooks.com
www.minotaurbooks.com

Library of Congress Cataloging-in-Publication Data

Alfieri, Annamaria.
    Strange gods : a mystery / Annamaria Alfieri.—First edition.
        pages cm
    "A Thomas Dunne book for Minotaur Books."
    ISBN 978-1-250-03971-2 (hardcover)
    ISBN 978-1-250-03972-9 (e-book)
    1. Women missionaries—Fiction.   2. Police—Fiction.
3. Murder—Investigation—Fiction.   4. Ethnic relations—
Fiction.   5. Race relations—Fiction.   6. Africa, East—
Fiction.   I. Title.
    PS3601.L3597S77 2014
    813'.6—dc23

                                                    2014008321

Minotaur books may be purchased for educational, business, or promotional use. For information on bulk purchases, please contact Macmillan Corporate and Premium Sales Department at 1-800-221-7945, extension 5442, or write specialmarkets@macmillan.com.

First Edition: June 2014

10   9   8   7   6   5   4   3   2   1

For John Norman Linder, dear friend and fellow traveler, who said, "Why don't you write about that Africa that you are so in love with?"

ACKNOWLEDGMENTS

I am grateful to:

Stanley Trollip, who understands and shares my love of Africa and who inspired me in writing this story. And to Stan and his writing partner, Michael Sears—the talented authors who write as Michael Stanley—for reading my draft and helping me make sure I got the details right for life in the bush.

Adrienne Rosado, my agent, who helped me choose this subject. I am incredibly fortunate to have her belief in and support for my work to keep me going.

Toni Kirkpatrick, my editor, who has been with me from my first novel. Her delicacy of spirit, her respect and insights see me through a process that could otherwise be daunting.

And as always Jay Barksdale and the staff of the great New York Public Library, Stephen A. Schwarzman Building.

Without the collection of this jewel on Fifth Avenue, none of my novels would have been possible. *SUPPORT YOUR LOCAL LIBRARY!*

"I am the Lord, thy God.
Thou shalt not have strange gods before me."

Africa, amongst the continents, will teach it to you:
that God and the Devil are one.

—Isak Dinesen, *Out of Africa,* 1937

Ex Africa semper aliquid novi.—
Out of Africa, new things always flow.

—Pliny (AD 23–79)

THE PROTECTORATE OF BRITISH EAST AFRICA

~~~ 1911 ~~~

I.

They never went out in the dark because of the animals. But if she was ever to escape the boredom of life confined to the mission compound, tonight determination had to win out over terror.

So, well before first light, she left her bedroom. The things she would need were packed and waiting for her in the Kikuyu village.

She went barefoot through the back door of the house and into the kitchen yard. Once outside she slipped on her boots and tried to step lightly. She stole past the mission office and the school. The moonlight was dim, but adequate. Her eyes were good.

All she wanted was a bit of adventure. To go on safari. She resented being kept at home while her brother, Otis, was allowed to go. She was nearly six years older, yet he had already gone more times than she. The Newlands had invited her as well as Otis, but her mother had refused to allow her leave. Her mother, who tried to control every minute of her time. Well, tomorrow morning she would tell Mr. and Mrs.

Newland that Mother had changed her mind. By the time her parents discovered what she had done, they would have no way to bring her back.

It was juvenile of her to be doing this. She was a grown woman, nearly twenty. But she would never have the chance to be an actual grownup, to make her own decisions. British rules of maidenhood did not allow for that.

Otis was already at the Newland farm, set to go off into the wilderness in the morning. After much cajoling, he had agreed to help her slip away and join the safari party. "We will leave at dawn," he had said before he went. "I will ask Mr. Newland to take us near the Kikuyu village, but you will have to be there and ready by six."

"That's easy enough."

"What will you say if they catch you?"

"I will go beforehand and put my rucksack and my rifle in Wangari's hut. That way, if they see me up in the night, they will not suspect the truth."

"Okay," he said, grave faced. "That's a good plan." She loved it that he pretended to be a man. He was such a serious boy.

The chill of the wee hours made her wish for the jacket that was already at the bottom of her pack. She scanned the shadows for the slightest movement as she crossed the bare packed earth of the mission grounds, listening with her ears, with her skin, for any sound of danger. Hippos might have come up from the river to graze. They were deadly but not quiet. The cats were silent but unlikely to be hunting here now. They came often to look for water in the dry season, but not after the long rains, when the land was moist and the water holes all round about were full.

Stupidly she thought of Tolliver. Whenever she moved from one place to another her thoughts always went to him, as if her bones and her blood vessels wanted her to move only in his direction, wherever else she was going. Tolliver, though, would never approve of her defying her parents. He was a proper Englishman. Men like him never expected a good girl to do anything but what she was told, even when she was an adult in every other way.

The moonlight threw a weak shadow beneath the thorn tree growing in the sward that separated the stone hospital from the grass and wattle school. A rustling in the under-brush halted her steps and her breath. She was between the river and whatever that was in the shadows near the chapel. If it was a hippo, it might kill her with one snap of its power-ful jaws just for blocking its way back to the water. Suddenly the night was full of sound. As many cicadas as there were stars, singing out near the hospital privies. The chilling cry of hyenas behind her, beyond the coffee groves. And then the long, deep, hollow vibration of a lion's roar that sounded as if it came from the core of the earth. The cat's night song did not frighten her. They made that noise when they mated. She thought of Justin Tolliver again but pushed her mind away from the mating call in her own blood.

She stole toward the stable, with her eyes to her right where the rustling in the undergrowth had come from. When she heard nothing, she ran flat out until she came to the veranda of the hospital. The windows of the building were dark. Not even a candle burned in the wards. She slipped into the gloom at the near-side stone wall, panting a bit, more from fear than from running. She breathed deeply to calm her nerves. The noise of something moving came again, nearer now. She was about to back away to try to get inside the building before the animal reached her when she saw a person carrying a lantern, approaching around the far corner. It could only be Otis, come back to help her. But why would he bring the lamp? She held her breath not to shout and scold him.

She crept in his direction.

The figure carrying the lantern became clear.

Vera gasped. "Mother!"

"Vera?"

"I— I—"

"Go to your room and stop this nonsense."

"But, Mother . . ."

"Immediately."

There was no disobeying her mother when she used that tone.

While, in the dark of night, Vera McIntosh returned to her bed, where she consoled herself with fantasies that involved kissing Justin Tolliver, the young man who was the object of her infatuation stood in the half-wrecked bar of the Masonic Hotel in Nairobi, his hands in the air and two revolvers aimed at his heart. His own weapon was still in the holster at his side. This was a tight spot where an assistant superintendent of police should never find himself, not even a neophyte like him. How he got here was as easy to explain as it was humiliating and exasperating.

His superior officer—District Superintendent of Police Jodrell—was off on home leave in England, making Tolliver answerable directly to Britain's top man in this sector—District Commissioner Cranford.

When Tolliver was called to the hotel to take control of two drunken Europeans who were tearing up the place, he brought with him a squad of his best askaris—African policemen who could be counted on to be brave and dutiful, including the best of the lot, Kwai Libazo.

But as they jogged at doubletime through the unpaved streets of the ramshackle young town, carrying flaming torches to light their way, Tolliver knew he was in danger of incurring D.C. Cranford's wrath. He was about to make the unforgivable mistake of using African policemen against Europeans. Cranford had the strongest opinions of such matters. So Tolliver had left his squad outside the corrugated iron and wood hotel and entered the bar alone. Unfortunately, he had failed to draw his pistol before he did so. Perhaps if he had not been exhausted from doing double work for days now, including fighting a fire last night in an Indian shop on Victoria Street, or if he had cared less about what Cranford thought and more about his own skin, he would not have let these louts get the advantage of him. As it was, he was completely at their mercy, unless the askaris outside came to his aid. But why would they if they had no idea how muddle-headed he had been?

"You are being damned fools," he said with more bravado

than his predicament warranted. "If you interfere with a police officer in the execution of his duty, you are risking many years of hard imprisonment. If you hurt me, you will be up before a firing squad."

"Bloody hell, we will," the bigger man said with a laugh. "Listen, you puppy, on the count of three you are turning tail outta here or you'll be picking lead outta your legs."

Tolliver gave them what he hoped looked like a careless, indulgent smile. "I am not leaving without putting the two of you under arrest. If you come with me peacefully, I'll not charge you with resisting." He took a quick step forward thinking that it might intimidate them.

The smaller of the two, a red-haired bloke with a vicious sneer, jammed his pistol into Tolliver's stomach and said, "Stop right there or it's the graveyard for you."

"If you shoot me, you will be joining me there," Tolliver said. He thought to add that the sound of a shot from inside the bar would bring in the squadron of policemen he had left guarding the entrance. But it suddenly occurred to him that all he had to do was get one of these drunks to fire a shot— not at him—but at something. Help would storm into the room forthwith.

He raised his hands higher and pulled himself up to his full height, so that he towered over the sly, little man. "How do I know that gun is loaded?" he asked.

"Easy," his assailant said. "See that whiskey bottle on the shelf?"

"Certainly," Tolliver said, as nonchalantly as he could. It was impossible to miss since it was the only one still standing. All the others, along with just about anything breakable in the bar, had been smashed to pieces before Tolliver arrived and lay littering the floor.

The man turned his pistol away from Tolliver and without taking aim, shot the top off the bottle. His big companion looked away to see the result, and in a flash Tolliver had his pistol out and leveled at them.

In two heartbeats, Kwai Libazo was smashing through the door, his rifle at the ready.

"That was some excellent shooting," Tolliver said as he relieved the bigger man of his weapon.

The other askaris were piling into the room.

"Libazo, handcuff these men and march them to the station." Tolliver knew when he gave that order that Cranford would disapprove. But he'd already almost gotten himself killed trying to appease Cranford, with his British ideas about keeping the natives in their place. Given the choice between death and the D.C.'s disfavor, he would take the latter, no matter how displeasing it would be.

2.

Two days later, as the sun rose, three dozen Kikuyu workers set out from their village to walk the mile and a half to their work in the coffee fields at the Scottish Mission. They were clad in *shukas*—cloths tied at the shoulder—of an orange-brown that matched almost exactly the soil beneath their bare feet. They moved along in silence, some not thinking of anything much at all, but some pondering but not speaking of the strange fact that this land on which their forebears had lived practically since the dawn of man now belonged to representatives of a foreign god. The women among them were past resenting that they were required to work for the privilege of farming the land of their ancestors. The men were more inclined to be resentful, since before the coming of the white men, they had not had to do fieldwork at all. Women did that. Men watched and remained at the ready to take up their warriors' shields and spears and defend their cattle, goats, sons, and women from attacks by other tribes.

The pairs of men who walked at the head and behind the column carried spears, like true defenders. But they watched, not for invading Maasai, but for jackals or leopards. All manner of predators might be out at this hour, hunting in the woods that separated their village from the white man's buildings. Such dangers were unlikely, since there were plenty of antelope and zebra, predators' prey, on the plains below these hills. Still, the guardsmen scanned the deep shade beneath the trees on either side of their path. Those in front held up their hands from time to time, if they heard noises that could mean danger. After a few seconds of intense listening, they gave the signal to proceed. More than a few of the farmworkers thought this action was for effect, to make the guards look and feel important. In the nearly twenty years of this mission's existence no farmworker had been attacked by an animal on this path.

As the ragtag column reached the edge of the plantation, the workers picked up hoes from a shed at the edge of the field and spread out between the rows of fragrant flowering coffee bushes. The long rains had come early and been very good this year. The lushness of the fields pleased the Kikuyu, though they had no use for the product that their labor would yield. During this time of the cycle, their job of work was to keep down the weeds that wanted to strangle the crop.

A scream pierced the silence.

It came from a place about midway between the stone hospital building and the river. An alarm such as one might expect from a woman attacked by a cobra, but it came from a man.

Several hundred yards away, in her bedroom in the missionary's house at the crest of the hill, Vera McIntosh was trying to hold on to a beautiful dream. She was waltzing with Justin Tolliver, who danced in that athletic way of his. In her dream, neither of them wore gloves. He held her right hand gently in his left. The white drill cloth of his tropical dress uniform felt smooth under her left palm. The song was not in the rather oom-pah-pah style of the usual King's African Rifles Band at the Nairobi Club, but the sweet strains of a full orchestra such as she had danced to at balls in Glasgow. That music had been one of the few compensations of her most recent visit to her maternal grandmother. In her sleep, Vera danced on tiptoes that barely touched the floor. Then the violins, from farther and farther away, began to make a screeching sound. Vera tried to put her arms around Tolliver's neck. And suddenly she was awake.

The screams were coming from down the hill. From the fields. And there were shouts at the front door. "Reverend Sahib!" And banging. She threw open the mosquito netting and pulled on a robe. The long hall outside her bedroom led to the noise. At the entrance, her father and Njui, their houseboy, were opening the door. She could not make out what the people on the veranda were saying. Her father groaned.

Her mother called from her bedroom door. "What has happened?"

"I don't know, Mother. I will find out." She ran back to her room, dressed quickly, and without even a splash of water on her face or a pause to lace up her boots, she ran out.

A knot of workers, whose shaved heads barely showed above the coffee plants, moved around, their arms raised in fright. She saw her father's pith helmet and the battered brown hat of Joe Morley, the farm manager. Vera ran to them.

"Father?"

"Stay back, lass."

She disobeyed, circled the knot of people, and pushed through the Kikuyu, who opened a path for her. A gasp shook her chest. Her uncle Josiah lay facedown between the rows. Dew clung to his khaki trousers as it did to the dark leaves of the plants. His left arm was half under his body, oddly askew. A native spear stood straight up in the middle of his back. His tan jacket had a slight stain of red-brown where the point of the spear had entered.

Her father was at her side. He put his arm over her shoulders.

"He's dead," she said. She had meant it as a question, but it came out as a statement, though she could hardly believe it.

Her father drew her to him and turned her head, shielding her eyes from the sight. "Ay," he said. "We'll have to tell your mother." He turned to Joe Morley. "You'll have to send someone to notify the police. Move the body into the hospital."

"You'll have to help me," Joe said. "None of this lot will touch a dead body."

It was a taboo Vera knew well. She had known the Kikuyu to burn a hut where a woman had died in childbirth. They never touched a dead person.

Joe Morley moved toward her uncle's head. He picked up Josiah Pennyman's hat, which had fallen off and lay beside his corpse. Her uncle's dark hair shone in the early morning sunlight.

Her father moved toward the dead man's feet. "Let's get it over with," he said and bent to lift the legs.

"I'll go to my mother," Vera said.

"No, lassie." Her father's voice was strangely commanding. "I will tell her. I will be there in a moment. Get yourself
a cup of tea, my girl. You're as pale as the coffee blossoms."

And the world is as bitter as their perfume, she thought. Her
uncle was dead. He, the pride of her granny. The handsome,
brilliant doctor. Someone everyone seemed to like and admire. Vera felt a tinge of guilt, realizing that she had doubted
how wonderful he was. In truth, though he was a member of
her small family, living in close proximity, she hardly knew
him. And now he was dead. And she was supposed to be
extremely sorry. And she was, even though he never took the
least interest in her.

She went to the kitchen and asked Njui to make a pot of
tea. In a little while, she heard her father coming in, his tread
heavier than usual, and his knock on her mother's door. "My
lass," he said softly. It was hard for Vera to think of her mother
as anyone's lass.

Later that morning, in the newly constructed Government
House in Nairobi, Kwai Libazo stood with his back to the
dark paneling of the district commissioner's office, trying to
seem inanimate, but listening carefully to what B'wana Cranford was saying to Assistant District Superintendent Tolliver. If Libazo had been naked and closed his eyes and mouth,
he would have been nearly invisible, his skin so exactly
matched the color of the wood behind him. As it was, the
khaki of his uniform shorts and shirt, the blue-black of his
puttees, and the dark orange shade of his leather sandals gave
him away. His red fez was the brightest thing in the room,

except for the British flag that stood behind District Commissioner Cranford.

The powerful man sitting at the desk was entirely gray, his clothing, his hair, his skin, his eyes. It occurred to Libazo that his grandfather, who had not lived ever to see a man so white, would have thought him a medicine man who had painted himself completely, even the pupils of his eyes, instead of just streaking his chest and cheeks with ash paste.

"So," Cranford was saying, "I am glad you were able to subdue those oafs last night. I understand the predicament you were in, but I have already had several complaints about the unseemly sight of handcuffed Europeans being marched to jail by natives with rifles. We cannot have this, my boy."

The district commissioner always called his white underlings "my boy." The blacks, he addressed just as "boy," if he spoke to them at all. The "my boy" in question was Libazo's commanding officer, who stood at attention facing Cranford across the desk, his khaki clothing unrumpled despite the stifling heat. The effort of the toto standing next to the Union Jack and pulling a cord to operate the punkah fan overhead was having no effect whatsoever on the temperature of the office.

Libazo focused intently. His captain had been a soldier before he was a policeman, and it showed in his posture and in his respect for his superior. These were things Libazo understood, as would any warrior tribesman. Not that Libazo had been admitted to the rank of warrior in any tribe.

Tolliver leaned slightly forward. "It is a circumstance we will find more and more difficult to avoid, sir, given the paucity of European policemen and the recent influx of undesirable white men. I cannot see—" A sharp knock at the door interrupted.

"Come," the district commissioner commanded.

Stocky, bow-legged Sergeant Hobson of the King's African Rifles came in and saluted. His small blue eyes were wide, his forehead sweatier than usual. "A runner has just come. There has been a killing," he said. "The doctor at the Scottish Mission hospital has been murdered by a native."

D.C. Cranford leapt to his feet. "Bloody savages!" His face had turned a shade of red almost as bright as that in the flag behind him.

Kwai Libazo remained wooden, stiff. He held his breath not to allow his chest to heave. The tribe that lived near the Scottish Mission were Kikuyu, his mother's people. His people. No matter the facts of the case, this would hurt them.

Captain Tolliver's fists clenched. He turned to the sergeant, who stood at attention with his head thrown slightly back, his back hair shiny with sweat. Tolliver had barely changed his position, but his body was suddenly energized. To Kwai Libazo it seemed as if Justin Tolliver already knew something about what was going on at the Scottish Mission. "Was anyone else hurt at the mission?"

Hobson glanced to D.C. Cranford and back to Tolliver with quizzical eyes. "No. The runner said everyone else was safe."

Tolliver let out his breath and unclenched his fists.

Libazo felt no such relief at the news that the mission family was otherwise safe. The hospital there was known far and wide, to the settlers and to the tribes. The doctor was the best in the district. He had cured Libazo's baby cousin who had rolled into a fire in the night and been badly burned. His death at the hands of a tribesman was a very dangerous thing.

Cranford sank back into his chair and shook his head as if he were trying to settle its contents. "Bloody savages." This time he growled the words. "Get out there immediately, my boy. Find the bastard, and we'll do for him."

Tolliver had started to inch toward the door before the order came. Sergeant Hobson opened it. Tolliver turned to his superior. "Sir," he said, "I will need to take Libazo here with me. Request permission to mount him on a pony for speed's sake."

Libazo did not move, even to blink his eyes. The D.C. flashed his habitual look of disapproval, ever ready when anyone proposed to ignore any protocol, especially one that blurred the distinction between the people he called the natives, who had lived in this land forever, and the British, who had so lately begun to flow in and act as if it really belonged to them.

The expectant look on Tolliver's face did not change in the too-long period it took Cranford to relent. "If you must," the district commissioner said at last.

"Follow me, Libazo," Tolliver ordered as he marched out the door that Sergeant Hobson still held by its brass knob.

Only then did Kwai Libazo let his muscles come to life and his tall, slender body to move. His mind was troubled by where these events would take him, but his bones and his muscles longed to race there on a steed.

Even as he spurred Bosworth, his chestnut stallion, toward a tragedy, A.D.S. Justin Tolliver could not help but be impressed by the beauty of the land they traversed. The long rains had been plentiful that year, and the area around them was rich with grasses and exotic wild flowers. As he and Kwai Libazo crested the last hill, the sun had nearly reached its zenith. They looked upon the Mission of the Church of Scotland. On that April morning, in a verdant valley beside a meandering river, the coffee fields that stretched just below them were in flower, acre upon acre of white blossoms against dark green leaves. Cattle grazed on the far hillside. Though Tolliver was troubled at the thought of how Vera McIntosh was reacting to her uncle's death, the vista lifted his heart. Something in his soul, his spirit, seemed to be expanding here in Africa. It was not what he had anticipated when he first traveled to South Africa with his Yorkshire regiment in 1909, the year the British colonies in the south were united. He had come to this continent a young lieutenant intent on doing his duty as an Englishman. He never expected his loyalties to change. England was his home. That "sceptered isle . . . earth of majesty" was where his heart was meant to belong. Back there, he had been a second son without prospects, and one itching for adventure, disinclined to settle down and marry a girl of means—his father's phrase, one he loathed, but one that his sort of life in England dictated.

After more than a year in Cape Town and Johannesburg, he had been reluctant to go back where his only choice was to find a girl with money who would have him. When he heard of the wonderful hunting, the richness of game to be had, the ease of life in the new British East African Protectorate, he had taken only a brief sojourn in England, and then come here to seek a change—here where living was cheap and opportunities abounded—to serve the Empire and to see what he might make of it all. Once his fortune was made, he had expected to take it home and rejoin society there, not as a poor sap on the lookout for a large dowry, but with money of his own, so that he would be able to let his heart, not his banker, choose his wife.

He had not expected this land to grow on him so. Nor had he thought a missionary's daughter would also find a place in his affections. But now, down somewhere among the picturesque buildings in this irresistible landscape was the niece of the dead man. His attraction to Vera McIntosh was another thing it would be better to resist.

He banged his heels into the flanks of the stallion that was, if he admitted it, one of the only truly loyal companions he had found in British East Africa. The horse skirted a hole filled with water from the recent rains.

"Careful here," he called to Kwai Libazo, behind him on a pony. The last thing Tolliver needed was for Libazo to lame the animal. Cranford was already in a difficult enough mood.

"I see it, B'wana," Libazo said.

"I have told you to call me sir."

"Yes, sir."

There was not a hint of irony in Libazo's tone. Tolliver did not understand why he disliked the term the natives always used when speaking to European settlers. But it rubbed him the wrong way. He liked Libazo. Perhaps it was their matching stature. Perhaps it was the innate elegance of the man. Libazo was only half Kikuyu. He was half Maasai, which accounted for his being six feet two and straight as a rod.

The native policeman's face always remained impassive, as if he little cared what happened, but the other night's enterprise in the Masonic Hotel was typical of Tolliver's experience of the man. Libazo could be counted to do the right and the intelligent thing. Whether they were sent to pick up the pieces after a drunken brawl or to fight a fire in the Arab trader's stores, Libazo's eyes often revealed that his thoughts tracked along with Tolliver's. The askari worked side by side with Justin, always on point for whatever came up, but he never revealed that his thinking ran ahead of Tolliver's. As it must have from time to time, considering Tolliver's relative inexperience and the native's superior knowledge of the territory and the people who inhabited it, even many of the white ones. Libazo's deference was only proper, of course, but it must have taken something for him to give it.

They dismounted at the stable near the house workers' huts. A toto ran up and took the reins and walked the horses into the shade.

"Wait here and water the horses," Tolliver ordered Libazo and walked toward the mission office, passing the McIntosh family's stone house on the way. He looked straight ahead, all the while worrying about what he would say to Vera about her and her family's terrible loss and wondering if she was looking out through the gauze curtains as he went by.

Before he reached the office, her father, Reverend Clement McIntosh, shouted to him from the veranda of the house. "Captain Tolliver." He always addressed Justin by the rank he had held in the army. It was a sign of respect that few British men accorded a young nobleman who had had the bad judgment to join the police force. And it endeared the Scot to him.

McIntosh beckoned with a sad smile. His ordinarily jolly, florid face was pale and troubled, as was to be expected.

Tolliver took the Scottish priest's offered hand. "I am so sorry for your loss. I will do everything I can to apprehend the culprit."

"A terrible business. Terrible." The reverend's chin sunk to his chest and he shook his head. His Scottish burr somehow made the word "terrible" sound worse than it otherwise would have. He sighed deeply and indicated a wicker chair beside a small white table laid with a lace cloth and teacups. He rang a little silver bell.

Glad of something to quench his thirst after the nearly hour's ride from Nairobi and for tea to brace him up for the ordeal ahead, Tolliver took the chair, which creaked when he sat.

"I hope the ride was not too long and hot," the reverend said, as if Tolliver had arrived for a social call.

With relief, Tolliver continued in that vein, knowing it could not be long before the business he had come to conduct would destroy any semblance of normalcy. "Not at all. The panorama from the crest of the hill is stunning on this lovely day."

"The Lord's rains have blessed the farmer this year," McIntosh said. Like all British missionaries, he had come to this land to fight slavery and to convert the heathens, but like all the clergy that Tolliver had met here in the Protectorate or in England for that matter, he showed as much enthusiasm for his plantation and his herd of cattle as he did for his flock of native converts.

A door opened behind Tolliver. Expecting a native in a white robe and red fez, he nudged his cup toward the approaching sound, but when he turned he found Vera carrying a tray. He jumped to his feet and overturned his chair in the process. His face heated up. It mortified him that at the age of twenty-three he could still blush to near purple just because of an awkward moment.

She looked up at him. The rims of her eyes were the color he was sure she saw on his cheeks. He took the tray from her and set it on the table. "Miss McIntosh, I am so sorry about your loss."

She blinked her eyes and for a moment he was afraid she would burst into tears. But she poured the tea instead and asked, "Have you seen the body?"

"Vera!" her father exclaimed. "Captain Tolliver will think . . ." He didn't finish.

She put down the teapot none too gently. "Well, isn't that why he came?" She took the third chair at the table while Tolliver righted his own and sat on it, trying not to blush again as it let out a sound like an injured cat and threatened to collapse under him.

"Let the man have his tea in peace for a moment, gal."

She gave her father a rather wan smile. "Captain, I believe you take it with cream and sugar." She did not wait for a reply before she took the tongs, dropped in two lumps, poured in cream from a blue and white china pitcher, and offered the cup, looking right into his eyes.

Tolliver took it from her hands. They were small and beautiful and had disappeared into his when they had waltzed at the Nairobi Club, when they had both been wearing gloves. He resisted drinking the tea in one long draught, as his mother had warned him never to do in company.

He did not want to send Vera away, but he also thought it quite inappropriate to talk about a murder in the presence of a young lady. She had, however, brought it up herself, and given the extreme gravity of such an act of violence as had occurred, there was a great deal of urgency in this matter. She might have information or insights that would be helpful to his inquiries. Those who disapproved of his choice of a profession were right about one thing: Sometimes the behavior of a gentleman and that of a policeman were mutually exclusive. "Perhaps Miss McIntosh is right, and if she will forgive us for speaking of such an unseemly matter in her presence, it might be best to get on with it."

Her father looked decidedly reluctant, but nodded his assent.

Tolliver drained his cup and drew his noisy chair forward. "Please tell me, Reverend, what you know about the discovery of Dr. Pennyman's body. The runner who came to Government House could not give us any details except for the fact that it—um, he was found at early light facedown in the coffee field with a native spear in his back."

"Yes, that is correct. The workers take to the fields just after dawn to get on with their work before the sun is too strong. They always have some stalwart native laddies with spears with them, in case there are night-prowling animals that might be in the groves, and they make a great noise to warn off any creatures lurking there. When their usual chanting turned to screams and shouts, I thought it might have been a hyena or even a lion. But when I got there, I saw it was Josiah." He looked away and blinked.

While her father was talking Vera had taken Tolliver's cup and refilled it from the china teapot and placed it in front of him. He gave her a fleeting smile of thanks and took a sip while he waited for her father to recover himself. Her pretty face was calm. Enigmatic girl that she was, she was holding her own against her grief. Perhaps D.C. Cranford was right about Vera, that having been born here and nursed by a Kikuyu woman, she was bred without the true delicacy of an English maiden.

"Forgive me, Reverend, but I must ask—please describe exactly what you saw with as many precise details as you can remember."

McIntosh coughed and took a long breath. "He was lying facedown, as if he had been speared whilst running away, and died instantly. One arm was underneath the body, the other was bent at the elbow. The spear was sticking straight up from the middle of his back." His head shook, more like a shudder than a negation of what he was saying. "The spear shaft threw a shadow, like a sun dial's."

Vera made a tiny noise.

Her father threw her a quizzical glance and stood up. "Perhaps, my dear, you should spare yourself this."

She stood, too, but made no move to leave them.

Tolliver rose. "Perhaps your father is right, Miss McIntosh."

They were all standing now. Her dark eyes pierced him with a troubled glance. "Yes. Excuse me. I will go to my mother. I do wish to speak to you before you leave, Captain."

Tolliver assented with a slight bow, and he watched her disappear through the green painted door of the house. The speed and determination in her gait made her small, slight frame seem strong and lithe as she moved, but light, as if she might as well hover over the ground as walk upon it. Tolliver pressed his lips together. Her flight from the subject of murder told him that she had not been as composed as she seemed on the surface. Somewhere in that African-born graceful figure lurked a real English—no, a Scottish girl, after all.

Vera's step slowed once she was out of Tolliver's disturbing sight and he out of hers. She had done her best to act the demure young lady in front of him, but she was sure she had done a bad job of it. Every time he turned that blue glance of his on her, she saw something in it that looked like shock, or at least like surprise. Never did she see attraction, much less affection. Every part of her was disturbed: by the discovery of her uncle's body, by her mother's outpouring of grief, the most emotional state she had ever seen in her mother, and even in the face of all that, more so by Justin Tolliver's presence. Who, what, how, everything he was overwhelmed her. Even his rosy lips and blushes, which were not supposed to impress a girl. Her father used the word "virile" to describe men he admired—like that other newcomer Denys Finch Hatton. People had used it when they talked about her dead uncle. She had never really understood the word. "Manly," her mother had said it meant. Tolliver was broad shouldered and tall. She came up only to his chin. And athletic. He had proved that even in the way he waltzed. Maybe it was his virility that disturbed her so. He seemed walking proof that a manly man could blush and have lips the color of strawberries. And now he was crossing the compound to examine her uncle's dead body.

She backed away from the window, slipped down the corridor, and knocked lightly on her mother's bedroom door. "Mother," she said barely above a whisper, half desiring, half dreading intimacy with her mother that she used to imagine would make her feel loved.

"Come in, Vera." Her voice was tired and resigned.

Vera turned the knob and opened the door silently as if she were playing the thief. Her mother lay on the bed fully clothed except for her boots, which stood side by side on the rag carpet beside the iron bedstead. Her father insisted that they always wear boots, frightened as he was of snakebites. It made no difference to him that the natives walked about barefoot and in Vera's memory none of them had been bitten.

Her mother stretched out a hand to her and moved over to make room for Vera to sit beside her on the bed. This in itself made Vera suspicious and anxious. The death of her uncle, her mother's only sibling, seemed to have softened her heart in a way Vera would have thought impossible.

Vera sat and took her mother's hand. Her angular face was ashen and her eyes puffy from her tears. "This is awful," Vera said.

Her mother squeezed her hand, let it go, and reached for a balled-up linen handkerchief that lay beside her on the damask bedspread. She patted her eyes and her nose. "I heard Captain Tolliver's voice. They have gone to see Josiah, I suppose." She sobbed and bit her lip, but the tears flowed anyway.

Vera twined her fingers in between her mother's. "Oh, Mama, I am so sorry. Shouldn't we try to send for Otis?" No one and nothing cheered her mother as much as the presence of Otis. Accustomed to her mother's strength and the depth of her habitual reserve, Vera found it intolerable, seeing her like this.

"I told you already, Vera, and you know as well as I that tracking him in that vast wilderness is neigh on to impossible. They have two days' head start. Kibene is our best tracker, and he has gone with them. Richard Newland said he and Berkeley Cole intend to end up at Berkeley's farm on the Naro Moru. There is absolutely no way to know what route they will take through all that trackless open space. We will send word to Cole's farm that they must bring Otis home forthwith. There is no need to break the news to him before he returns."

A.D.S. Tolliver followed Clement McIntosh toward the stone-built hospital on the other side of the mission compound. They mounted two steps, crossed the flagstone veranda, and entered through a heavy door carved with native symbols. Tolliver removed his pith helmet and placed it under his arm as he entered. The walls of the interior were whitewashed and the rooms impeccably clean. A nursing sister approached them immediately and greeted them with a Scots burr so thick Tolliver could barely make out what she was saying. He nodded gravely to her, and she led them down a corridor lined with waist-high wainscoting. Though the exterior of the building was typical of such a place in the Protectorate, the interior was arranged very like any hospital in Tolliver's native Yorkshire. The sister closed her eyes and bowed her head as she opened the door and let them into a small room where Dr. Josiah Pennyman's body lay under a sheet on the table where he used to perform operations.

As Tolliver approached the corpse, McIntosh drew back the sheet. The dead doctor's hair was the exact rich brown color of Vera's, which gave Tolliver a start. He concentrated on his work. In the seven months that Tolliver had been in British East Africa he had never had occasion to visit the doctor and had seen him only in large crowds at Nairobi Club dances and at sporting events. In life, from afar, the doctor's statuesque form and countenance had confirmed his reputation of enormous appeal. His face, though a bit round-ish, had pleasant regular features, a bright complexion, a quick, handsome smile, a hardy laugh. Here, even in death, there was a gentleness about the face of the corpse that made it easy to see why he had been so well liked, even loved.

Clement McIntosh woke Tolliver from his reverie with a touch on his arm. "Do you want to see the wound?"

"Yes."

It took all their strength and the nursing sister's assistance to keep the inert body from falling on the operating room floor while they turned it. A gash about three or four inches wide traversed the man's spine just below the shoulder blades. The wound was clean, the flesh inside it white.

McIntosh's open hand indicated the nurse. "Sister and I washed him once we brought him here," he said.

The woman in white pursed her lips and nodded but did not speak.

"I'll want to see the place where you found him," Tolliver said.

"I will show you." McIntosh started for the door.

Tolliver held up his hand. "In a moment." He turned to the nurse. "I suppose the spear pierced his heart and that is what killed him."

The woman's rigid face darkened; her lips pursed again. "We could not say that with any certainty. The spear most likely severed the spinal cord. That might have been enough to kill him. A qualified doctor performing an autopsy would be able to determine that but—" She glanced back at the dead man. "But we no longer have such a person here."

"I don't suppose it much matters," Tolliver said. "One way or another the spear killed him. How long do you suppose he had been dead when they found him?"

"Again, it would be difficult to be certain. But his clothing was quite damp. It did not rain in the night, so the wet must have come from dew. I would imagine that he was lying there most of the night. A few hours at least."

Tolliver studied her. She was sturdy and no nonsense, as one would expect of a Scottish woman who volunteered to work in an African mission hospital. But there was also a spark of intelligence and pride in her eyes. She merited his confidence, which her denials of certitude belied.

He extended his hand to her. "Thank you very much, Nurse—"

"Nurse Freemantle," she said. Her handshake was firm but very brief.

"If you think of anything else that might be helpful, please let me know."

The look she gave him was almost a smile.

Tolliver followed the missionary to the door. As they left, he saw the nurse covering the dead man with the white sheet, an act of gentleness not all nursing sisters spared for the living.

Tolliver signaled to Kwai Libazo, who was waiting in the shade of an acacia tree near the horses. He would need Libazo to translate as he questioned the Kikuyu who had found the body. McIntosh led them across the center of the compound and into the flowering coffee fields that sloped gently down to the river. Here and there, natives, mostly women, worked with hoes. The plants stretched far to their left and right. The myriad blossoms were as white as clouds and gave off a bittersweet fragrance. Tolliver had read somewhere that a death by arsenic gave off a bitter almond smell. But that could have no relevance here. McIntosh stopped in a spot that seemed undistinguished from any other in the expansive plantation and pointed to the ground. "Just there," he said.

The reddishness of the earth was the color of all the ground thereabouts—not a sign of blood. Tolliver examined it carefully. It held no clues.

"It has been well cleaned," McIntosh said.

Tolliver could not help but frown. If he had been Sherlock Holmes, the fictional detective whose stories had been all the rage in England since Tolliver was a babe in arms, he would have cursed this statement and gone back to his apartment to work out his anger playing the violin, except that in his case it would be a cello.

"The Kikuyu despise and fear death," a lovely voice from behind Tolliver said. He turned to see Vera's grave face. She was standing beside Libazo and looked up to him, seemingly for confirmation. The native policeman might have been carved out of wood for all his expression altered.

The girl shrugged and went on. "They burn down a hut if someone dies inside it. They will not touch a dead body. My father and Joe Morley had to move my uncle to the operating room." She spoke the words without distaste or judgment, straightforwardly, as no proper English girl ever would have.

"Joe Morley?" Tolliver asked.

"The manager of the plantation," the missionary explained.

Libazo looked down. Tolliver saw in his eyes that it was costing him some effort to maintain his lack of expression.

"My workers would have refused to come into the fields where a dead body was found," the Reverend McIntosh said. "Morley had to call in Gichinga Mbura to cleanse the area. At this time of year the weeds want to turn the field wild again. And it is hard enough to get the workers to give us enough time to keep nature at bay."

"Who is this Gichinga Mbura?" Tolliver asked. The very

mention of the name had set the muscles in Libazo's jaw working.

"The local witch doctor," McIntosh said, his voice ever more apologetic. "Much as I regret it, I sometimes have no choice but to give the local religion, if you can call it that, its due. Otherwise nothing would get done on the farm and the mission cannot survive without the income from the coffee. The faithful of Scotland cannot be expected to support hundreds and hundreds all over Africa."

"Libazo," Tolliver said, "go into the Kikuyu village and find this Mbura. Perhaps he noticed something while he was doing his spells that might help us?"

Libazo stared at Tolliver as if he expected him to explode. "B'wana, the medicine man—"

Tolliver held up his hand. "How many times do I have to tell you to call me 'sir.' Now please just do as I have asked. Go and find Mbura and bring him to me." Tolliver turned back to the missionary. "Reverend McIntosh, where is the spear? I would like to look at it."

"I put it in my study with the hunting rifles and shotguns, for safekeeping. I thought you would want to confiscate it. It will be evidence, no?"

"Certainly." Tolliver's voice was deep and resonant. Vera loved the sound of it, with its barest hint of Yorkshire. He had got that from his nanny, she imagined. She shook her head in a vain attempt to dislodge her thoughts. She would either have to give up dreaming of him or to make herself into the kind of girl he would think attractive. Neither course seemed at all possible at this moment.

He turned and led the way up toward the house.

Vera tramped through the fields following her father and Tolliver in a state of complete confusion. Ever since she last saw Tolliver at the Nairobi Club dance, whenever she enjoyed something, she had imagined how much it would enhance her joy to have him with her enjoying it, too. Once the coffee came into blossom a week ago, she had fantasized about walking with him among all this beauty—the tall clouds sailing in the blue sky, the blossoms in matching white profusion, their heady perfume, the lightness of the air above. She wanted Tolliver to know this place at its most beautiful. Anyone with a human soul would find a thrill in this. She knew from the way he had spoken to her at the club dances that the wonder of British East Africa had surprised him. Until this morning, whenever she thought of him that was how she thought, of the places she wanted to take him, of the native crafts she wanted to show him. There were stories her Kikuyu nanny had told her, splendid vistas— Oh, what was the use? Now he would look at her only as the niece of a murder victim. Happiness for him would never attach itself to her. And if he could read her thoughts now, he would think her horrid for dwelling on such a subject when her uncle lay dead.

With her head lowered, she nearly walked right into his back as they approached the veranda of the house.

In spite of her confusion of feelings, Vera could not help going with him into her father's study. He stood aside and let her enter first. Her father took the long spear, which stood in the corner, and brought it to Tolliver. Its one-piece head of iron had a leaf-shaped blade and cylindrical base into which the long wooden shaft was fitted. The point of the blade shone brightly; it had been cleansed of any blood from the stabbing.

Tolliver stood it next to him and glanced up at the tip. "A bit taller than I. Six feet and four inches I would say."

Vera's father nodded. "The blade was in his back up to about there." He pointed to a spot on about two inches from the top.

Tolliver glanced at Vera. His round blue eyes held concern and something else that might have been disapproval of her. Ladies were supposed to faint if they heard such things. "I have seen a Kikuyu kill a warthog with a spear," she said as if to defend herself. "And a Maasai kill a lion with one very like that." If anything, his look of disapproval deepened.

She turned away, went to the window. "Your man is returning with Gichinga Mbura." She did not bother to tell him that Mbura was gesticulating wildly and that the black policeman in the red fez was having to push the medicine man along the path with a hand at the middle of his back.

Kwai Libazo knew he had no choice but to deliver the medicine man to A.D.S. Tolliver. He was unsure if the rules also required him to reveal what he had just learned: that Mbura hated the Scottish doctor with a passion most Kikuyu reserved for their worst enemy—the Maasai.

When Libazo had arrived at the medicine man's hut, the

villagers had stood mute and suspicious, as was their wont with him ever since the British government had hired him to be a policeman. Not that he had ever been completely accepted by the Kikuyu, his mother's tribe, or by the Maasai, his father's. He had asked both his father's and his mother's brothers to include him in the circumcision ceremony of their respective tribes. Becoming a full-fledged man in either would have freed him from the limbo in which he had lived his life. But neither group would accept him. Once he turned fifteen and it was clear he would never get his wish from either tribe, he had confronted his mother. Why had she lain with an enemy of her people to make him? Why had she brought into the world a son who had no place in it? She had looked up into his face and walked away from his anger and his pain.

One of the old men who sat around in his mother's village watching the women do the farmwork had suggested that his mother might have been raped during a Maasai raid to steal goats and cattle. The old grandfather had told him to ask his father. But his father was dead—eaten by a lion. And his father's brother denied it, and said the old man was just trying to get Kwai to hate his own father. He had never gotten the truth about why he had been born.

Kwai pushed the medicine man forward as if he had a right to command the second-most powerful man in his mother's tribe, after the chief, Kinanjui. "Your tribesman Kamante told me that you have been cursing the white doctor, that you have said he deserved to die because he was trying to steal the Kikuyus' spirits for his god."

Gichinga Mbura contorted his torso to shrug off Libazo's hand on his back. His skin still bore the remains of the red mud and white ash with which he had painted himself for the ritual cleansing of the coffee field. "That dwarf Kamante is a twisted monster. No one follows his words. What does he know of the power of Small-knife-no-spear?"

Libazo kept his face in neutral though the Scottish doctor's nickname made him want to smile. His mother's people did this: They gave names to the white settlers that described something about them, usually a physical attribute or an article of clothing, derogatory if they disliked the person, complimentary if they found the person pleasing. Libazo had briefly worked for the red-haired Berkeley Cole and called him Sunset-shines-on-head.

Libazo pressed harder on the medicine man's back. "Move faster."

Gichinga twisted away from Libazo's hand again and began to walk very fast. "You give the white man's orders, but you are not a white man. You are not a Kikuyu. You are not a Maasai. You are not as much of man even as Kamante."

Kwai Libazo's Maasai father's height and strength gave him an advantage over the smaller, slighter Kikuyu. Libazo now grabbed Mbura by his upper arm and held him fast. "You would be better to think how you will answer B'wana Tolliver's questions."

"You would be better to think why you take the side of your B'wana against your own people."

Libazo did not remind Gichinga that he was just after saying that Kwai Libazo did not belong to those people. He decided at that moment that he would tell A.D.S. Tolliver about Mbura's threats against the British doctor.

Justin Tolliver had seen an African witch doctor only once, in full regalia, during a ceremony to greet the former American president Teddy Roosevelt, who had come to the Protectorate to hunt and to explore. That was almost two years ago on a brief visit with a schoolmate and fellow army officer, Granville Stokes. They had come from South Africa to transport polo ponies and see the new British territory. The memory brought back powerful images. Tolliver suppressed a wave of desire that wanted to wash over him. He and Gran had met two women at a polo match. They had stayed with them for two months. Lillian, Lady Gresham, had introduced him around as her nephew. In private she had called him Candy. She had nearly consumed him. Almost old enough to be his mother but slender and lively, with skin soft and warm, the heady air of the African highlands and the scent of her French perfume, his first real affair. Barely past his twenty-first year, he had spent that leave lost in a stupor of sex and whiskey. Until she ran away south with a German, and he went back to Johannesburg to grow out of his infatuation. And he did. He now thought of her as debauched, rather than delicious. Except sometimes in the night. When the urge came over him to make love and that lecherous woman seemed the ideal partner.

He shook off those thoughts and stood beside Vera McIntosh on the veranda, waiting for Libazo to cross the mission compound with the witch doctor in tow. Clement McIntosh had left them and gone to see how his wife was faring in her grief.

Tolliver tried not to think of what it would be to lift Vera's body and kiss her mouth and find out what she was like without that silly split skirt and boyish khaki shirt. She was not a predatory woman looking for nothing but pleasure. Neither was she a prim and proper English girl who would faint at the slightest provocation. Somehow, at this second, that made her more desirable than any woman he had ever known.

Libazo let go of Mbura's arm as they approached. Tolliver stepped forward and with Libazo translating asked the native to describe exactly what he had removed from the site where the body was found and if there had been anything left behind that might help them discover who had killed the doctor.

Libazo dutifully asked the questions his captain had requested. He wanted to reveal his suspicions to Tolliver, but he was not sure that Mbura was as ignorant of the British language as he claimed to be. No matter what the English may say, he knew there was reason to fear the medicine man's curses. And the lady who was standing by, he knew, spoke perfect Kikuyu, so she understood all that passed between him and the medicine man.

Tolliver grunted. "This is not helpful at all." There was an edge of frustration in his voice.

"Perhaps," Vera suggested, "Gichinga Mbura will look at the spear and tell us if he knows who the owner might be. Even if he does not know its owner, he may know which iron monger made it."

Tolliver turned his blue gaze on her. It went through her heart. "I'll go inside, Miss McIntosh, with your permission, and get it."

She held his eyes with hers and nodded. While he was gone, she asked Libazo in English why Gichinga was so agitated. He told her in Kikuyu about the witch doctor's anger at her uncle. He wanted Mbura to understand that his true feelings were being revealed.

Tolliver returned before she could ask anything further. He stood the spear upright in front of Mbura, who looked carefully at the blade, pointed to it, and spoke animatedly to Vera.

Tolliver interrupted. "Ask him if he knows who owned this," he said to Libazo.

Kwai nodded and spoke at length to the witch doctor, who answered with a torrent of words.

"What is he saying?"

Libazo raised a hand to quiet Mbura. "He says that this is a Maasai spear."

It seemed an entirely inadequate report of a conversation that had taken more than two minutes. "How does he know that?"

Libazo pointed to the blade. "Do you see here, sir? This shape of the leaf, how it curves abruptly into the shaft? Well, that is the shape of Maasai blade. A Kikuyu blacksmith would make a blade where the bottom of the leaf slants more gradually into the shaft. Like this." He traced a finger along the blade to demonstrate the difference between Maasai and Kikuyu spearheads.

"But there are over a million Kikuyu in the Protectorate.

There must be hundreds of blacksmiths in the tribal areas. Do you mean to tell me they all make their spearheads the same way and all the Maasai make theirs a different way?"

Vera put a hand on his arm. "Englishmen," she said, "often lump all the natives together as if they must all have the same attitudes and traits. They do not. One tribe is as different from another as the French are from the English or the English from the Italians. Each tribe's artisans have their own signature way of making things like baskets or wood carvings, or songs and dances for that matter."

Tolliver gave her another assessing look and then addressed Libazo. "Is this a Maasai spear?"

Libazo nodded. "Yes. And, sir, you see these lines cut into the blade." He turned the blade over to show Tolliver both sides. "I have never seen anything like these. Both the Kikuyu and the Maasai might make a design there, but always something that resembles a snake. I have never seen a spear that looked exactly like this."

Tolliver examined the spearhead. Incised in it on one side was a squared-off design that resembled a Greek key. On the other side was a zigzag that looked very like something found among Egyptian hieroglyphics.

"Also, sir," Libazo said, "I think you ought—" he began hesitantly.

Vera interjected, speaking to Libazo in English. "Let me explain to the captain." She knew it would be best for Libazo if she, rather than he, revealed the witch doctor's possible connection to the murder. She turned to Tolliver. "May I ask Mbura some questions?"

"About?"

She drew near and put her lips close to his ear. "I think Gichinga Mbura knows more about my uncle's death than he is saying. Kikuyu do not easily answer direct questions from strangers, but they are usually more open with people they know. Mbura is being evasive with Libazo. It seems to me he has something to hide. He has known me from birth. Perhaps he will be more forthcoming with me. Shall I ask him?"

Tolliver gestured with an open palm for her to proceed and waited while she spoke rapidly, but in a polite voice. The witch doctor accorded her no such civility. His tone was harsh, and he even stamped his foot at one point. At length she hushed him up with a gesture and turned back to Tolliver. "Mbura says that he has lost face with his people because they began to look to my uncle to cure their ills whereas in the past he was the one who could help them. From the way he spoke, he resented my uncle quite vehemently."

Tolliver looked from her to the blade of the spear to Mbura. "It is likely then that he killed your uncle."

Vera seemed about to object when her mother suddenly appeared in the doorway. Her father stood a few feet behind his wife in the hall. Mrs. McIntosh gave a slight bow to Tolliver in lieu of a greeting. "I think you should know that my brother was carrying on an affair with Lucy Buxton," she said. "I do not like to reveal Josiah's sins, but Kirk Buxton recently found out about his wife's—" She grimaced. "Shall we say, *activities?*" Her lips pursed with disapproval.

Tolliver glanced from the witch doctor to Blanche McIntosh. Kirk Buxton was the manager of the Standard Bank of India's branch in Nairobi. Tolliver was well aware from his previous visit to the Protectorate of what went on among certain European settlers, had been part of it himself. He tightened his grip on the spear he still held. "But your brother was killed with a native weapon. And I have just this moment discovered that this Mbura had a motive to kill him."

Blanche McIntosh's gray eyes widened. She looked down, and her shoulders sagged. Tolliver could not tell if she felt disappointment or just grief.

In the dim light of the hallway, Clement McIntosh stepped forward. "Anyone could take a native spear and kill someone with it," he said. "If a settler wanted to conceal what he had done, it would be the weapon to choose."

"I think, sir," Libazo said, speaking out of turn, "that a Kikuyu medicine man would never choose a Maasai spear to reclaim his power. Mbura said this himself just now. The Kikuyu and the Maasai have been enemies since they found themselves together in this valley."

Tolliver let Libazo's insolence pass. He was already struggling to keep control of his own thoughts. For a moment, it had seemed that this murder was going to be a straightforward case of resentment and a savage's way of reasserting his power. Now he was not so sure. British interests required not only that the police force show that English law now ruled this land, but also that the British Empire stood for true justice. If they did not take the moral high ground and teach the natives the righteousness of British ways, the best of England would never prevail.

"Ask him if he killed your uncle," he said to Vera.

She moved a step closer to Tolliver's side. Her mother

turned away and walked toward her bedroom with her head hanging. Her husband followed her.

Gichinga Mbura's answer to Vera's question poured forth with such violent temper that Tolliver felt the need to step between her and the witch doctor.

3.

Back in Nairobi, Justin Tolliver's steps slowed as he left the stable, on the back street near Government House. What he was about to tell D.C. Cranford played in his head. He had not taken Gichinga Mbura into custody. In the hour's ride from the mission to town, he had not determined where to start in explaining why he had not arrested the witch doctor. He cursed the fact that this murder had taken place while the district superintendent of police was away.

Cranford was a formidable man and too like Tolliver's own father, the Earl of Bilbrough. And Tolliver was many ranks beneath Cranford in the local hierarchy. Perhaps the district commissioner resented Tolliver's bloodlines; he lacked such distinction himself. Maybe that was why he went all toffee-nosed with Tolliver when he got the chance of it. Though jolly on the surface, the D.C. was completely certain of his own opinions and sure to be unyielding on the very point Justin wanted to make: that there was more to this murder than at first met the eye. Tolliver was not prepared to risk a native dying for a crime he did not commit. The

Tolliver family's antislavery position and the fervent conviction of his student days moved him more than ever. The natives must have the same consideration as an Englishman when it came to the law. He was not at all sure Cranford would see it his way.

On a whim, he turned away from Government House, went instead toward the bustling main street, and dodging a dogcart as he crossed, made for the offices of the Standard Bank of India. There he hoped a preliminary chat with Kirk Buxton would give him some ammunition to convince Cranford that they needed to eliminate the other possibility before arresting Gichinga Mbura.

The building that housed the third largest bank in British East Africa looked nothing like any bank Tolliver would have expected to encounter in his native York. There, banks were palacelike granite affairs meant to inspire absolute confidence in their financial solidity. This was a corrugated iron and wood building, the window frames painted a strange, muddy golden color. Only its stone stoop and heavy oak door gave any impression the bank might outlast the decade. The cramped interior smelled of pipe smoke and spicy hair tonic.

Tolliver asked the Indian clerk on the ground floor for Buxton and found him at a desk on a loft that overlooked the complete lack of activity below. The manager had an accounting journal open before him, but he was reading the day's copy of *The Leader*, the local paper. Gossip spread with the speed of sound in this town. Buxton might already know of Pennyman's death. But at least, he could not yet have read it in the newspaper.

"Halloo, Tolliver, my boy," Buxton called out as Justin

mounted the short wooden staircase. It was what all the sporting supporters called him. They admired his prowess at cricket and polo, and especially at tennis. And they thought their cheering for him at matches made him a chum. But calling him "my boy" also established the superiority of Buxton's social position, at least according to local rules. The thing Tolliver most disliked about the Protectorate—the only thing he disliked really—was that the officials hereabouts had, like Buxton, served first in India. They brought with them the strict social stratification of the Raj, a detestable snobbery based only on administrative rank and salary. When Justin first arrived to stay, he came as an English nobleman, albeit a younger son. He was welcomed everywhere and included in the best gatherings. But he soon had to give up the idea of farming. At the instigation of a fellow army officer, he had volunteered for the understaffed and desperate police force, at which point the social structure pushed him down into a limbo. His invitations to dine with the tonier settler families, especially those with eligible daughters, had all but dried up. The only reason he was still welcomed at the Nairobi Club was that they wanted him for their cricket team. Without sport, Tolliver would have been tantamount to a social pariah.

Buxton extended his hand, and Tolliver endured his crushing handshake. The banker was a broad, sturdy man, built more solidly than the office of the business he ran. Like almost every European settler, he wore a light-colored gabardine suit and a shirt of heavy cotton that was, in this climate, no more comfortable than Tolliver's uniform khaki.

Buxton indicated the chair beside his desk. "Can I offer you a whiskey?"

Tolliver took the seat. "No, but I would gladly take some quinine water." He nodded toward the bottle on the sideboard.

Buxton poured the water into a glass and, without asking, put in a splash of gin. He grinned at Tolliver. "Only thing that makes the vile stuff tolerable," he said and handed over the drink.

Tolliver took a sip. "Thank you. I've had a hot ride just now, coming back from the Scottish Mission." He watched Buxton's eyes, but Buxton acted as if he didn't know the news. Tolliver decided he would blurt it out when the moment was right and see how the man reacted when he heard.

Buxton's face took on an expression of apprehension. "The hospital? You aren't ill, are you? Have you fever? Do you think it's malaria?"

"No, no. I am afraid I have awful news. Dr. Pennyman has been murdered."

Shock froze Buxton's heavy aquiline features. "Good God, man. How could such a thing have happened?"

If he was acting, he was doing a good job of it. Tolliver sipped his drink and waited for the banker to ask a real question. Before he did, there came the sound of a woman's voice from below and a foot on the stair.

Lucy Buxton's face appeared coming up from the ground floor. Tolliver had met her before, danced with her once or twice at socials. It was evident that the news of her lover's death had reached her. The pale, normally perfect skin of her face was blotched with red, her eyes shone with tears; her usually rosy lips were pale and drawn. She barely looked at Tolliver, who had risen from his seat as soon as he saw her on the steps. Kirk Buxton remained seated. "You've heard," she said to her husband.

He showed none of the warmth with which he had greeted Tolliver, a man he barely knew. "Just now. Evidently, you have too."

Mrs. Buxton went straight to the credenza, poured herself a generous whiskey from the cut crystal decanter, and drank down a large gulp. She sank into a chair in the corner and stared into her glass.

Tolliver knew the couple would have preferred that he leave and let them get on with whatever hostilities might ensue, but in this situation he was a policeman and sometimes that took precedence over gentlemanly behavior. He had been tripped up in the past by watching his manners rather than the people he was investigating. This was a case of murder and finding the real culprit was the only way to do what he had joined the police force to do: help Britain bring peace and prosperity and civilization to this beautiful but savage land. Half-justice was no way to accomplish that.

Now that the lady, if she qualified for that description, was seated, he sat back down, sipped his drink, and waited to see how this man and wife would behave while being observed by an officer of the law.

He gleaned no clues, only embarrassment for his trouble. Buxton also helped himself to a very large whiskey. Lucy gave him a look she might have bestowed on a cockroach.

"Don't worry," her husband said with distain. "If I know you, you won't be in mourning for long."

"Quite right." She drained her glass.

Her husband took it, refilled it, and left it on the credenza for her to take. "Sometimes, Lucy," he said, "I think you should have been born a man."

She grabbed her drink. "That's funny. I always think that of you."

Her husband rounded on her and said, in too loud a voice, "Why don't you just go back to Berkeley Cole?" At which point, Lucy launched what was left in her glass at Buxton. Much of it ended up on Tolliver's uniform jumper.

He stood up and mumbled apologies, all of which were drowned out by the biting, venomous words they spat at each other. There was nothing for it but to leave. He would now have to go back to his room at the officers' barracks and change. He could not report to the D.C. smelling like a Scottish distillery. He was glad of the delay, though he was sure no amount of forethought would increase his chances of convincing Cranford of anything.

4.

Even in the highlands around Nairobi, far away from the torrid tropical climate of the coast, by noontime the heat became oppressive, so it was best to bury the dead quickly. The Kikuyu had no rituals connected with interment of a corpse. They ordinarily left bodies out in the bush; the hyenas cleaned up whatever remained of a tribesman after life was gone. The Christian converts at the mission, of course, learned to put their dead in the churchyard like any other believer in the one true God and in Jesus their savior, for they anticipated—one day—the resurrection of the body. The nonbelieving tribesmen thought such a hope ghoulish at best.

Barely eight hours after the discovery of his brother-in-law's murder, Clement McIntosh was arranging rites for the next morning. Nurse Freemantle had dressed the body in Pennyman's best frock coat and striped trousers, not worn since he had left Edinburgh. The mission boys were building a coffin and digging a grave.

Vera and her mother stayed close to one another, but mostly in silence. Her father was dismayed at the fact that his wife would not go to see her brother's body. He worried that this decision meant she was having a great deal of trouble dealing with her grief, and that it would weigh on her for a long time. "I do not want to say good-bye to him," was all Blanche would say in response to her husband's pleas.

All the many novels and stories Vera had read told her that women were the softhearted sex, that they were the ones who would express their emotions, wanted love and tenderness, were vulnerable to hurt. In her family, however, it was not that way at all. It was her father who wept when he listened to the mission children singing carols at Christmastide, who touched her hair and fondly kissed her cheek when he said goodnight, who wrote to her almost daily during that six months when she went to stay with her grandmother in Glasgow when she was ten years old. It was her mother who had insisted that she go "home," to her home, to be brought up a lady. And it was her father who responded to her pleading letters and decided to bring her back from that luxurious and intensely cold place, where the warmest beings were the dogs and the butler.

Vera sat on the veranda and did not grieve over her uncle. When he first arrived in the Protectorate, he had caused a stir in the country—a real Scottish doctor, someone to care for the colonists' ills with up-to-date medicine, unlike the doctor in Nairobi who was drunk most of the time. Josiah Pennyman was handsome and exceedingly charming, tall and slender, with shining dark hair, very like Vera's and her mother's. Otis had taken after their father—red-haired, florid, and big-boned. Uncle Josiah had a beautiful voice, perfect teeth, and a joke and a smile for everyone—white or black, gentry or civil servant, attractive or plain. Everyone loved him. But he was not a good person, and Vera had learned that he used that magnetism of his not just to conquer the souls of the natives but also the hearts of other white men's wives. Proper maidens were not meant to know such things, but not even Blanche McIntosh could shield Vera from knowing her uncle Josiah's reputation. And that was not the only reason she had to think of him as other than a good man.

She wished she could ask her father if a man like her uncle could have gone to heaven. Her father seldom mentioned hell in his sermons. It was more the promise of eternal happiness that he used to motivate goodness in his children and his converts. Surely, though, a just God would not welcome a fornicator like Josiah Pennyman to his side.

Vera got up and walked across the mission compound to the huts of the natives between the back of the hospital and the roadway that led to the railroad stop at Athi River. She went to the only person, other than her father, whom she ever sought out when troubled: Wangari, the Kikuyu woman her mother called her governess and her father called her nanny. The Kikuyu had no word for such a relationship. Wangari called herself Vera and Otis's *nyukwa*, their mother. Vera found the statuesque, vital woman outside her hut, peeling a pumpkin. Vera embraced her.

"You are sad, *mwari*," Wangari said.

"Not as sad as I think I should be," Vera said.

"That is sadder than just being sad."

Vera smiled. She had come here, as she always had even after she was grown, whenever she needed comfort and wisdom, and, as ever, Wangari started to dole them out even before Vera had a chance to sit down. "I think I am supposed to feel a dreadful loss, but I hardly knew my uncle. When I was in Scotland with my granny, he was away living in Edinburgh. By the time he returned to Glasgow I was packed and ready to come home. Since he came here I have never really had a conversation with him—just overheard what he spoke of with my parents. My heart does not know which way to turn."

With a quick stroke of her iron knife, Wangari split the pumpkin and began to scrape out the seeds. "What can I tell you that will help you choose your way?"

"The police investigator wants to think Gichinga Mbura killed my uncle."

Wangari's handsome brown face broke into a smile. "Is this the same English policeman who stirred up your blood by dancing with you?"

The very description stirred Vera's blood again, in ways she was sure a ladylike missionary's daughter was not meant to be stirred. "Yes, the same. Kwai Libazo told Captain Tolliver that Gichinga hated my uncle."

"Yes. That is true. He cursed your uncle. He despises all of us who have taken the water of Christianity. He says we betray our own people by taking the white man's God. But your uncle—" She broke off for a second and shook her head. She began to cut the pumpkin into large cubes, which she tossed into a clay cooking pot. "He says that your uncle robbed him."

"Robbed him of what?"

"Think, my daughter. Before your uncle came here, the old Scottish doctor worked to heal the people, but he was not loved by many. Your uncle was like a warrior king. The people thought he could do anything. All came to your uncle for medicine and many took the baptism because he had healed them or their children. Your uncle took away the people's fear and need for Gichinga Mbura."

"Do you think Gichinga hated my uncle enough to kill him?"

Wangari took a jug of the salty water the Kikuyu made by charring certain plants. She poured a little into the pot with the pumpkin and placed the pot over the fire burning in a ring of stones on the bare ground. "I cannot say. Mbura must believe that he was fighting your uncle for his own life. He does not know anything but the power of a medicine man. He was losing his position in the world."

"My uncle was killed with a Maasai spear. Do you think Gichinga Mbura would have used a Maasai spear to kill his worst enemy?"

"No," Wangari said emphatically.

"Never?"

"Never. He would risk losing his own powers if he betrayed the Kikuyu way with such an act."

5.

By the time Justin Tolliver had changed his clothes, he was called back to the police station. An Indian storekeeper was being held hostage at knifepoint by his brother-in-law over a business dispute. Tolliver much preferred a Hindu with a cutlass to facing the D.C. But soon the welcome distraction was settled and the brother-in-law disarmed and locked up until he cooled off. Evening had descended, in that sudden way it did in Africa. Tolliver knew he could no longer avoid reporting to Cranford, and he knew exactly where to find him at this hour.

As soon as Tolliver entered the Nairobi Club, he found the district commissioner descending the broad central stairway.

He approached. "Sir?"

"My boy! What have you found out about that hideous business of Pennyman?"

"I wonder, sir, if I might have a private word."

"Certainly. What are you drinking?"

"Gin and quinine water, please, sir."

"Always good to take your quinine." Cranford led Tolliver through the airy gentlemen's bar and stopped to order drinks from Arjan, the red-turbaned majordomo.

He took Tolliver into the small, dark-paneled library, which was blessedly empty. They drew leather armchairs into a pool of light under a standing hurricane lamp. It had a leather shade on which the big five game animals had been drawn in black. Other lamps were lighted in the corners.

Cranford took out a pipe and silver pipe tool and began his ritual of reaming out the bowl. "Tell me then, do we know which bloody savage robbed the good doctor of his young life?" He dumped the contents of the pipe bowl into a marble ashtray on the square mahogany table between their chairs. "I'll see him swing." He rapped the pipe on the tray with a sharp tap as if it were the gavel of a judge pronouncing the death sentence.

"Well, District Commissioner, I don't think this will be the open-and-shut case we wish it were. The circumstances don't lend themselves to an immediate conclusion."

Cranford paused to fill his pipe from his tobacco pouch. "We must have a quick conclusion. We can't ruin the reputation of the whole country by allowing people to believe that an important European doctor can be slaughtered with impunity. Find the native who owns the spear and let's get on with it, man."

A tall, slender servant in a white robe, brown brocade vest, and red fez entered. Tolliver and Cranford waited in silence while he drew a wide leather hassock in front of them and set the drinks tray on it.

Tolliver took up his glass but did not drink. "You see, sir, the natives thereabouts around the mission are Kikuyu, but the doctor was killed with a Maasai spear. The only native in the area who had a motive to kill Dr. Pennyman is a Kikuyu witch doctor. There is considerable doubt that he would have used a Maasai weapon to do the deed."

The D.C. lit and puffed on his pipe. Fragrant blue-gray smoke swirled around his head. It matched the color of his hair and of his eyes, which at this second were wide with disbelief. "Why ever not?"

Tolliver sat forward with his forearms on his knees, holding the cut crystal tumbler in both hands. "It seems his motive for the killing would have been a matter of honor. Evidently, he would never use the weapon of an enemy tribe to defend his honor."

"Poppycock! I know full well that a lot of those settlers down there in the Kikuyu territory ignore that tribe's faults. They say they are scoundrels only on surface, that deep down they are one solid mass of virtues. I disagree, completely. If you told me that story about a Maasai, I might be inclined to accept it. Your Maasai are a violent bunch of beggars, but they are courageous and straightforward. But except for their fecundity and a certain amount of intelligence, the Kikuyu are a blight on our society. They lie, they steal, they poison, they conspire, they are intensely lazy and callously cruel." He picked up his glass, drained the inch or so of whiskey in the bottom, and poured himself another from the decanter on the tray. He sat back and sighed. "No. Your murderer is the Kikuyu mumbo-jumbo man. You can be sure of it."

Tolliver kept his head down to hide his dismay. In a way, he tended to agree with Cranford that swift justice in such a case as this would be best. Local savages mustn't be allowed to harm subjects of the crown with impunity, but faulty justice was no way to truly civilize the African people. "Certainly, your conclusions are likely to be justified, sir, but hadn't we better prove we have the right man to show the natives the fairness of His Majesty's government?"

Cranford did not hide his annoyance. "Curse it, Tolliver, who else could have done such a dastardly deed but some barbarian with vengeance on his mind?" He looked into his empty glass as if he wanted another refill, but he did not take one.

Tolliver steeled himself for the outburst his next revelation was likely to provoke. "There is another possibility, as it happens, sir, and if we are to be completely thorough we must consider it." Tolliver took a deep breath and finished off his drink.

"Out with it, man."

"Pennyman, it seems, was having an affair with Lucy Buxton. Perhaps—"

"Now, just wait a minute."

Tolliver did just that, though the intervening silence made him want to say something, anything.

"You have heard of Pandora's box."

"Yes, sir, I have, but I—"

"She is a beauty, that Lucy Buxton."

"Yes, sir, she is, and very, very sad at the moment."

"You saw her out there?" Cranford looked into the bowl of his pipe, which had gone out.

"No, sir. I stopped by Buxton's office for a moment when

I came back to town, just to get an inkling of where he stood on this."

"And?"

"Mrs. Buxton came in, and they had a row."

Cranford sucked on his pipe, and looked into the bowl again. He tapped out the dead ashes and put the pipe in the breast pocket of his jacket. He looked disappointedly into his empty glass and rose. "Have it your way if you must, but do it with the least amount of noise and trouble. Eliminate that business as quietly and quickly as you can and get the native bugger into custody. The sooner we hang him for this, the less damage it will do."

"Yes, sir," Tolliver said with less enthusiasm than the D.C.'s exalted rank warranted.

Passing through the lobby of the club on his way to his quarters, Tolliver was dismayed to be accosted by Lucy Buxton, herself, tipsy and teary.

"I have to talk to you," she said. Before he could say a word in response, she drew him into the deserted tearoom, lit only by one lamp that sat on a table near the door. She threw her arms around him and started to weep openly.

He tried to pry her from around his neck. "Mrs. Buxton, please, may I get you some water? A coffee?"

She held on so tightly that he was sure he would hurt her if he tried to drag her off him. "You saw my husband, what a plain old fat man he has become? He was beautiful when we met. He's Irish, you know. He was handsome in that way that only Irish men can be."

She threw her head back and looked up at him. He had

his hands on her forearms. Her eyes were bright, the shade of blue he saw in his own mirror when he shaved. "Let us try to find you a coffee, Mrs. Buxton."

"You are not Irish, are you?"

"No."

"You are beautiful, though. You are very beautiful." She lifted her knee and rubbed it up the inside of his thigh.

He tightened his grip on her forearms.

At that moment, D.C. Cranford and Lord Delamere came to the darkened doorway. "Why in God's name are you doing that in here?" Delamere demanded.

"Tolliver," Cranford said with a smirk. "I will ask you to be in my office at eight in the morning. We will speak before we go to that confounded funeral."

6.

Once he had extricated himself from the alternately weeping and seductive Lucy Buxton, Justin Tolliver spent the night composing explanations he might deliver to Cranford and to his superior in the Protectorate's police chain of command, if it came to an inquiry that serious. He also had to fight off remembrances—which brought on desire—of his afternoons in the arms of Lillian, Lady Gresham, a woman not unlike Lucy in physique: fair and blond, statuesque, the type who would dress as Diana the huntress in a tableau. Just before dawn, his thoughts turned to Vera McIntosh, the antithesis of those hungry women—dark-haired, olive-skinned, slight, and graceful as a fairy forest creature.

When Ndege, his manservant, woke him at seven, he thought matters through again and decided he'd best not open the conversation by defending himself to Cranford in the matter of Lucy Buxton. He would let the D.C. speak his disapproval and then counter with the facts. There was enough gossip in the town about Lucy's drinking to make Cranford see sense.

By the time Tolliver marched into Government House and to Cranford's office on the cool and shaded south side of the building, he had changed his mind six or seven times on how to defend himself. Cranford gave him no time to further consider the topic. His grin when Tolliver entered soon turned to a chuckle, accompanied by dancing bushy gray eyebrows. "Bit enthusiastic, our Lucy girl, wouldn't you say, Tolliver?" Uncharacteristically, he reached his hand across the desk, as if Justin were an equal and not someone who should salute on entering.

Tolliver shook the D.C.'s hand and smiled, he hoped just a bit apologetically. Whatever else Delamere and Cranford's "discovery" did, it seemed to have raised his reputation with the higher-ups in British East African society.

"The African air does make the ladies frisky. I rather enjoy that myself." With a gesture, Cranford invited Tolliver to sit. He reached for the silver bell on his desk. "Shall I get us some tea?"

"No thank you." Tolliver left off the "sir." "I have just breakfasted."

Glancing over Tolliver's white dress uniform, Cranford got to the point. "You are going to the funeral, I see."

"Of course, sir. I am acquainted with the family."

"Take a squad with you to stand by until after the service," Cranford said. The jolly tone had left his voice. "Whilst you are out there, I want you to arrest that witch doctor."

Tolliver squared his shoulders. "With all due respect, sir, we have not investigated enough to conclude that he is guilty. As I said yesterday, it would be best if we gathered enough evidence to convict him as we would any Englishman. Conciliatory treatment will keep the situation calm. If we stir up resentment—"

Cranford shooed away his words. "The creature dresses up in feathers and dances around to drumbeats. What does he know of English justice? Confound it, man, the little barbarian killed our doctor. Does your conciliatory approach extend to letting them get away with murder?"

Tolliver wished he had asked for the tea. Sipping it would give him precious seconds to think at this moment. "Please, sir, I am not saying we should not prosecute the villain. Only that we should be absolutely certain we have the right man before we hang him. We want to show the natives how much better off they will be if they adopt our way of life. Isn't that right?"

Cranford grimaced. "I'll have none of these philosophical questions muddying up the waters, Tolliver. Strong measures backed by force are the only thing these treacherous bush dwellers understand. You must know that."

Tolliver knew he was on thin ice, but this was a point he could not concede. If he was not in his current line of work to make the world a better place, why was he here at all? He could have taken his father's advice and gone to New York to woo an heiress. "If we destroy an important tribesman, we may find ourselves putting down a rebellion. I know I owe it to you to do as you say, but please, sir, am I then forbidden to consider other explanations for what might have happened before we destroy Gichinga Mbura's life?"

Cranford stood up. He was dressed in black for the funeral.

It made him look like an executioner. "You can get your proof after he is in jail. Lock him up first and ask questions later. I state this as a direct order."

Funerals were meant to be sad, Vera knew, but there was something about this one that made it extremely so. It surprised her what a great number of settlers had come to the service. Practically every British person for miles around, and a huge contingent from the town had journeyed out to the mission. The intensity of the grief they expressed took her completely by surprise. Their sad faces contrasted with the surpassing beauty of the setting: with the flowering coffee fields, the delicate and deep greens of the hills and forests, luxuriant after the long rains. Everything around them was vibrant with life and fecundity, yet the mourners focused only on the wooden box, draped with the blue and white flag of the Church of Scotland and on her tragic-faced father, who could barely get out the words of the service.

In the chapel, the Kikuyu Christians, whom Vera knew to be saddened and terribly frightened, had yielded their customary places to the European settlers who crowded in on this singular occasion. The natives, wrapped in their cloths of red or orange-brown, stood at the sides and the back of the chapel, a phalanx of color framing the black-clad white people. Vera bowed her head, ashamed of her own amusing thought that if the natives had dressed in white, her uncle's funeral might have been attended by whites in black and blacks in white.

Vera had taken her mother's place at the organ. She pumped the bellows with her feet and played "Nearer, My God, to Thee," without glancing at the notes in the hymnal that stood before her on the oak music stand. She wondered again, as she had over and over during the past twenty-four hours, whether her arrantly seductive uncle could possibly be nearer to any god whatsoever. A god who would welcome him would be nothing like the benign, but chaste one her father had taught her to love.

At end of the prayers for the dead, the elders of the Scots community of Nairobi served as pallbearers. Her mother, silent tears running down her cheeks, followed the coffin out of the chapel to the tiny churchyard that separated the house of worship from the hospital. She stood beside Vera at the grave. As soon as her husband closed his prayer book, Blanche McIntosh took a handful of dirt, dropped it onto the coffin, and with only the briefest bow and no words at all for those who had come to comfort her in her grief, she left the assembled mourners and walked straight into her house without even a backward glance. That left Vera and her father to greet and console those who had, in theory, come to console them. The natives filed away to their circle of huts at the edge of the wood. The black-clad Europeans then stood about and whispered to one another.

There was a table covered with a snow-white linen cloth set up in the shade near the veranda. Two of the houseboys ferried between it and the knots of guests on the lawn with trays of teacups, glasses of lemonade, and little sandwiches. Vera was sure some of the people would have preferred a tumbler of something much stronger, but her father had refused that idea. "Not even a Scot as patriotic as I would serve whiskey at a funeral at eleven in the morning."

Justin Tolliver, whose presence Vera had noted immediately, from her perch on the organ bench, approached her and her father as they stood side by side. He was in the white uniform he always wore in her dreams. He spoke to her father so softly that she could barely hear what he said, but he looked at her all the while he was speaking. Then he came to her and took her fingers in his gloved hand, very much as he had the first time she agreed to dance with him. "I am so sorry for your loss," he said. "I wonder if I might come back later. Right now, I must go and meet Kwai Libazo at the stable. I have an order to follow."

The look in his eyes was disturbed, and the intensity with which he looked into hers disturbing. "Please do." She could feel how crooked and fleeting her smile must look.

"I will come back as soon as I can." He was still holding her hand. He bowed over it and for a second, she thought he was going to kiss it. But he let it go and marched away.

Vera turned away, shook hands with, and accepted kind words from D.C. Cranford, Lord and Lady Delamere, Berkeley Cole who was Lady Delamere's brother, and a newcomer who turned out to be a Swedish baron named Bror von Blixen-Finecke, just arrived in the Protectorate. Vera wondered why he had come to a perfect stranger's funeral. He took her hand and did kiss it. "Did you know my uncle?"

"We played cards a few times at the club." He had a lilting accent that went up at the end of his sentence, making it sound something between a statement and a question. Their little group went, then, to speak with some others near the refreshments table. Vera glanced at the house, half expecting her grief-stricken mother to be watching out from the window.

A few at a time, the mourners eventually made their way off on their ponies, carts, and buggies. When there were only a few left, Vera found herself alone. She took a plate of sandwiches and a cup of tea to the veranda to wait for Tolliver to return. She was sitting, wondering if the order he had to follow had to do with Gichinga Mbura, when Denys Finch Hatton left a group that was heading for the stable and came toward her.

"May I sit with you? I am in sore need of tea and you look as if you are just as much in need of sympathy."

"Certainly," she said. She started to stand to serve him the tea.

"No. No. I can help myself."

He was an athletic-looking man, not unlike Tolliver in that way, or her uncle. She knew that since he arrived a few months ago, he had been very much admired by all the settlers. Well, by all of the women, and if not all, by many of the men. He was handsome and graceful and had lovely manners. But there was something about the intense and intimate way he spoke to her that Vera found disturbing. As disturbing as she found being near Justin Tolliver, but not the same. There was nothing at all sinister about this man, and yet she felt in danger just being near him.

Assistant District Superintendent Justin Tolliver led Constable Kwai Libazo and his contingent of young native policemen along the path the farmworkers took to go back and forth to their village. "Do you think that Gichinga Mbura killed Josiah Pennyman, Libazo?" He hoped the other men did not understand English. Ostensibly, they knew the language, but few spoke it fluently. Kwai always spoke to them in Swahili or Kikuyu, but Tolliver could not be sure if the askaris understood what he was saying. He was trying his best to learn the native languages, but there were many of them, and they remained an absolute muddle to him. He feared his French teacher at Harrow had been correct when he said, "Tolliver, you are hopeless at foreign languages."

Libazo's back stiffened at the question. "I cannot know if Mbura is guilty, sir." He continued to march.

It was the kind of answer Tolliver expected. One could never get any of these boys to hazard a guess at anything. They were too afraid of being wrong. "Do you think it likely?" He heard too much frustration and even a tinge of fear coming out with his own words. He did not want to do an injustice. In fact, he feared that was exactly what the arrest he was about to make would be.

"Gichinga Mbura has a lot to lose," Libazo said. Enigmatic and vague as ever.

"It is going to be up to us to make sure justice is done here."

"Yes, sir." Libazo's answer was crisp and strong. As if he were mimicking the voice of the sergeant who had taught him the proper response to an officer.

The Kikuyu village near the Scottish mission was a neat collection of round huts thatched with grass surrounded by fields of maize, sweet potatoes, and sorghum. On the hillside above them goats and cattle grazed. Cooking fires burned in shallow pits in front of each doorway. On a few, clay cooking vessels sat on circles of stones. Acacia trees, with their flat umbrellas of foliage, shaded the hard-packed bare ground between the dwellings. There was not a person in sight. Tolliver was sure word of their coming had preceded them, though how that could be, he did not know.

"Which one is his?"

Libazo pointed to the other end of the village.

As they neared the witch doctor's doorway, Tolliver heard a kind of low, mumbling chanting. "Libazo, you come with me," he said quietly. "Tell the others to stand by the entrance and stop him if he tries to escape." He waited while Libazo translated. He unsnapped the flap that held his pistol in its leather holster, looked Libazo in the eye, and nodded. Together, they ducked their heads and entered the hut.

Gichinga Mbura stood swaying before a fire inside the small round room. The temperature in the hut was stifling. Mbura was no longer wearing the dark orange cloth he had had on the day before. In fact, he was hardy recognizable. He was naked except for a short grass skirt and a ruff around his neck of what looked like the remnants of a lace tablecloth decorated with colorful bird's feathers. He had smeared his dark brown face with a black paste of some sort, and then dabbed chalk-white designs on top of the black. There were three white lines above his nose and three on each cheek. Smeared above and below his lips were a white chalk mustache and beard. On his head he wore a crown of ostrich feathers that swayed gently with the movements of his body. He crooned to the fire in a low-pitched hum, as if he were adoring it or pleading with it. The sound seemed to carry a threat. He could have been chanting words or just random sounds. Tolliver could not tell. He slipped his hand under the flap of his holster and felt the metal of his pistol, but did not remove it. He was sure that what he was about to do, what he had been ordered to do, would not have a good outcome. "Tell him what we are here to do," Tolliver ordered Libazo.

Kwai spoke with a commanding tone, too loud for the small space, but his words seemed to have no effect whatsoever on Mbura. Libazo looked inquiringly at Tolliver.

"Repeat it," Tolliver said. He reached up and unbuttoned the brass button that held down the epaulette of his khaki shirt. He removed the coil of brown hemp cord that hung from his right shoulder.

Libazo spoke the lilting words even louder the second time. Mbura still paid them no mind, continued to sway and chant.

"Listen, man," Tolliver said, speaking to the witch doctor in English, keeping his voice even, having no idea if the savage would understand a word. "We are here to arrest you for the murder of Dr. Josiah Pennyman. You must come with us. If you did not kill B'wana Pennyman, you will not be punished." The last sentence fell out of his mouth before he quite knew it was coming.

Libazo looked shocked when he heard it.

Gichinga Mbura straightened his body, put his head back, and laughed—a gleeful, satiric laugh that seemed to come from deep within him. Against the deep black of his painted face, his perfect teeth looked bright and as white as milk, matching the streaks that decorated his face. His broad tongue was surprisingly pink.

Without being asked, Libazo spoke to him again, sharply, and after Mbura stopped laughing continued with some sort of long explanation. The only part Tolliver understood was that Libazo pointed to the holster, which immediately subdued Mbura's mirth.

Tolliver waited and thought about something the district superintendent of police had said to him when he was working hard to recruit Justin to the force—that whatever happened, the English would prevail, because they had firearms and the natives did not. It did not seem to Tolliver the proper way to convert the primitive world to civilization.

Mbura raised his fists, and for a moment, Tolliver thought he might have to use the pistol, but then the witch doctor held out his hands over the fire and opened them. A powder of some sort fell into the flames and startled all but Mbura by causing a green flare and a slight explosive sound.

Before Tolliver could recoup and react, Libazo, taller, more physically powerful than Mbura—leapt forward and took the witch doctor by the wrists. Kwai said something low and guttural that made the usually musical native language sound like the hiss of a snake. Mbura answered him in kind.

Tolliver took the cord and tied Mbura's wrists. He placed the end of the lead in Libazo's hand. Seeing Mbura's hatred and anger gave him hope that what he was doing might very well turn out to be the right thing. Tolliver had no idea what sort of god or gods these Kikuyu worshipped, if any, but it was clear from Gichinga Mbura's action that he was filled with exactly the sort of resentment Vera had described. The European settlers had brought their god as well as their rule of law to this place and in doing so had supplanted whatever deities endowed Mbura with his power over his people.

"Tie the cord to your belt, Kwai," he said. "Take him to the police station and lock him up. I will meet you there. And remember what happened when that boy who shot those other children was allowed to escape. If Mbura gets away from you, the district commissioner will assume you let him go on purpose, and I will have no way to defend you without District Superintendent Jodrell to back me up."

Before exiting, Tolliver looked around the hut and found two native spears. Their blades were as Libazo had described a Kikuyu spear point: leaf-shaped, but with a long taper into the shaft, more oval, whereas the blade that killed Penny-man was more triangular. He took the spears and handed them to Libazo. "Lock these up with the murder weapon in the storage room in the police station."

When they ducked out of the hut, Tolliver was blinded for a moment by the bright sunlight.

Ordinarily, the ground between the random arrangement of small, round thatched huts would be alive with noisy children, scolding mothers, the sound of grain being ground in stone mortars. Now, though it was no longer deserted, it was silent but for the breeze rattling through the fronds of the banana plants. At least two dozen Kikuyu stood, here and there, in twos or threes, still as statues—even the children—and watched with wide eyes as Tolliver and his squadron marched their medicine man along the path that led through the forest back to the Scottish Mission.

Tolliver saw Libazo and the other men off, with Mbura

in tow. "Go directly to the jail. Be seen by as few people as possible."

Libazo nodded knowingly. He understood the problem. Not only was he a black constable mounted on a pony, but his prisoner was mounted in front of him. Tolliver judged this the best method for ensuring that Mbura would not escape, but if Cranford got word of it, Tolliver would be on the carpet. The rest of the askaris would run alongside, as was the norm for natives with parties of black and white policemen on duty.

Tolliver went to the pump beside the stable, washed his hands, and rubbed the back of his neck with cool water. He dried off with his handkerchief and fitted his pith helmet back onto his damp hair. Vera McIntosh would give him a cup of tea and perhaps some lunch. The eggs and sausages and bread with marmalade that he had for breakfast had long since worn off. The soothing thought of sitting with her on her veranda and sipping tea quickened his step.

As he rounded the corner of the house, he heard her speaking in an earnest voice. "What right have we to walk in and act as if we own it?"

"We do that wherever we go," a man's voice responded with a laugh.

Tolliver hesitated and then grimaced. Finch Hatton. He was talking with Vera. For a second, Tolliver thought of turning on his heel and leaving her to the charming interloper. Ever since Denys Finch Hatton had arrived in the Protectorate, at every social gathering, he was there, taking an interest in her. Tolliver could not imagine what he was about.

Like Tolliver he was the younger son of a nobleman without enough in the way of funds to live well in England. Like Tolliver, he was here trying to make some sort of life for himself. But unlike Tolliver, he did not seem at all the type to take a serious interest in a missionary's daughter, however gentlemanly her reverend father might be. He'd marry a fortune. Or not at all.

Well, Tolliver was not about to leave the field to the charming Denys. He stiffened his spine and rounded the corner.

Both Vera and her guest were facing away from him. Finch Hatton was sitting in the noisy wicker chair, which was keeping quiet for him, as it had not for Justin. He was much too close to Vera McIntosh, leaning toward her in that insinuating way of his. He was making a sweeping gesture taking in the panorama of flowering coffee fields, cattle grazing on the far hillside, the meandering river, and across it, the vast plains, bright with new green growth after the rains. "Besides, who wouldn't want to own that?"

"The Kikuyu do not believe anyone can own it," Vera said. Her voice was wistful. "And now that the British government are here, it will never be the same."

Tolliver took off his hat, stepped forward, and cleared his throat. "Nothing ever stays the same." He heard the sharpness in his voice, which he had no way of controlling. She was changing before his eyes now that Finch Hatton was paying court to her.

"Tolliver," Finch Hatton said and extended his hand.

Tolliver took it.

"I have been here at the feet of my instructress, learning the lore and philosophy of the native," Finch Hatton said.

Vera turned her deep brown gaze on Justin. "May I offer you some refreshment? Some sandwiches? Tea?"

It was what Tolliver had been hoping for, but he could not remain with her while Finch Hatton hovered. Nor did he want to leave just yet.

"I would like to speak with the Reverend McIntosh."

"I will find him for you," she said and whisked through the door, in that light, quick way of hers, as if her feet hardly touched the ground.

"What do you make of this business with her uncle?" Finch Hatton asked as soon as she was out of earshot. "Everyone is saying it was the witch doctor."

Tolliver had no wish whatsoever to discuss his work with this man. They ought to have been allies. Finch Hatton had an easy way about him. Tolliver had thought they had a lot in common when they first met, but any hopes that they might be friends were blotted out by their rival interest in Vera McIntosh. In the past month, the chaps at the club had begun to notice how Tolliver prickled in Finch Hatton's presence. Tolliver joked with them that Denys was Eton and Oxford and he was Harrow and Cambridge. Besides, they played for different polo teams. Among British men, it was enough of an excuse to be plausible.

"We have just arrested Gichinga Mbura," Tolliver answered, despite himself. Word of that would get around soon enough in the tight society of European Nairobi. "The proof of his guilt is still in play, however." This also slipped out against his will. Instinct told him that the Kikuyu medicine man was not the murderer, but he had no reason to let his rival know that.

Finch Hatton's blue eyes narrowed. "If not, who?"

Tolliver got control of his tongue. Bringing up Kirk Buxton was much too much to reveal. He was saved by Vera's returning with her father.

Clement McIntosh was a big-boned and florid man with a lumbering walk, and as unlike Vera as Tolliver's father was unlike him. The missionary took Tolliver's shoulders in his hands and squeezed them in greeting. It was a purely fatherly gesture of the kind Tolliver had never received from his own papa. "My dear chap, what are we to make of this dreadful business?"

Tolliver put on his helmet and indicated the lawn that sloped toward the coffee fields. "Let's walk out for a moment," he said. "There are some things I wanted to ask you."

The missionary picked up a pale straw hat with a black band from a table next to the door, put it on, and followed Tolliver. Vera gave them a look of curiosity and disappointment that Tolliver enjoyed.

When they were across the lawn and close enough to the fields to hear the natives chanting as they worked, Tolliver stopped in the shade of a thorn tree. "I wanted to ask you some questions about your brother-in-law's private life," he said. "I thought it would not be proper to speak of it in the presence of Miss McIntosh."

"Quite right," her father said, as if he understood already what the subject of this conversation would be.

"On orders from D.C. Cranford, I have sent Gichinga Mbura to the jail in the Nairobi police station, but I am not convinced that he murdered Dr. Pennyman."

"Nor am I, if the truth be known."

"The truth is what I am after. I feel very strongly that if we do injustice to the natives, we will never succeed at what we came here to accomplish."

McIntosh looked into Tolliver's face not without surprise. "You are more sensible than many a policeman, and I could not agree with you more, my lad. Ours is not an extremely popular point of view with the settlers or the crown's administrators, however. Many would give lip service to the notion but find ways to ignore it when it suits their purposes."

Tolliver could not see how he could respond without criticizing his superior, so he redirected the course of the conversation. "Why is it that you are not convinced of Mbura's guilt, sir?"

"First of all, I agree with what Vera said about the spear. She knows whereof she speaks when it comes to the native way of life. She not only understands their style of thinking, but she sympathizes with it on many points."

"I have noticed that, sir." Tolliver did not always find her opinions acceptable, much less admirable, but he was not about to say that to her father. "What else?"

"Well, many of our fellow subjects of the king think that the natives are simple or even stupid. I do not think that at all the case. My experience with them tells me that they are canny and actually quite good at understanding where their best interests lie. I have known Gichinga Mbura since I built this mission, nearly twenty years ago. He is certainly capable of hating my brother-in-law with all his soul. I believe he did despise him."

"But not kill him."

"Mbura's quarrel with Josiah, if you can call it that, was

over who was seen as the more powerful by the natives here-abouts. Josiah was the kind of man who attracted admiration. His cures, of course, worked much better than Mbura's. Quite a number of Kikuyu came to the hospital to be treated, and at Josiah's urging stayed to be baptized. Also . . ." McIntosh paused. His eyes said he was reluctant to go on.

Tolliver waited.

"You see, my lad, my brother-in-law was a very confident man, sometimes overly so. He made it a point to ridicule Mbura's spells and potions. He made sport of him right to his face. Some of the other natives laughed at Mbura with Josiah."

"You are making it sound as if Mbura had every reason to kill him."

"Yes, I understand that, but first of all, it is a very grave thing for one of these natives to take a settler's life. Mbura did not seem the sort of man who would ever cross that line."

"Not even if he lost all control?"

McIntosh took off his hat for a moment and scratched the tuft of red hair on his balding pate. "That is another fallacy about the natives—that they are a bundle of unbridled emotions. I have never seen that in them, especially not the men. They are as controlled in their emotions as any Englishman, if not more so. And second, Mbura was very open in his resentment of Josiah. He made no secret at all of that. He may have wanted him dead, but he would not have killed him, especially not that way. He was sly enough to know that he would be suspected. If he planned to murder Josiah, he would have hidden his true feelings."

"The fact that it was a Maasai spear? Could he have done

it and been sly enough to use a rival tribe's spear to throw suspicion away from himself?"

"Perhaps," McIntosh said, but he shook his head at the same time, as if he did not believe his own word. "Mbura has faith in his own spells and curses. If he wanted to destroy Josiah, he would have tried to prove his power by doing it with a spell, not with a spear."

Tolliver gazed out upon the plains on the other side of the river. A herd of zebra mixed in with wildebeests had come out of the woods and were grazing on the grasses. He wanted to ask more details about the dead doctor's sexual exploits, but he did not know how to bring that up without blushing crimson. "Mrs. McIntosh spoke of Kirk Buxton. Is there anyone else who would have had a reason to kill him? Perhaps someone who had nothing to do with his—um—personal habits? Could it have been a Maasai, for instance? Do you think one of them could have had a reason?"

"I thought about that, too, in the sleepless nights I have just spent. Could Josiah have treated a patient who did not fare well? Such a situation might have aroused hatred against him, especially by a Maasai. But the Maasai do not come to the hospital. They have been moved away from this area, as a way of keeping down the tribal rivalries and maintaining the peace. No . . ."

McIntosh paused again. He, too, looked out at the scene before them. The sun had shifted just enough that the trees that spotted the plain were beginning to cast shadows toward the east. "I do not want to speak ill of the dead," he said at length.

"In my work, sir, we must speak of the dead so frequently

that it would be impossible to obey that maxim." Tolliver stood very still and waited. This was the sort of moment that often led to information that could be most valuable in solving a crime. Despite his upbringing, he was getting used to making other people uncomfortable.

McIntosh sighed and looked at Tolliver. "Josiah Pennyman was a fine doctor. He was a man who brought many souls to Christ by bringing them to baptism. But he was not a worshipful man. Nor a very good one." He paused and pursed his lips.

Tolliver kept his face neutral and his eyes on the scene in the distance.

The missionary lowered his head. "Josiah's god was not my god. His god was himself. He was completely self-indulgent when it came to his sexual appetite. He—"

"I don't hear much of that sort of gossip," Tolliver said quietly and then held his breath.

"Mrs. Buxton was the latest in a long line of his conquests, if you can call them that. It was his lack of self-control that forced him to come here in the first place. In a sense he was too good a doctor for this backwater. You know he took his training with the best doctors in Edinburgh. His patients were from the top echelon of Scottish society. He treated one of the princes when the royal family was at Balmoral. There was talk of his going to London to care for the royal family there. Then, his behavior became known—that he was taking advantage of his position to seduce the young women of the families he cared for. There was hardly a house that he visited where he did not use his— He had to leave the country or be put in the dock. He came here to retrench."

McIntosh's voice had become more and more strangled. When Tolliver turned to look at him, there were tears in his blue eyes. He looked back toward the house. Tolliver continued to face the view. The grazing animals were disappearing back into the woods.

McIntosh got control of himself. "The Scottish Mission Society thought they were doing us a great favor by sending us such a skilled physician. We could not refuse him without revealing to them why. Blanche could not bring herself to do that. I prayed Josiah would have learned to overcome his venal self. God is stronger than the devil. But He does not always reveal Himself to us in that way."

Tolliver glanced into the missionary's eyes. "I am sorry to say, sir, that in my line of work, I almost never see that side of God."

"I watched him like a hawk with Vera," McIntosh said. He was looking at the ground again now, kicking at a clump of weeds like a schoolboy who'd been reprimanded. "Her mother and I both did."

Apprehension pricked the back of Tolliver's neck, but he gave no voice to the question in his mind.

McIntosh squared his shoulders and gave Justin a brief smile. "No, lad. No. He did not touch her. We can thank our merciful God for that at least."

Tolliver wondered if Vera's safety didn't have more to do with her parents' watchfulness than with the mercy of some faraway deity. "Do you know which of the settler women he was involved with, besides Lucy Buxton, that is?"

"No other that I know of. When it was going on, I tried not to think about it. Mrs. Buxton came to see him too often, supposedly about some ailment—trumped up if you ask me. That woman looks the picture of health." He kicked at the weed again. "But I must say she looked a good deal better when she came out of the hospital than when she went in." His face took on an embarrassed look, half grimace, half grin. It was the kind of thing men might joke about among themselves, but not under these circumstances.

"But there were others?"

"Not that came to the hospital here to see him as often as Lucy Buxton. But he was out all night quite a bit. Can't see how he could go on with his work considering how little he seemed to rest. But he did, somehow."

"He didn't keep a room at the club." It was a statement, not a question.

McIntosh shook his head and turned to glance back at the house.

Vera was coming toward them. She wore what all the women here wore in the daytime—a double terai, a double-thick dark brown felt hat, gabardine breeches that looked two sizes too big covered by a sort of khaki kilt, a loose tan shirt, and heavy boots. All that cloth was meant to protect them from sunstroke. Tall, statuesque, fair women like Lillian Gresham and Lucy Buxton managed to look vital and strong in such clothing. Vera looked like a lovely girl playing Julia in a local version of *The Two Gentlemen of Verona*, dressing up in boy's clothing to follow her love. Tolliver could not understand why he would desire such a person. But he did. Far too much.

She took her father's hand and stood next to him holding it. "Papa, you look done in."

"That I am, lass. I think I will go and have a lie down."

They stood and watched him walk up the slight slope toward the house. His carriage was the picture of a soldier leaving a dreadful defeat.

"Would you come to the veranda and have something to eat and drink?" Vera asked.

"Finch Hatton?"

"He's gone." Her voice was perfectly neutral.

"Then, yes," Tolliver said, aware that his tone of voice had revealed more than he wanted but relieved he was not blushing.

Back in town that evening, Tolliver checked on Gichinga Mbura in his cell at the police station and then went to report to Cranford, who, true to form, insisted that the case was solved and that they could proceed to try and then as quickly as possible execute the culprit. Tolliver managed to convince him that they needed to follow protocol and procedure in order to satisfy the home authorities. The last thing Cranford, or the governor of the Protectorate for that matter, wanted to do was run afoul of their overseers in the colonial administration in London, whom officials on the ground in Africa considered bleeding hearts and a thorn in the side of the king's hardworking empire builders.

While Tolliver was changing for dinner, a boy arrived at the barracks, asking for him. Ndege went to the door and brought back a blue envelope. The script that said "A.D.S. Justin Tolliver" was decidedly feminine. He tore it open, wondering what Vera would be trying to tell him. Instead he read,

"Meet me at the Carlton Lounge tomorrow for luncheon." It was signed "Lucy."

Tolliver shoved the note into the pocket of his jacket and dropped his hands so Ndege could tie his tie.

7.

The next day, a Sunday, Kwai Libazo dressed as he would to visit his mother, in a Kikuyu's traditional dark orange cloth shuka, but he sported a tan linen jacket over it and instead of bare feet, wore the leather sandals that were part of his police uniform. He thought he looked quite handsome.

But he was not going to visit his mother's village. Instead of taking the train one stop north from Nairobi to Kikuyu, he spent his half a rupee to go one stop south to Athi River. From that station, it would be just a three-and-a-half-mile walk on the red dirt road to the Scottish Mission and its neighboring tribal village. As it turned out, one of the mission boys driving an oxcart gave him a ride, and he arrived at the mission workers' village half an hour sooner than he would otherwise have expected.

He spoke to Kamante and to Gichinga Mbura's brothers, and to the old women of the clan that lived there. The men told him, as expected, what they wanted him to believe. The old mothers, who knew everything, said very little to him at all except to remind him that he worked for the British. One of them laughed a gleeful cackle. "Who will speak to you now, Kwai Libazo? You were not born a fish. You were not born a chicken. But at least you were born an African. But now you have given yourself to the British for wages. So now you are not black and you are not white. No one will talk to you."

Libazo knew another person who did not really belong to any group: Vera McIntosh was the person he must speak to because she was nearly as much of a stranger in the world as he. She was born here so she was not a settler, but not an African either. He could tell by the way she looked at the British people that she did not feel herself to be one of them. After her uncle's funeral, he had watched from under a tree at the edge of the lawn and seen how the settlers had spoken to her with false expressions on their faces, as if they expected her to say the wrong thing and were bracing themselves not to show their disapproval. She could not read what they were thinking and did not know how to play with them. Looking from far away was often the best way to see the reality of a place.

He left the Kikuyu village and went first to Wangari—who had been Vera McIntosh's second mother—to secure an introduction to the lady. He took the path from the Kikuyu village to the huts where the house staff lived, behind the hospital building. He found Wangari tending her sweet potato plants in the shamba.

She was a handsome woman, still lithe; she seemed very much younger than Vera's actual mother. She was the third wife of a prosperous man, who had sold many, many daughters and now had many goats and cattle to show for it. When

Kwai greeted her, she gave him a puzzled look at first, but then seemed to understand what he wanted. She led him to the open ground in front of her hut and offered him water in a pottery cup. He took it and they sat on the ground in the shade of tall trees at the edge of the forest.

"You are a constable now, Kwai Libazo." She spoke in Kikuyu, but she used the British word to describe his work, since there was no such word in the native tongue.

"Yes, *nyina*." As a mark of respect, he addressed her with the Kikuyu word for another person's mother.

"Being a policeman must be hard work for you."

"Yes, it is very hard."

"Why do you do it?"

"You, too, work for the white man." A white man would consider his answer rude, he thought. He was beginning to learn how many ways of answering a question the British thought to be rude. But the African people knew many ways to answer a question, or to avoid answering it. They thought it rude to answer when the response would be hurtful.

Wangari smiled. She did not think him rude. "I took care of his children. I came to nurse Miss Vera when my first child died. My son Kibene shared my milk with her brother. She still comes to me when she is troubled."

"She is very troubled now."

She paused a moment and nodded, but not in complete agreement, he could see.

"It is her brother, I have come to ask about," he said. "He is not here. There is no talk of him."

"No," she said, matter-of-factly. "He went away on a shooting safari two days before the doctor died. Kibene went with him. They rode to Too-many-hats' farm." Too-many-hats was the nickname the local people had for Richard Newland, because of his habit of changing his hat several times a day. "The safari party left from there." She nodded her head toward the end of the path that led to the field-workers' village. "Some of the local men have also gone as porters and gun bearers."

"Ah, I see," Libazo said. "The district commissioner believes Gichinga Mbura killed the white doctor. Do you think that, too?"

"Gichinga hated the doctor because the doctor laughed at his dances and called his spells mumbo jumbo." She said the English words with which the British belittled tribal ways.

"Do you think the English doctor was right? That the medicine man has no real medicine?"

"Scottish," she said and grinned. "They prefer to be called by their own tribal names. You know that they have tribes, too, like us."

He nodded. "Some tribesmen become angry because the settlers think their English tribe is the best in the world. But all people think their own tribe is the best."

Wangari raised her eyebrows, but she smiled at him. He repeated his question about Mbura's powers. This time he wanted the kind of answer a European would expect. She eyed him, not entirely trusting why he asked to know this. He sipped his water and waited.

"I am a Christian now." She was not going to make it easy.

He just sat and waited, looking into the empty cup and bearing the silence.

Finally she sighed and gave in. "I believe the doctor cured the hurts of the body better than Gichinga Mbura. But I think our medicine man does more for the hurts of the spirit."

It was not what Libazo expected to hear. "Medicine men can hurt people's spirits, too." He had seen strong, healthy Kikuyu and Maasai wither and die because they believed they were cursed by a medicine man.

"You are right, Constable," she said. She made it a point to address him by his title and not his name, but her voice was gentle, her eyes sympathetic, as if she knew that he had been hurt in his spirit by a curse against a child who was not Kikuyu and not Maasai.

"Sometimes," he said, "hard work is what a man needs most." And he asked her to take him to speak to her white daughter.

Justin Tolliver shook his head at his own reflection. He had shaved carefully, brushed his dark blond hair till it stayed slicked back and in place and looked almost brown. He reached for the bottle of lime tonic on the shelf above his circular shaving mirror but thought better of using cologne this day and withdrew it. It was the sort of thing a man would put on his face if he wanted to kiss the girl he was about to meet.

He had spent the morning playing tennis and distracted by thoughts of Vera McIntosh, and also of Lucy Buxton. The celibate life he had led since coming to British East Africa in the fall of the previous year was playing on his nerves. He would not risk catching a disease from an easy woman.

Such ailments were all too prevalent here. But his body still had its desires. And, in physique, Lucy was too like Lillian Gresham, who had provided such delectable pleasures in his past days in Nairobi.

Lillian had also been another man's wife. Justin knew that many of his fellow soldiers much preferred the carefree satisfactions of taking their pleasure wherever they found it. He had reined in his libido and not only because he feared venereal disease. He wanted deeper satisfaction, lovemaking that meant more than momentary release. The match he had played that morning reminded him of how far from certain he was ever to find such a love. His tennis opponent that morning had been Denys Finch Hatton. The match had been fierce. They should have been making friends, given their common love of sport, but their rivalry over Vera reigned paramount in Tolliver's mind.

The other settlers might admire Finch Hatton a great deal. But Tolliver could only resent his annoying attentions to Vera McIntosh and found nothing much to like in the man.

If the morning's tennis match had been a struggle for supremacy in that regard, Finch Hatton would have won the territory. Tolliver had played with all his heart and strength, to deuce and back to game point, over and over, winning and losing game after long game, set after set. In the end he lost the match.

He reached for the lime tonic water on his shaving stand and patted some on his face after all. Lucy Buxton was beginning to seem more and more like the antidote to being crossed at every turn.

Tolliver left the barracks and turned right, slightly uphill and onto Government Road toward the Carlton Lounge. The day was bright and the early afternoon sun had burned off the cool of the morning. The street was thronged with Hindu traders and Africans carrying small purchases. The heat was gathering like an army on the attack.

In front of the Indian and Swahili shops that lined the street, poles and cables lay along the green verges between the red dirt walkway and the red dirt road. A sign declared works being done by the Nairobi Electric Lighting and Power Company, which was wiring the town. But the Hindu workers who strung the cables were nowhere in sight on a Sunday, when work stopped no matter what the workers' religion. Except for himself and two or three other settlers, also making their way under the eucalyptus trees to luncheon, the hot back street was deserted.

The entryway of the lounge provided a welcome cool. The dark wood-paneled bar was full of European men— government functionaries, bankers, businessmen. At the back of the building in the main dining room, some tables were already filled with women in daytime frocks, light and summery as any group of women in England might look on the finest day of June. Their escorts, like Tolliver, wore tan or white linen, but in too many layers to give them any relief from the weather.

To Justin's dismay, though it was fifteen minutes before the appointed time, Lucy Buxton had already arrived and taken a table. She stood up and called to him from near the doors that opened onto the patio. Her gauzy dress clung to her curves. The distress of the other day was gone from her lovely face. When she raised her hands to wave to him, her breasts rose, too, and Tolliver imagined them bared. He was in terrible trouble of forgetting himself.

"I've ordered you a gin and quinine water," she said without further greeting. She sat, and he took the chair opposite hers. There was quite enough enthusiasm in her eyes. She did not need to smell his cologne water just yet.

"I must say you look just as fetching in a linen lounge suit as you do in your khaki uniform," she said.

He should have complimented her on her ensemble, but he blushed instead and stared down at the green glass tumbler that stood at the place next to her. She picked it up and handed it to him. Her hands were lovely. "Go on. Drink it. It will do you good. Must take our quinine." She raised her own glass to him and drank. He did, too. Despite its reputed medicinal purpose, the drink was mostly gin. Now he was in danger of getting drunk as well as letting himself be seduced.

This meeting can serve as part of my investigation into the murder of Josiah Pennyman, he thought. But he knew full well what a sham of an idea that was. It would take a lot more gin before he would be able to fool himself into believing that. No matter what the demands of his work, he would not have the audacity to bring up a former illicit liaison with this lady who was trying to seduce him. Especially one whose offer he was so sorely tempted to accept. He warned himself to hide how willing he might be. He took another gulp of his drink.

When he looked across the table and into her round blue eyes, she lowered her voice and said the last thing he expected. "I fancy that you think my dolt of a husband killed Josiah Pennyman in a fit of jealousy."

He sputtered and nearly choked.

She leaned toward him. He could see halfway down the front of her dress. "Well, if that is what you think, you are wrong. Kirk wouldn't. He doesn't have enough fire in him to get that worked up about anything." She considered her statement and then said, "Well, not about sex with me anyway." She drained her glass and smiled beguilingly. "About money, perhaps."

Tolliver realized that he had not spoken since he arrived. He still could not. What with her breasts, the sparkle in her eyes, and the shocking things she was saying, he could not put a coherent sentence together.

She waved her empty glass at a passing waiter dressed in a dark jacket, white pantaloons, and snow-white turban. He bowed and took away the glass. "The same again, please Binder. And for my friend as well."

"Well, darling," she said once the waiter had gone away, "my husband is not much use to me, as a woman, if you know what I mean." She leaned over the table again and made a gesture with the fingers of both hands toward her torso. "You don't think I should allow all this to go to waste, do you?"

Tolliver might have said no, but he finished his drink instead. If the glass had contained any quinine water, he couldn't taste it. And gin, though it might be known to make quinine tolerable, could not ward off malaria all on its own. It was, however, sure to make him drunk if he continued to consume it in such quantities on an empty stomach. He reached for the menu that lay on the table between them. "Perhaps we should order something," he suggested.

She smiled indulgently. "Yes," she said. "Men your age

are always hungry, aren't they? Must keep up your strength." She hiked her chair forward. Tolliver felt her toes trying to crawl under his left trouser leg, and he wondered how many drinks she had drunk before he arrived. He looked at her, and she actually batted her eyelashes at him. Perhaps it was the alcohol she was using to drown her grief over the loss of her lover, but she portrayed the picture of a music hall comedienne's farcical seductress. Suddenly any temptation he felt from her evaporated.

He shifted his entire attention to the bill of fare, which was precisely the menu he would have expected to find on offer at a dining establishment in Cambridge or Surrey— roast beef, roasted chicken, lamb stew, all one hundred percent English.

When Binder returned with the drinks, Tolliver ordered the chicken, to avoid the Yorkshire pudding, which came with the roast beef. This far from home it would never please a true Yorkshireman like him.

"The same," she said, handing the menu to the waiter. "And a bottle of claret," she added. Her toes seemed to be trying unsuccessfully to pull down his sock, which reached to his knee. There was a pleading look in her eye of such intense desperation and pending disappointment that he could not look at her.

He was saved when a flurry of activity at the doorway to the dining room distracted them and Lord and Lady Delamere entered. They approached the table. Delamere's words from two nights ago at the club rang in Tolliver's memory— "Why the devil are you doing that in here?" The toes were removed from Justin Tolliver's leg.

"Oh, jolly," Lady Delamere said. "You won't mind if we join you."

Tolliver rose to his feet. "Not at all," he said, trying to sound like a man who knew how to keep his composure. "We have just this moment ordered."

"The chicken, I hope," Delamere said.

"Oh, Hugh," Augusta Delamere said, "must you be such a creature of habit?" She took a seat, and she and Lucy Buxton immediately put their heads together and began to discuss how exhausting it was finding and having to break in new servants. Once the Delameres had ordered, everyone who passed the table stopped to talk to Lord Delamere—about the fine rains that year, about land speculation, and yesterday's polo match. One of them also brought up "the dreadful business of that barbarian murdering poor Josiah Pennyman."

Lord Delamere gave an all but imperceptible shake of his head and quick, surreptitious gesture of his thumb in the direction of Lucy, who was still deep in conversation with his wife. The passerby raised his eyebrows, coughed, and beat a quick retreat.

The waiters appeared with their plates, and Binder poured the wine. The conversation at the table quieted while they began to eat. Lucy sipped wine more than she picked at her food.

"Lovely claret this," Lady Delamere said.

"So it is." Delamere lifted his glass and admired the color of the wine. "Must tell Berkeley to lay in a few cases for us. Great connoisseur, my brother-in-law." He directed his last sentence at Justin Tolliver. Lady Delamere gave her husband an arch look.

Tolliver, who was trying to drink as little wine as possible after the two double gins, then remembered what that warning look was about. In that dreadful argument between Kirk Buxton and Lucy, Buxton had intimated that Lucy had also been involved with Lady Delamere's brother, Berkeley Cole. Could Cole, a bachelor and one of the best-liked members of the Protectorate's social set, have been jealous enough to commit murder when his lover took up with the handsomer Scottish doctor?

Justin looked across at the lovely Lucy, who had been staring into her wineglass. She raised her glance to his. Her eyes were filled with pain that had not been there before anyone mentioned Josiah Pennyman and Berkeley Cole.

The noon meal was already over at the missionary's house south of the town. There, Vera McIntosh followed Njui through the back of the house. The houseboy had come to tell her that Constable Kwai Libazo had asked for her at the back door. "I do not think, Msabu, that he is here on business. He is not wearing his uniform."

Vera could not imagine what, besides the business of her uncle's death, could bring the African policeman to her door. When she went out, Libazo was standing at attention in the kitchen yard with Wangari at his side. The stance made him look strange, as did the European man's jacket he wore over his typical Kikuyu shuka. He wore sandals, which in her life Vera had never seen on an ordinary tribesman's feet. From the looks of him, she had surmised that he was not a full-blooded

Kikuyu. There was something Maasai about him, too. And in that getup he was neither purely a tribesman nor a policeman. Wangari bowed, said nothing, and went away.

"Hello, Constable Libazo," Vera said as if he had been properly introduced to her. Native workers were never introduced to Europeans. Most settlers acted as if they were invisible, or machines, but not people.

"I would like to speak to you, Msabu, if it would not trouble you too much. I am sorry to interrupt your time. I need to— I have some—" Vera wasn't sure if it was the fact that he was uncomfortable speaking English or the unusual fact of his calling on her that made his speech so hesitant.

"I will speak with you," she said in Kikuyu and smiled at him. She wished she could invite him to sit on the veranda, to take a cup of tea with her. At moments like this, she felt neither fish nor flesh herself. She could sit down and eat and drink with any white person no matter how intimidating or unsympathetic to her, but she could never invite a native to a comfortable conversation. It just wasn't done, her mother told her. Yet she felt much more comfortable with the tribespeople, who, after all, had been her only playmates growing up. She would much rather sit on her veranda with Kwai Libazo than with Lady Delamere or Mrs. D.C. Cranford. European women spent more time looking disapprovingly at her fingernails than at her face, which was probably equally dirty anyway. She glanced at the windows of the house. Neither her mother nor her father was looking out at her. "Come with me," she said.

She walked between the house and the mission office to a tree that stood on a little knoll between the woods and the house workers' huts. It was one of those days when the light was remarkably beautiful—silver, not the usual golden yellow. The blue sky was streaked with long wisps of clouds and the banana plants in the workers' shamba, the stone hospital, the river at the bottom of the coffee plantation all seemed to glow and shimmer. "Sit with me here, Kwai Libazo," she said. She took a place in the shade of the tree on the log that Joe Morley, the plantation manager, had placed there for her, so she could come here to sit and read or sketch. Libazo sat on the ground before her with his back to the loveliness of the view. "What is it that you have come to talk to me about?" she asked.

Libazo crossed his legs and put his elbows on his knees. He was tall and powerfully built and though she sat up on the log, his face was just about even with hers. "I have a fear about Gichinga Mbura," he said. He reached out and pulled up a blade of grass. He glanced into her face and looked away. His English was quite good. Whoever the missionary was that had taught him had done a very good job of it. Most natives who could, usually spoke English to settlers, even to those who could, like her, speak their native tongue. She thought it was a point of pride with him. That he liked to show how well he did it.

She respected his choice. "You fear that Gichinga Mbura is being wrongly accused?" It was what Tolliver had said he also thought.

"Perhaps he is not guilty. But that is not what I came to

speak to you about. When we went to arrest him yesterday, he was in a trance."

It was what the medicine men did when they were communicating with the spirits—good and bad. "Did he speak in the trance?"

"I knew you would know why this is bad," Libazo said. "Yes. He put a curse on Justin Tolliver." He crushed the blade of grass between his fingers and flicked the remains of it away.

A shiver went up Vera's back despite the denial that rose to her lips. "Those curses work only if the victim believes in them. I doubt very much that Captain Tolliver would believe in Gichinga Mbura's magic."

"I did not tell Captain Tolliver." The way Libazo said it, Vera saw that he had not translated the curse because he wanted to protect Tolliver from it.

"So, then he is safe," she said.

"I hope so, Msabu," Libazo said. "When I was taking Gichinga Mbura into town to the jail, I told him that his words did not reach Tolliver's ears. I wanted to tell him that his curse was useless, but he laughed and said it did not matter if Tolliver heard the curse, that when he threw some powder into the fire, he saw shock in Tolliver's eyes. That was the curse entering into Tolliver's heart. It frightened me, because I, too, saw the shock in Tolliver." He hung his head and pulled another blade of grass.

"You respect Captain Tolliver?" It was half a question, half a statement. Vera did not know why she cared what this relative stranger thought of Tolliver. How could that matter to her? But it did matter, and she wanted to know. "Tell me what you see in him?"

Libazo shifted his position so that he was no longer facing her, but looking away in the direction of the banana plants behind the workers' huts. "He does not understand Africa," he said, "but his heart is good." He looked sidelong, right into her eyes. "His heart is very good."

For whatever reason, Vera found Libazo's pronouncement disturbing. A British policeman would have to be very good indeed to elicit such a compliment. The last time Tolliver was here he had acted cool and distant—all business. She did not want her heart to leap upon hearing what a good man he was. She stood up. The constable jumped to his feet, like a proper English gentleman.

"Please, Constable Libazo, do not tell Captain Tolliver of Gichinga Mbura's curse." She did not think it at all likely that Tolliver would put any store by what he would undoubtedly call mumbo jumbo, but she had seen the medicine man's curses work. She wanted to make sure Tolliver would not be Mbura's victim. Not knowing he had been cursed could not hurt Tolliver, but there was the slightest chance that if he did know of it, the spell could work against him. Vera did not want to leave that to fate.

If Vera could have seen the intimate way Lucy Buxton slipped into the chair next to Tolliver after the Delameres left the luncheon table, and the way she put her lovely white hand on his knee beneath the tablecloth, she might have thought twice about preserving him from the medicine man's curse.

Before leaving the table Lord Delamere had surprised Tolliver by whispering that he would be glad to discuss the matter of the Pennyman murder investigation any time Tolliver would like. Delamere then followed his wife and most of the other Sunday luncheon diners as they drifted out the French doors to take chairs on the shaded patio and under the trees on the lawn beyond, where they drank coffee and continued with their chat about the prospects of harvesting minerals from Lake Magadi or complaints about the vagaries of rule from the government in London, which they invariably referred to as "home."

To Lucy's consternation, even after all he had drunk, Tolliver was still sober enough to resist the spell the lovely lady in the gauzy frock was attempting to cast. She rose from the table with a languid air.

He stood quickly, and were the truth known, felt quite lightheaded with the sudden motion. That surprised him. Granted he had not indulged to this extent in a long while, but even as a lad at Cambridge, he was able to hold his alcohol better than this. He had drunk two gins, but that shouldn't have been enough to have this effect. He must have drunk more of the claret than he imagined, and all that food he had eaten had not been enough to absorb it.

"I am sorry, Mrs. Buxton," he said. "I have very much enjoyed this luncheon, but I do have urgent official matters to attend to."

Lucy studied him for a moment and then bowed awkwardly

almost as if she were trying to curtsy. "It is Sunday, Mr. Tolliver," she said with surprising sobriety, "and you are wearing a linen lounge suit. What 'official business' could be calling you away?"

"Begging your pardon, but I have a prisoner—" He cut himself off, remembering just in time to avoid bringing up a murder that seemed to have all but broken her heart, and that might have been the result of her affair with the dead man. "Enforcing the law must happen every day. It does not take the Lord's day off." He sounded like a prig, and he knew it.

She turned and walked before him to the desk between the lounge and the dining room, where guests saw to their tab. Though Lucy Buxton had invited him, Tolliver stepped forward to pay the bill.

"You have been Lord Delamere's guests," the desk clerk said.

Tolliver was about to feel guilty and obligated over that when Lucy smirked and said, "Well, it's about time." She turned and kissed him quickly on the mouth. "I hope one day, you'll change your mind," she whispered and slipped away to the powder room. Tolliver went to the gents, gave up an unconscionable amount of water, and loosened his belt a notch. In the mirror, he felt as if he was seeing a stranger.

He went out toward the men-only bar. He needed coffee almost as badly as he needed to escape Lucy Buxton's sad desperation. After downing two strong coffees in rapid succession, he took his hat from the hatcheck boy and made his way out to the street. The sun was still high and hot as blazes, bearing down with a vengeance on the facade of the Carlton Lounge. The street was empty.

Tolliver was crossing onto the shady side and formulating a plan to change into his uniform and go to the jail to question Gichinga Mbura, when, without warning, he fell into a dead faint and collapsed facedown in the middle of the road.

8.

"Malaria, I imagine," D.C. Cranford was saying to Clement McIntosh two days later. They were sitting on McIntosh's veranda, facing the marvelous view. "One of the town doctors is seeing to him. He's keeping to his room. No point in moving him here." He gestured toward the mission hospital building, that had for nearly a week now been without a doctor to run it. "And you know how beastly malaria is? Could take him a while to be up on his feet again. But I wanted to assure you that the matter of your brother-in-law's death, though it will have to be somewhat postponed, will be seen to. That savage will taste British justice."

Vera was making a show of playing the dutiful daughter, serving the tea and cakes because it gave her a chance to listen in on her father's conversation with the district commissioner.

"I hope it is not malaria," her father said. "It can turn to black water fever all too easily. I will pray for Tolliver. And for Gichinga Mbura, too. That poor savage does not know the evil of his ways."

"Quite right," Cranford said. "But that mustn't stop us doing away with him for killing the good doctor. Have to be made an example of, these bloody barbarians." He glanced at Vera, as if in the hopes that she had not heard him fairly bellow out a rude word. Cranford was, to Vera, the worst kind of Englishman: entirely certain of every opinion he held, however misguided, and inclined to express them in a voice like a trumpet.

She bit into a buttered muffin. It was as good as the muffins in her grandmother's house in Glasgow. And no butter in Scotland could compare with that of the mission's cows.

The D.C. kept on with his opinions. "Rum business, this delay, but Tolliver is right about one thing. Those lily livers in the home office will have us laid out in lavender if we give you and your family satisfaction before we have turned over every stone looking for anyone else we might accuse. I am afraid I have to let the idealistic young policeman play out his hand. Be unwise to stir up London over this."

He pressed on the arms of his wicker chair, which squealed and creaked as he hoisted himself into a standing position. He took a gold watch out of his vest pocket. "Must be off. Catching the train back to Nairobi. Eleven twenty. Can't stand the roads in the buggy. About killed my kidneys on the way out here. I'll send it back empty. Anything or anyone you want to send back to town in it, just say. Glad to put it at your disposal."

"No, thank you," her father was in the course of saying, when Vera chimed in.

"I wonder, Father, if I might take District Commissioner

Cranford up on his offer and go into Nairobi with Nurse Freemantle. Perhaps she can be helpful to Captain Tolliver." She looked down at her teacup, hoping that she seemed like a demure Scottish girl, not like a woman desperate to see for herself how ill Tolliver was.

"Capital idea," Cranford said, before her father had the chance to respond. "I'll have the boy drive you back here after tea. Still enough moonlight. He will get back to town with the rig with no trouble tonight."

"Very well," her father said, rather belatedly.

Vera rose from her chair, trying not to flutter about.

Cranford looked at his watch again. "I'll get the boy to run me down to the station at Athi River. He will come back for you." He shook hands with her father and started across the lawn without further ceremony.

The cello and the music stand in the corner distracted Vera McIntosh from her trepidation about entering Justin Tolliver's room. All her reasons to feel anxious about this encounter were still there, but those thoughts were completely over-whelmed by her surprise that Tolliver played music. It was the only possible conclusion one could draw from the pres-ence of the instrument and the sheet music. This was the last thing Vera wanted to know about the man she already found irresistible, whose interest in her seemed to wax and wane for reasons she could not fathom. Those swings in his attentions made her enthrallment stronger: pushing her by turns from hope to despair, enflaming her desire and her resolve to captivate him one moment and then, the next, dousing her hopes and threatening to break her heart. Now she would have to add to her fantasies pictures of him at the cello and her at the piano.

Nurse Freemantle, prim in her white uniform and blue cape, cleared her throat. Tolliver's manservant closed the door and went to stand in the corner. Vera began to introduce the man in the bed to the nurse.

"We have met," Tolliver said; his voice was weak, his skin pale. He was sitting up, resting against white pillows, covered up to his waist with a thick linen sheet. He wore a blue and white striped nightshirt, open at the collar, revealing hair on his chest the same dark blond color as that on his head.

"Oh, yes, of course," Vera said. "At the hospital. I remember now." She took a couple of tentative steps forward. "I hope you will forgive the intrusion, Captain Tolliver, but my father and I thought perhaps Nurse Freemantle might be helpful. She served in the Boer War. She has a great deal of experience in African diseases."

He smiled faintly. She saw how little energy he had. If Gichinga Mbura could see him, he would be sure his curse was working. What he said next all but confirmed her fears. "At first, the doctor thought it was malaria, but now he is not sure. He seems perplexed about what it could be. I have been taking my quinine." He blushed a bit at the last sentence, as if there were some shame connected with the taking of quinine. Vera looked away from his eyes, afraid he would see how much she cared for him.

Nurse Freemantle went to the bed and felt his forehead, as if his flushed face was a signal of fever, which of course it must be. "Quinine does not always work," she said. "May I take your pulse?" She took him by the wrist before he had a chance to respond. She reached under his chin and lifted his face to hers. "Show me your tongue."

The tongue he showed was pink but pale down the center.

Nurse Freemantle's efficient hands palpated his neck under his jaw. Not for the first time in her life, Vera thought it would be romantic to become a nurse.

"No sign of infection in the glands. Have you had the sweats?"

"No," he said, his voice a bit livelier, as if the nurse touching him had made him feel better. "That was why the doctor began to doubt malaria."

"It is not malaria. Definitely not," Nurse Freemantle said.

The skin on Vera's shoulders prickled. She did not want to believe it was Gichinga Mbura's curse that had made him ill. She had never believed in those things. Even Wangari, who was baptized only a few years ago, now laughed at people who feared the medicine man. Except when they believed the curse. She and Wangari both understood that there was some way that a victim's belief in a curse gave it power. But Justin Tolliver could not believe in a curse that he had no idea had been placed on him.

"When exactly did you collapse?" the nurse asked.

"When I woke up, I could not at first remember what had

happened. They told me it was Sunday afternoon about three-thirty. Just this morning, it all started to come back to me."

"Sunday was an unusually hot day for this altitude. Tell me what you did during that day, before you collapsed."

Tolliver pulled his sheet up over his shoulders and blushed again. Something told Vera he was not going to tell the whole truth. She kept her eyes away from his.

"I went to luncheon at the Carlton. I fell in the street as I was leaving." He sounded like a man pleading innocent to a crime he had committed.

"Start at the beginning of the day." Nurse Freemantle was giving him no quarter. She was frequently like this, seemed to be looking for what her patient had done wrong to bring disease upon himself.

"I went to the Gymkhana Club in the morning and played tennis." Now, he was a frightened boy, defending himself against his nanny's suspicions.

"Was it a long and difficult match?"

"Look here," he said. They were the words Vera wanted to say. She felt a terrible urge to defend him, too, against Nurse Freemantle's prying. She was suddenly more afraid of finding out something that would dash her hopes of him than she was of Gichinga Mbura's curse.

"Well, then, if you will not be forthcoming, let me guess." Nurse Fremantle's examining hands had gone to her hips. She quickly folded them in front of her, but her voice remained impatient. "Your tennis match was a particularly strenuous one. You sweated quite profusely during the match, but not for the rest of the day, despite the intemperate heat. Without any rest in between, you changed after your match and went to luncheon where you ate quite heavily and consumed quite a bit of alcohol—more than you are used to—and almost no water. You also may have drunk more coffee than you are used to. You felt light-headed and may have attributed it to the drink. You collapsed without other warning."

He laughed then. "You sound like Sherlock Holmes in a story in *The Strand Magazine*."

Now Nurse Freemantle smiled triumphantly. "Then I am correct." It was not a question.

Tolliver pulled his arms out from under the sheet and sat up straighter against his pillows. "You are. And I am happy to know you have discovered what is ailing me. What exactly is it?"

"Completely obvious actually," she said, still not quite approving of him. "Though we are very near the equator here, cases of heat stroke are not that frequent in Nairobi, as we are over a mile above sea level. Given your age and how fit you are, you would have had to do absolutely everything wrong on a particularly hot day to have managed it. But evidently you did." She looked at the manservant who still stood unmoving in the corner. "See to it that your master drinks a great deal of water. I will deliver some salt pills to the desk at the front door shortly after I leave. He must take one with every gallon of water he drinks for the rest of today and all of tomorrow."

She turned back to Tolliver. "You are lucky that your case is not a very bad one. You have regained your memory quickly. Some people do not for many, many months. An older man or one not so strong might never have recovered. I trust you have learned your lesson."

Despite the scolding he was taking, Tolliver looked positively gleeful. "I have. I have."

"You must stay in bed until Thursday. Eat sparingly for the rest of today—just broth." She gave his manservant a look that was half commanding, half conspiratorial. "After that you should keep your diet and your exercise light for a few days. And you may have one glass of wine per day, but no strong spirits until Saturday at the earliest. No coffee or tea for the rest of the next week. Alcohol and coffee and tea are diuretics—make you lose water. They are mainly what got you into trouble in the first place. The altitude seems to contribute to the water loss somehow, even for persons who seem otherwise to be well acclimated." She gave a curt bow of her head, as if to put an exclamation point on her instructions.

"Thank you very much, Nurse Freemantle," Tolliver said with a broad, handsome smile, properly chastened, but obviously sincerely grateful. "It's a wonder to me the doctor did not better understand the problem."

The nurse folded her arms across her chest again. "The British-trained doctors are okay as far as injuries are concerned. But it takes one a while to understand how English people react to conditions in Africa." She straightened the cape that had been part of her uniform in the South African war.

Vera had watched the proceedings with relief, keeping quiet for fear of revealing the intensity of her feelings.

Nurse Freemantle walked toward the door. "I think, Miss McIntosh," she said, "that you can put aside your worries about that disgusting witch doctor and his silly curse."

Vera was mortified by Freemantle's revelation of her fears. "Curse?" Tolliver asked. "What curse?"

9.

Out of bed at last, on the following Thursday, Justin Tolliver shaved carefully, put on his uniform for the first time in too many days, and went to work. He went through the charge room and straight to the cells, taking Kwai Libazo with him to interrogate the prisoner. No matter how many times he told himself that the savage witch doctor's curse meant nothing to his investigation, he could not banish the thought of it. He asked himself what the detective Sherlock Holmes, a thoroughly logical man, would say, and laughed at himself for comparing his thoughts to those of a fictional character.

When he came face to face with his native prisoner, he found the man arrogant in the extreme. The Somali askaris had forced him to wash off the markings on his face and body. But rather than subduing him, that seemed to have heightened his pride. "You must translate everything," Tolliver told Kwai Libazo. "None of your editing of what he says."

Libazo stood at attention the entire time. He never let Mbura go on for very long before he interrupted and translated for Tolliver.

Still, at the end of the interview, Tolliver came away unsure that Libazo had followed his instructions. Worse yet, he was more convinced than ever that Mbura might be innocent. That aside, Tolliver realized he intensely disliked Mbura. It was a new emotion to him. He had been in the Protectorate for nearly half a year now. He had visited it for several months, once before, but in all that time, he had not felt any strong emotion, one way or another, toward any native. As a whole, he found the Africans interesting, had been a bit discomfited by their nakedness at first, was sometimes amused by their naïve ways, but he had never held any real admiration or intense dislike regarding any single native person.

Mbura had repeated his curse; Libazo had translated faithfully enough to tell Tolliver that. Tolliver blamed himself for reacting at all to silly savage superstitions. He wanted to be rid of the witch doctor's laughter and wagging, too-pink tongue. But that was not a reason to hang him. Certainly, there was the death penalty if Mbura had actually murdered the Scottish doctor, but no one, under English law, would be hanged for making mumbo jumbo and putting a curse on a man. Tolliver was, after all, a man who had dragged the witch doctor off to jail for a crime he may not have committed. And Tolliver was also a member of the group that had, for all intents and purposes, invaded Mbura's territory.

Tolliver realized that, when it came to his opinion of the British presence in East Africa, he had just had a thought that was more normal for Vera McIntosh than it ought to be for a policeman.

The only way to appease the livid D.C. Cranford was to

close the case as soon as possible. Cranford had the power to make Tolliver's life here intolerable. If Justin did not want to be forced back to England, he had to end his investigation without further delay. Therefore, his next step must be to turn his full attention to the only other suspect in the crime: Kirk Buxton.

Tolliver's spirits drooped at that thought. Such a line of inquiry would take him back into the path of Lucy—a woman far too attractive, overly willing, and whom, deep in his heart, he pitied. And pity was dangerous—too tender a feeling by half.

A much more pleasant line of attack at the moment was a detour, but it might prove productive. He would take Lord Delamere up on his offer of information. There was a serious-ness in the way Delamere had spoken on Sunday that hinted he knew something important that might guide Tolliver to the truth.

Kwai Libazo was standing at Tolliver's desk in the middle of the police station offering a large glass of water. He was in cahoots with Ndege to drown his superior officer. Tolliver took the glass, drank it down, and set off to find Delamere. As he expected, he discovered the social doyen of the settlers in the first place he looked—the bar at the Nairobi Club— reading *The Leader* and sipping a cup of tea.

"Do sit down." Delamere indicated the brown leather club chair opposite his own. "Will you have one?" Delamere asked, pointing to his cup.

Much as Tolliver longed for tea, he was mindful of Nurse Freemantle's interdiction. "Thank you, no. Nothing for me. I wondered if you would mind—"

Delamere raised a hand to signal an approaching waiter. "Bring Captain Tolliver a glass and a pitcher of water," he ordered. Evidently everyone in the town knew the exact nature of Justin Tolliver's ailment and its recommended treatment. If he drank all the pitchers of water being forced on him wherever he went, he would surely end by spending most of the day in the loo.

Delamere folded his newspaper and slipped it under his chair. "I'm glad of the chance to chat," he said. "We haven't had a proper opportunity to get to know one another. You came here under unusual circumstances for a man like yourself. How is it that you are in the line of work you are?"

It was a question Tolliver knew was talked about. Policing was not the done thing for the son of an earl, not even for a second son. Men like Tolliver were meant to find their own way in the world. That had always been the case. But Delamere knew, as well as Justin Tolliver, that things had changed drastically in Britain since Tolliver's birth. Landed families' futures were no longer assured. Bankrolls for second sons had vanished from many families. Delamere himself had come here, as many of their class had, to try to preserve some sort of life they could call dignified.

Tolliver had taken a commission in the army—perfectly normal for a nobleman. Once in Africa, his next step ought to have been to take land and become a farmer. But that required some capital, and Justin had not even that rather paltry amount. Still, even in his impecunious state, he had chosen to do something completely out of the ordinary. Men of his bloodlines and education were meant to ensure their futures by marrying women with money, not by becoming policemen. Tolliver delayed his response by accepting a glass of water and sipping it for a moment. "I had been here in East Africa once before you may remember, Lord Delamere."

Delamere chuckled. "I remember it well. You and your friend, what was his name?"

"Granville Stokes."

Delamere laughed again. "I remember him well. You two cut a very wide swath through the available ladies as I recall."

Tolliver looked at the Turkish carpet and tried his best not to blush. "I wanted to come back here, but I had learned my lesson the first time. I am not suited to an idle life. I was not happy with myself on my first visit. I found myself at sixes and sevens, and too much taken up by distractions."

"So it wasn't Lillian Gresham you came back to find."

"No, sir. After spending some time at home, I began to realize that I longed to be back in Africa. The main chance for chaps like me who settle here is to take a farm but I wanted a bit more adventure, a bit more of a challenge than trying to avoid bankruptcy. At least for a couple of years. Frankly, sir, I did not expect people's attitudes to be so negative about my joining the police force. In South Africa there were many such as I serving as quasi-military policemen." He realized how close he had come to insinuating that Delamere was one of the snobs. At least, he didn't blush about it. "At any rate, I am very happy to be here in Africa."

Delamere smiled. "I understand very well how this place draws one. It gets into one's blood." A wistfulness had come into Lord Delamere's ordinarily lively voice.

"I chose the police service because it was desperate for

staff, and I thought it would give me the chance to serve king and country and to be off in the wilderness from time to time when duty drew me there. I started out knowing almost nothing of the law or how a policeman is meant to do his work. I wish I could speak more of the local languages, but in the main I am not at all unhappy with my assignment."

"It suits you, I think," Delamere said. "But you do have one failing at it."

"What is that, sir?" Tolliver was on edge now. Delamere's expression turned mischievous.

"You do not participate sufficiently in the local gossip, son. Half the clues you will ever find among the Europeans you will learn from gossip."

It was Tolliver's turn to chuckle.

"I am not being entirely facetious," Delamere said. He raised his hand to the waiter in the corner and signaled for another cup of tea. "Many people come here with hopes that lead them into all sorts of unsavory activity, and I don't mean merely of the sexual kind." He hiked his chair closer to Tolliver's and leaned toward him. "Let me tell you something worth knowing." Delamere proceeded softly but clearly. "Shortly after Pennyman arrived, he took a leasehold on a farm. You know, I suppose, that any European can take a ninety-nine year lease at very good terms, but one cannot be awarded a land grant unless one can prove to the land officer that he has at least four hundred British pounds to spend to develop the property—build, plant, that sort of thing. Do you know all this?"

Tolliver knew it very well. It was the discovery of these rules that had dashed his hopes of taking land for himself, given his practically nonexistent allowance from his father. "Yes, sir, I do."

Delamere picked up the tea, saucer and all, as soon as the waiter put it down.

Tolliver's mouth watered at the aroma. It would be two more days before he would have a cuppa.

"At any rate," Delamere said, "from what I heard, Pennyman was well-named. He barely had the five pounds to pay the application fee. He had lost his nest egg in some scandal in Edinburgh. The Church of Scotland paid his way here if he promised to work two years at the hospital.

"But he applied for land?"

"Yes. Maybe he thought his sister would stake him. She has an inheritance from their father. But his sister would not give him a sou. Yet, he somehow convinced Buxton to stake him a loan. The land officer will accept an assurance from a banker."

Tolliver was nonplussed. "I didn't know one could borrow the money." The sentence slipped unbidden off his tongue, revealing more about his own circumstances than he wanted to.

"But when Pennyman went to Buxton for the cash, he was refused the funds because by then—"

Tolliver heard the evidence coming. "By then Pennyman had taken up with Lucy."

Delamere's cup rattled as he replaced it on the table. "The man was foolish, Tolliver, just foolish. Of all the willing women in the Protectorate, he went for the wife of the man whose approval he most needed to get on in this world."

"Because Buxton had found out."

"Everyone knew by then. My sister in Hampstead Heath knew. Our Lucy is not what anyone would call discreet."

Tolliver looked back at the carpet. He hadn't known. Delamere was right. He avoided gossip because he thought it trivial and because knowing others' secrets made him uncomfortable. But if he wanted to be serious about his work, he would have to get used to knowing other people's embarrassments.

"In the end," Delamere said, "Buxton reneged on the loan. Without the means to make improvements, Pennyman's land had to be confiscated." Delamere stood up. "So you see, Tolliver, Buxton is unlikely to be your man. He had already had his revenge. Under the circumstances, Pennyman was more likely to have wanted to kill Buxton than vice versa."

Tolliver didn't know what to think of such a statement. Though he could not imagine it ever being a thought he could think about himself, he knew there were many of the gentlemanly class in England who cared more about their money interests than they did about who might be sleeping with their wives. Perhaps Buxton thought ruining Pennyman financially was adequate satisfaction for Pennyman's seducing Lucy.

At the moment, however, Delamere was looking very like a man who had had enough of this conversation, and Tolliver had another pressing question he wanted to ask. Not having the faintest idea how to couch it politely, he found himself blurting it out. "Lord Delamere, did Berkeley Cole also have an affair with Lucy Buxton?"

Delamere looked puzzled for a second but then understood. "Ah, I see. You think my brother-in-law might have been jealous of Pennyman's affair with Lucy. No such thing. Berkeley had finished with Lucy before Pennyman came on the scene. Cole is the most sought after social companion in the Protectorate. He would not need to pine away for the likes of Lucy. Besides, he doesn't have a combative bone in his body. He shoots big game, but otherwise he wouldn't hurt a fly." Delamere guffawed at his own joke.

Tolliver smiled though he did not feel at all amused by any of what Delamere had told him. And what Delamere said next sank his heart.

"I don't like to have to say this to you, Tolliver, but under the circumstances, I don't think it at all right that you have been seen around the town in the company of Mrs. Buxton." He trundled off in the direction of the club's front door.

Kwai Libazo rode a pony for the third time in his life as he again followed behind A.D.S. Tolliver to the Scottish Mission. After months of running with the other native policemen whenever they went out on the Protectorate's business, Libazo found himself in an enviable position. He had become Tolliver's translator of choice. Tolliver had said it was because his English was the best of all the others in the native police corps. He had also complimented Kwai on his swift action when they arrested Gichinga Mbura, but Libazo knew it was more than just the words and his strength. Libazo was beginning to understand his English masters and their ways. Many of his fellow policemen still found them quite puzzling and were daunted by the need to translate, not just words, but ideas that did not make any sense to the tribal people. For instance, Libazo knew now that they were on their way to the Kikuyu village near the mission to look for proof.

It had taken Kwai himself several months of working with Tolliver to really understand the concept of proof—that they needed to establish the person responsible for a crime by collecting facts. The words "proof" and "fact" did not exist in any tribal language that Libazo knew. He had never heard of such a need before he began the work he now enjoyed so much. The ideas that governed the British were hard to fathom, but Libazo was proud to say that he was better at understanding them than any of his rivals in the native corps. And for him it was enough of a reward that, because he was the best, Captain Tolliver also saw to it that Kwai rode this pony.

The desire to ride horses was something he found very easy to understand about the British. It gave great joy to do it. And not just because it put a person up high where he could see so much better what he passed as he moved along. Also the feeling of speed when the horse ran and being one with the animal, and controlling the beast so much bigger and stronger than oneself. It was making his work wonderful to him. Then there was his learning about the people who had come to live here. To see how a foreign people thought was something one could learn when one acquired their language and tried to understand what they really meant when they spoke their words. That knowing was in itself a source of pleasure. The English were here, and they were not going to go away. They built buildings of stone. They expected to stay as long as those buildings would last, which was a very long while. Much longer than a person could live. Knowing how they thought would always be important.

As he had the day they first rode here together, Captain Tolliver paused at the crest of the hill and studied the view: the coffee fields, the glistening river where eight or ten kudu were drinking, and the plain beyond where a herd of Cape buffalo grazed, the purple hills in the distance.

"Can you still see the beauty of it?" Tolliver asked. "You have seen it all of your life. What does it look like to you, Kwai Libazo?"

"It looks like home, sir." When the British said the word "home," they said it like a prayer. To them "home" meant England. But to Kwai Libazo, this was the place whose name should be a prayer.

"Mmmm." Tolliver made a sound like a very thirsty man drinking water. As if this scene looked like home to him, too. But Libazo knew that England did not look like this. He had seen pictures of it in the books in the English Mission where he had gone to learn to read and write as a young boy. Those pictures did not look at all like this.

This day, they did not ride into the mission when they arrived. They went directly to the Kikuyu village where Libazo followed Tolliver's orders and tried to get the people there to tell him if Gichinga Mbura had left the village during the afternoon or the night before the white doctor was found dead. Over and over, Libazo asked the question and got the same sort of response: one that showed that the person he was asking did not understand why he was asking this, did not know the answer, or would not say. Those same two old women laughed at him again for asking. In the end, Kwai did his best to try to explain to Tolliver that the people of the village would not be what Tolliver wanted them to be, people he would call "reliable witnesses." It was not in their nature to remark upon or to speak clearly about such things.

Tolliver became more and more frustrated by this and kept insisting for more than an hour past the time he should have given up. It was not the first time, while working with Tolliver, that Kwai Libazo thought that it must not be a pleasure for a British man, as it was for him, to learn and understand how a foreign people thought.

In the end, Tolliver had no choice but to stop asking.

As they walked with their horses along the path to the mission, Kwai asked Tolliver, "Do you think that the medicine man did kill the Scottish doctor?"

"I am not sure," Tolliver said, "and in order to accuse him, I have to be sure."

"You must have proof," Libazo said.

"Exactly so." Tolliver gave him a look of mild surprise mixed with respect.

"Then why must you try so hard to find out where he did not go?"

Tolliver stopped in a shady spot along the path. He dropped his horse's reins and the animal immediately began to eat the bright green grasses that grew along the edge of the path. Kwai Libazo did the same with his reins, and his pony also followed suit. He felt a little anxious that it would run off if he did not hold on to it or tie it to a tree, but it did not. Perhaps the pony was like him and would stay at his work, though it might be hard. It must find its work difficult. It was not as large as A.D.S. Tolliver's stallion, and Kwai was only a bit more slender than the captain. Perhaps like Kwai, the pony found enjoyment doing his job.

"We have this word in English," Captain Tolliver said in the voice he always used when he was teaching Libazo something. Not like the way he spoke when he gave an order or asked a question. "The word is 'alibi.' It means that the person who might have committed a crime can show that he could not have done it because he could prove he was elsewhere when the crime was committed."

"So this is why you asked if the villagers had seen Mbura leave or were with him. If he had been with them the whole time, you would know that he could not have been the murderer."

"Precisely." Tolliver gave Kwai one of his approving nods.

"So we are trying to see if he can prove himself innocent, even though the law says that we have to believe he is innocent unless we can prove him guilty." This was one of those times that Libazo found it very difficult to tell what the English really meant with their words.

Tolliver looked as if he wanted to take back that approving nod. "Well, we *do* have to prove him guilty, but if he had an alibi that we believed in, we would not try to do so."

"And the alibi would be that the others in the village say that he was with them?"

Tolliver smiled but did not nod.

"But if the villagers knew this and they wanted to save him, they would say what you want to hear, whether it was true or not. They certainly would."

"That is why I asked you to talk to so many of them. If some said no, he had never left, and others said yes, he did, we would not trust the ones who said no. We would know that they were not all telling the truth, that some were trying to save him."

"But suppose some of them hated him because he had helped their enemies put a curse on them. Then they would say that he had left, when he hadn't. What then?"

Tolliver reached for his horse's reins and started to walk again. "This is what I find so exasperating," he said. "It is almost impossible with you people to get at the truth."

Kwai took his pony and followed. "Exasperating" was a word he liked very much. It helped him understand how he himself felt when this sort of thing happened. The British talked about respect for the "truth" but they did not always tell it themselves. Otherwise, why would their laws spend so much time trying to find out who was lying and who was not? Tolliver found it "exasperating" that the tribal people did not always tell "the truth." The tribal people knew that the truth was different things to different people. At least that was what Kwai Libazo, who was not a member of any tribe really, knew to be the case.

Vera McIntosh watched Justin Tolliver as he approached her veranda across the packed earth center of the mission compound. His face carried that same expression as when he discovered her deep in conversation with Denys Finch Hatton.

She had read enough novels to know that his disapproval of her conversations with Finch Hatton could be based on jealousy, which pleased her in a way. If he was jealous, that would mean he cared for her. Which gave her hope. On the other hand, when she was in town visiting him with Nurse Freemantle, she had heard gossip about him and Lucy Buxton, whom her mother called a hussy. So maybe she should be the one who was jealous. What she could not fathom was how Tolliver could think that Denys Finch Hatton, who by all reports could have had almost any girl in the Protectorate or, for that matter, in all of England, would want her. Men like Finch Hatton did not marry missionary's daughters, not even ones like her who had a decent pedigree. Men like him married girls with a great deal of money, even if their fathers were in trade.

Besides, as attractive as everyone thought the desirable Denys, she preferred Tolliver, thought him handsomer, much handsomer, even if not so easy in his manners.

"Good morning, Captain Tolliver," she said, getting up and meeting him at the low privet hedge that surrounded their lawn and garden.

He handed the reins of his horse to his lieutenant, Kwai Libazo. She saw him take notice of the nod and smile that passed between her and Libazo. "Take the horses back to the stable and get them some water."

"Njui will give you something for yourself," Vera said to Libazo. She wondered if Tolliver knew his policeman had come to talk to her privately. She rather thought not.

Tolliver indicated the chairs on her veranda with a hand that still held a riding crop. "Do you mind if I ask you a question?" he asked.

Ask me to marry you, she thought. Make love to me not that hussy Lucy. She smiled and said, "Certainly. May I tell my mother that you will stay to luncheon?"

He took a gold watch from the deep pocket of his khaki uniform trousers, looked at it, and said, "Yes, please."

When they were settled in the wicker chairs and she had served him a glass of water, she expected him to tell her about his progress in the investigation into her uncle's death. Instead he said, "Tell me about your brother."

"Otis?" It was a silly question. She had only one brother. But it was such a surprising subject. "Surely you have met him."

"In a manner of speaking. I have seen him at the horse trials and cricket matches at the club. I have never really had a conversation with him."

"He's like any other almost-fourteen-year-old boy, I imagine," she said. Not that she knew very many British boys Otis's age. They were all sent back to England to school by the time they reached ten years of age. "He went back home to attend Saint Andrews for a time, but he grew ill, in his lungs. The damp, my uncle said. Uncle Josiah brought him back to Africa when he came out last fall. He said Otis should not pass another winter in the wind and rain of the Scottish coast." She looked into Tolliver's blue eyes. "Why do you ask?"

"Your father said he left on a safari two days before your uncle's—" He didn't seem to want to say the word "murder."

"Yes," she said. "I wanted to go, too. I actually tried to run off with them early on the morning that he left. But my mother caught me and stopped me." The blue eyes registered shock, but only for a second. "I suppose you think me wicked for trying to go against my mother's wishes," she said.

"Not entirely. How is it that he was allowed to go and you were not?"

"You don't know my mother. She believes that women must be kept as busy as possible. She has me constantly working on things. She said that she could not spare me when I asked to go. It wasn't true. She didn't think it ladylike, is all."

She was aware that she sounded petulant. She was just happy that she had not revealed to him that her mother was trying to make her look properly marriageable before June when she would turn twenty and, if her mother were to be believed, shortly thereafter turn into an old maid.

Tolliver didn't respond, which Vera liked a great deal. Finch Hatton would have said something clever, at which she would have had to laugh, but she didn't think this subject at all funny.

Tolliver, on the other hand, made her feel comfortable, and when she thought he liked her, it seemed to be for things about her and not what she did or did not represent. "My mother believes that proper young British girls do not spend their time shooting buffaloes and rhinoceros."

Now he did laugh. "Oh, I think proper English girls might do so, if there were such animals on the Downs or lurking in the hedgerows."

She grinned. "Well here I am being dull. And Otis has gone off to have his adventure." She picked a piece of lint off her skirt. "I am glad for him actually. He has been spared this sadness. Oh, he'll have to hear of it when he returns, certainly, but the shock will have worn off the rest of us a bit by then."

"He'll be gone at least a month, I imagine."

She nodded. "And it is better, under the circumstances, that I have stayed behind. To be here with my mother and father at this moment."

He put his hands together and squeezed them between his knees, leaning toward her. He smelled of lemons and leather. "I wonder," he asked, "if you would like to come to watch the polo match next Sunday afternoon at the Gymkhana?"

Her heart wobbled. Every ounce of her wanted to say yes. "I don't think I can. I think my mother expects me to be in mourning." She bit on her lip. She hated having to say that. He might take it as a criticism of himself.

He blushed, something she had begun to find extremely endearing. "Oh, of course. How could I be so stupid?"

"Not stupid. It was a lovely idea," she said. "I do hope you will ask me again." Her longing for his company got the better of her. "I would ask you to come for a visit here, instead of my coming to the club that day, but you will be playing in the match, I imagine."

"I will. By then I will be free of Nurse Fremantle's dictums."

"If you are free on Saturday," she said, desperately trying to sound matter-of-fact and only lightly interested, "perhaps you would like to come for a picnic on the Kikuyu reserve. It should be fine weather. We could ride out with a basket." She did not say "just the two of us."

The look he gave her was analytical and made her apprehensive, but then he smiled and said, "That would be lovely. What time shall I come?"

"It will be getting dark by six, and the ride out to the nicest spot will take nearly an hour. Shall we say you arrive around noon?"

"I shall."

She could not resist a tiny tease. "And no overdoing tennis early in the day and having a relapse."

He appraised her again. "Will your father let us go alone, just the two of us?"

10.

Early on the next day, Tolliver made for Kirk Buxton's office at the Standard Bank of India. He needed to interview the bank manager, and he wanted to avoid any encounter with Lucy. As much as she drank, Tolliver imagined that she was not an early riser. As for himself, minding Nurse Freemantle's warnings, he was taking his quinine water straight these days, though it tasted quite vile without the gin to sweeten it.

He found Buxton at his desk, reading the newspaper, and with but a halfhearted showing of polite chitchat, got directly to the point. "I am sure you understand that I must rule out any involvement of yours in the death of Josiah Pennyman. I am afraid I will have to know where you were and whom you were with on the evening of Wednesday and the wee hours of Thursday, a week ago."

Buxton sighed, but did not object. He seemed such a lethargic, cynical man, it was hard to imagine him becoming worked up enough to kill a snake, much less a fellow human being. He lifted an appointments calendar on his desk and thumbed it back a page. "On Wednesday evening, I was involved in a bridge tournament at the Nairobi Club. That newcomer Baron Blixen was my partner. We won all of our rubbers until the final, when we were defeated by the team of Sir Percy Girouard and Mr. John Ainsworth." Buxton said the names of the victors quite triumphantly, which made absolute sense, since Sir Percy was the Governor of the Protectorate, the highest authority in the land, and his partner one of its provincial commissioners.

"I see," Justin managed to say. The answer prickled him. He did not want to have to accuse Buxton of murder, but he did not like to be stopped cold in his tracks in his pursuit of the truth. "At what time did the tournament end?"

Buxton looked even smugger. "At about two in the morning. And then the final foursome passed nearly an hour standing one another drinks in the bar before staggering home."

Tolliver thanked Buxton as politely as he could and left. Since Pennyman had died sometime between midnight and three in the morning, according to the formidable Nurse Freemantle, Buxton had an alibi—if his story held.

Without permission from D.C. Cranford, Tolliver could hardly approach Sir Percy, given his exalted position. He could not just walk in and question Ainsworth either for that matter. Cranford would never allow it. "Protocol, my boy," he would say. But Tolliver was determined to dot every "i" and cross every "t." And there was nothing stopping him from getting corroborating evidence from Baron Blixen, who was barely an acquaintance, but was a fellow tennis player, who often took his luncheon in the club's dining room. Dinners, rumor had it, he took with whichever of the socialites of the Protectorate wanted him on any particular evening. Tolliver had also had many such invitations when he arrived, when, being the son of the 7th Earl of Bilbrough and the great-grandson of Admiral Wentworth, hero of the Napoleonic Wars, gave him some cachet with the settlers. That soon wore off once he joined the police force, and when the recent influx of new settlers brought them bigger fish—like the Swede with a title in addition to the right bloodlines.

Tolliver found Bror Blixen just sitting down in the club dining room. He was a rather slope-shouldered man with thinning light brown hair, but a pleasant face and a ready smile. "I beg your pardon," Tolliver said, extending his hand and introducing himself.

The baron, holding his napkin, rose half out of his chair and shook Justin's hand with a warm, firm grip. "Of course. I have admired your skills at polo. You are a wonderful rider."

"Thank you. I enjoy the sport. I wonder if I could trouble you to have a coffee with me after your meal?"

"Please," Blixen said, indicating the chair opposite him. "Won't you join me? I have yet to order."

"If you don't mind?"

"Not at all," the baron said. "I will be glad of your company. There is a match on Sunday I believe."

"Yes. I am looking forward to it, Baron."

"Call me Blix. Everyone else does."

They ordered their meal, and the conversation continued much as it had begun. Blix turned out to be a friendly and charming man. His accent made him sound decidedly German, which would not have put him in good stead in the Protectorate. The British had had, from the outset, a conflicted and uneasy relationship with German East Africa to its south. Many of the decisions Britain had made of how to comport itself in this part of Africa were based on that rivalry. But Bror Blixen had none of the arrogance Tolliver would have expected from a German. He was easy company and surprisingly full of wit for a man who was not speaking his native language.

"Now," Blix said, as they were served cheese plates toward the end of the meal, "I imagine, by the way you first approached me, that you must have a question you wanted to ask."

Tolliver asked him about the bridge tournament.

He shook his head and looked crestfallen. "Buxton and I lost in the last rubber. I can tell you this," he said with a chuckle. "If Sir Percy pursues the rights of the British crown in East Africa with half the determination and sangfroid with which he went after the Nairobi Club bridge championship, your king has nothing to fear."

Tolliver smiled despite the seriousness of the questions in his mind. "Can you tell me what happened after the game was over?"

Blixen gave him a questioning look but answered readily. "I am afraid Sir Percy and John Ainsworth also won the drinks-buying contest in the bar afterward. I overindulged in the extreme. I had a terrible headache and a meeting with the land officer the next morning, to go out and inspect a farm I am hoping to take to grow coffee. I remember wishing that the coffee was already there for the drinking."

Tolliver was sorry to have to spoil Blixen's fun. "What time would you say the party broke up?"

Blix's expression turned serious. He nodded knowingly. "I see. This is official business." He held up a hand to stop Tolliver's apology. "It was nearly three when I went to bed. Arjan, the majordomo, had to put Buxton in a rickshaw. He could barely walk when he left."

Approaching her father's study door, Vera heard her mother say, in a voice much louder than she usually used, "He could not have known until recently. Otherwise, why would he have come here, " she said. "He was a monster."

Vera slowed her step, but her mother said nothing more. Her father said something, but so quietly she could not hear his words, so she knocked on the door.

"Come." They spoke in unison. It was not the first time she had heard them do that.

"Come in, lass," her father said as the door opened. "You might as well know about this."

She took a seat on the ottoman near her father's desk. "What is it, father?" There was a metal box open on the desk in front of him, and he held a sheaf of papers in his hand. He put them in the box, locked it, and put the key in his vest pocket.

"We have been going through your uncle's effects," her mother said, her voice even, carrying none of the emotion Vera had heard from the hallway. But something in her father's expression made Vera wary.

"You have found something upsetting."

A look that ought to have gone with a dropped gauntlet passed from her mother to her father.

He pulled his chair closer to Vera. "Your uncle has squandered every penny of his inheritance," he said. "He was a brilliant doctor, but the rest of his conduct was not in the same league."

"What does that matter to us?"

Her mother said, "I had had hopes for what he might do for Otis, since it seemed your uncle would never marry."

"Why would he never marry? Women seemed to like him very much. He wasn't so very old."

"He was forty-four," she said. And now Vera knew the answer to a question her mother would never give her. Her mother's age—thirty-nine. She had told Vera she was five years younger than Josiah. That meant that her mother had been barely twenty when Vera was born. And it explained why she was so focused on Vera not becoming an old maid on her next birthday.

She wondered how her mother felt, having lost her only brother. She knew how bereft she would be if she ever lost Otis. She had adored him from the moment he was born, felt part sister, part mother to him, though he was less than six years younger than she. She wondered if her uncle had had similar feelings for his baby sister. Perhaps men did not have those instincts. No one ever spoke of male instincts as far as Vera knew. They spoke only of women's, and then only of maternal ones. But she did not think her mother felt about her what she felt about Otis. She could not find a maternal instinct in her mother. When it came to Vera, anyway, Blanche McIntosh seemed more interested in having her always at her side to get things done. She was much more loving toward Otis, always bragging about how much he looked like his father. There was no doubt that her mother loved her father, practically revered him.

"What made you think my uncle would never marry?"

Blanche McIntosh looked away from her daughter. "He told me; that's all. And I believed him." Vera recognized that the lightness in her mother's voice was forced and thought she really must have loved her brother and missed him. She went and sat on the floor beside the armchair at her mother's feet. "I am so sorry for your loss, mama," she said. She wished there was something she could say that would comfort her mother, but what that might be was completely beyond her.

Her mother did something she had never done before. She put her hand on Vera's head and caressed her hair.

Vera looked up at her and smiled. "I have news I think you will like," she said. "I know how happy you were that Captain Tolliver asked me to dance so often. Well, tomorrow he is coming to go picnicking with me on the Kikuyu Reserve. He particularly asked if we could go, just the two of us." Behind her, her father stirred, but before he had a chance to speak, she looked imploringly into her mother's face. "It will be alright, won't it, Mother. You know you can trust him. He is such a gentleman. And perhaps he has something to say that he would want to say to me alone."

Her father stood up quickly, but not before her mother had said, "Yes."

The coffee blossoms were beginning to fade, but the view of the Scottish Mission still lifted Justin Tolliver's heart. He felt this panorama would thrill him for the rest of his life no matter how many times he saw it. And today he would ride out into it with Vera McIntosh, which also lifted his heart. He had desired other women's bodies, but with her he also desired her company. She held opinions with which he could never agree, and she amazed him by frankly expressing them, despite his disagreement. Her complete lack of self-consciousness about this made him like her more and more. He could see that she might yield her body to him in the right circumstances, but never her mind. That made her more inter-esting than a girl who would always agree because she saw being agreeable as the quickest way to win him. Even Lillian Gresham had pretended to think that everything he said was biblically important. Vera was genuine.

He picked his way down the horse trail from the top of the hill to the veranda of her house. She was already sitting there with a colorful Kikuyu basket next to her chair.

Vera watched him approach and let her heart revel in the fact that she would be alone with him for hours. She wanted him to try to kiss her. She wanted him to want her, and she was afraid he might not.

"Just be yourself," her mother had advised. And Wangari had taken the advice one step further. "In Africa, we do not have this kind of love that you talk about," she had said. "We want to know how a husband and wife will work together for their family. You want him to think of you as a woman who will be useful. Your mother is right. You must be with him the girl you will always be. If he thinks you are someone else besides yourself, and he marries the woman you show him to attract him, you will have to spend the rest of your life trying to be that person." That all sounded very wise indeed, but Vera thought that she absolutely wanted to spend the rest of her life being the girl Justin Tolliver desired.

"It is a beautiful day, as I promised you it would be," she said and smiled up at him as he slid off his horse. She handed him a tumbler of water without his having to ask. He polished it off in three gulps.

Her father came out of the house. It occurred to Justin that perhaps, later in the day, he would tell the Reverend McIntosh about his investigation, but he would not spoil Vera's fun in the meanwhile.

"Good afternoon, my lad," the missionary said. He looked at Tolliver's horse. "Good, you have a rifle," he said.

"A must," Tolliver replied. "The shortest way here, as you know, passes through some pretty dense woods."

McIntosh nodded. "Vera, girl, you take a rifle, too. Better to be safe than sorry in case you run into anything out there that's hungry for something larger than a sandwich."

"It's already on my saddle on Patience, Father. Here we go then." She took back the glass and handed Tolliver the basket.

Her father put a hand on Tolliver's shoulder and said more with one glance into the younger man's eyes than he could have with a month of Sunday sermons.

"I'll take every care of her," Tolliver said, hoping her father took that as a vow of honorable intentions.

They went to fetch her horse, which waited in the shade between the stable and the hay shed. "My father gave her to me as a gift," Vera said. "He named her Patience. He said he wanted to give me the gift of patience." She chuckled at her own failings.

With barely a boost from the groom she mounted, with that fairy grace of hers, as if she could fly if she set her mind to it. She sat the horse astride, as girls always rode here in Africa, not sidesaddle like proper women in England. Tolliver liked this better. In foxhunts at home, he always thought the ladies looked too precarious to take the jumps. He had seen men astride fall many times. He could not fathom how the ladies kept their seat. He did not have any such worry about Vera. He imagined that if her horse stumbled, she would just rise up a few feet and then come down gently on her toes.

"Why are you smiling so?" she asked as they set out, with the picnic basket attached behind her saddle.

He felt the confounded blush, which he was sure gave the lie to what he said, "Who could fail to smile on such a day as this, in such a place as this?"

"Not I." She turned her horse through the rows of the plantation, toward the river. Natives in their dark orange shukas sang as they worked between the phalanxes of plants. The blossoms were brown at the edges, their bittersweet scent muted. With Vera in the lead, they easily forded the narrow river at a shallow spot near the coffee processing shed.

On the other side, the grassy plain stretched out like a great, vivid green sea, dotted here and there with acacias. The April growth was short and emerald, and it smelled of spice and moisture. Off to their left, a couple of hunting hawks circled in the blue, looking for their luncheon meal. In the distance, antelope he could not name moved in single file, silhouetted against the gray-blue hills. On a day such as this, the snow-covered peaks of Mount Kenya were visible, so high their white might have been clouds. Justin Tolliver gazed out for miles and miles and felt his heart swell, as if it were trying to take all of this vast landscape into itself. Vera looked back at him, and he was afraid that she saw he was on the verge of weeping from the beauty of it. "It's wonderful," he managed to say.

"It makes me so happy that you can see that."

"How could anyone with a soul not see it?"

She gave a little regretful grin. "Then there are many people who have no souls." She looked around her again and back into his eyes. She pointed to an outcropping where a pair of trees huddled against a rocky spur. "That's my favorite picnic spot," she said. "At this season of year, there is a spring to water the horses. I want to show you the view from there." She turned her mare and trotted off in that direction.

The sun was on them, and he was grateful for the breeze of moving along at a pace. When they had climbed up and reached the shade of the trees, she alit, more like a butterfly than a person.

They tied up the horses where they could drink from a little pool formed by water trickling down a rock. Tolliver soaked his neckerchief and cooled the back of his neck. Vera took off her hat and shook out her damp, dark curls. She put her hands in the cool water and patted some on her face. "Hot work, this picnicking," she said with a laugh.

She took the basket and spread a muslin cloth on the grass in the shade. She went and got her rifle from the holster on her saddle and laid it beside the tree trunk. Justin realized he would not have thought to do that, but he took his and did the same.

She pointed behind Tolliver. "Look," she said.

He turned. From this angle, they could see back to the river that glittered like a silver ribbon, and beyond it, the plantation, the hospital, and the little mission chapel. Even those man-made things took on a majesty from their surroundings, a loveliness he never expected to find outside his own beautiful home in England. But this, this was greater even than that. That was all tamed and manicured; this was more thrilling. The things people put here gave a bit of contrast and emphasized the beauty of the purely wild.

He pointed. "What animals are they? I can't tell from here."

She looked up from setting out the food and shaded her eyes. "Hartebeests. They have a muzzle kind of like a horse's. That large group farther on are Cape buffalo. You want to give them plenty of space. They don't want to eat you, but they do not like intruders. Their horns are sharp and their hooves are deadly."

"I'll remember that," he said, though he already knew the warning from the hunting safaris he had taken.

She took his hand to lead him to the picnic spread. It startled him when she touched him.

She drew her hand away quickly. "I am sorry. I— I—"

"Don't be," he said.

"I'll never be a proper British lady," she said. She sat down on a little hummock at the base of the tree where she had spread the cloth. He sat upon the ground across from her. She was flustered, fussing now with bread rolls and little dishes.

He reached across and put his fingers on the back of her

right hand. "Please," he said, "you mustn't worry about me, about that sort of thing with me, I mean."

"My mother is always warning me," she said with a tinge of exasperation in her voice. She handed him a plate with four little sandwiches. "They are chicken. Is that alright?"

"Yes, thank you." He also accepted a glass of lemonade.

"Good. I brought lots. That's one of the things Mother says. That I am always too hungry, like a boy. I suppose boys are ordinarily the hungry ones." She could hear herself prattling on and sounding foolish. This was nothing like the conversation she had been daydreaming about for the past two days. "Mother means well."

He finished chewing and swallowed the buttery bite in his mouth. It was really quite delicious. "Mothers usually do," he said, "but that does not mean that they are always right."

"Mine wants me to think like a girl who was born and bred in the Scottish upper classes, which was how she was raised." She gestured out to the panorama below them. "But I was born here. I have spent but five months in Scotland on two visits, and I hated it there. Everything was cold, the weather, the beds, even my granny and her friends."

"You feel a part of this then?" He gestured, too. The sun was past its zenith, and the scene below them was bathed in a golden light. The shadows of a few puffy clouds fell here and there in the green expanse. At some point, a herd of impala had come out of the woods to graze between them and the river.

"Not only feel a part of it. I am a part of it," she said. Her eyes followed his as he took it all in. She wanted to ask him if that made her as desirable as the land before him, but even she knew one didn't ask such a question.

"You are part of it. And that is lovely." There was a sincerity in his eyes that made her heart ache.

"Actually, I do feel a part of it, but not entirely," she said. And then words poured out of her: all her fears about who she was and who she wasn't. "The Africans have their tribes. They know where they belong. The white people all have their cliques, the civil servants, businessmen, and bankers; the farmers, settlers, and safari men. Each group has its little circle. Even the missionaries, I suppose, but they all call Scotland or England home. I want to call this home. I do call it home, but the European farmers and gentry don't think much of the missionaries, so they don't want me. I don't feel a part of them. I often feel as if I don't belong anywhere."

He reached for another sandwich, but the plate was empty. He had eaten them up while she was talking.

She laughed and reached into the basket for another plateful. "I brought tons." She passed them to him and then took one for herself. "I am afraid I have been boring you."

"Not in the least. Actually, I feel very much the same," he said.

"You? That cannot be. You are—" She was going to say "perfect," but she stopped herself just in time. She was sure if she went in that direction more than just her feelings about herself would come pouring out of her, things she would never have the courage to say to him, about how much she wanted him. She ate her sandwich instead. There was something so beautiful about the nape of his neck that she ached to kiss it. She loved him. Another thing she could never say to him.

He stretched out beside the picnic cloth with his head propped up on his hand. "What were you going to say I am?" *A prig*, he thought. Or a stuffed shirt.

"Nothing," she said. "It's just that you'd fit in anywhere."

"Which means I really don't belong anywhere," he said. "Like you. Oh, I have all the right bloodlines, but I spoiled it all by deciding to come here and serve in my present capacity. If I had acquired land, that sort of thing, they would have thought nothing of it. I would have been one of a group very like me in background. But I am not . . ." He stumbled over what to reveal. "I am not ready for that yet." He didn't say that he wanted to be married before he settled into a life like that, as he sometimes said to his male friends. He needed to get to know her better before he started that sort of talk. And he would never say how poverty stricken he was.

"At least you have your work," she said. "That gives you a position in life."

"Yes," he said. "And sport. I do fit in with the lads when I play cricket or polo."

She was rummaging in the basket, bringing out a tin of little cakes.

"On the playing field is where I have always felt most at home," he was saying and reaching for one of the sweets. "In sport the rules are clear and—"

"Shh—" She patted the air in front of her with her palms.

He sat up. One of the horses whinnied.

She stood and reached for the rifles behind her. He stood, too. "Back up," she said.

The horses stomped and kicked, dragged on the reins that bound them to the tree that shaded them.

She handed him his rifle. He moved in front of her. "Hyena," she said very quietly and evenly. "Do you see it?"

Just as she asked, he did: large and spotted, moving very quickly down the rock escarpment, making for them. He raised his rifle.

"There's another and another. Shoot," she said and raised her rifle, too.

He took the first shot, and the lead animal fell. A few feet off from the fallen hyena, the horses were in turmoil. He reloaded. She was ready but paused. The second animal turned tail and ran. A third, farther up, never came into full view but also made a hasty retreat. He kept his rifle aimed in their direction. She lowered hers and put her trigger hand on his shoulder. They stood perfectly still, as close together as they had been when they danced. "They are gone, I think," he said.

Her hand squeezed his upper arm. He heard her take in a deep breath. "I hate them. They are so ugly," she said. "My father tells me they are God's creatures, that they rarely attack people. The Kikuyu say they keep the land clean. But I have seen them take down a buffalo. One of them took the baby brother of a Kikuyu girl who was my playmate, when I was five years old. A sleeping infant."

He lowered the rifle. The danger had passed, but his thudding heart did not settle. It would take only the slightest movement for him to turn and take her in his arms. It took a great effort for him not to.

She let go of his arm. "Perhaps we had better go before their relatives descend on us," she said. Her voice, ordinarily low for a girl so slight, had turned husky.

"Are you alright? You've had a scare."

She laughed, making a silvery sound. "Not for the first time. My home," she said, "is quite a bit more beautiful, but also a lot more dangerous than the place my parents call by that name."

They wrapped up the picnic things in the cloth. Vera popped another sweet into Tolliver's mouth. She did not seem to realize what a gesture of intimacy that was to him.

They rode home with the sun lowering behind them and their shadows astride their horses side by side leading them along as they went. The way back seemed to take but a fraction of the time it had taken them to reach the picnic spot.

"Thank you," they said to each other simultaneously as they dismounted near the stable.

He looked up at the sky. "I'll have just enough light to make it home," he said. He hoped she heard the regret in his voice.

"Go on then," she said. "You have your match tomorrow."

"Yes." He wanted to linger but knew he could not.

"For luck," she said, and stood on tiptoe and gave him a swift kiss on the lips and ran away home.

II.

Both Justin Tolliver and Vera McIntosh thought often about that kiss over the next two days. If she had given it for luck, Tolliver made the most of it and saw to it that his team won the polo match on Sunday.

At the celebratory dinner that followed, Lucy Buxton approached him.

Tolliver had at that point completely abandoned Nurse Freemantle's prohibitions and accepted more than one too many whiskeys offered him by his team's supporters. In his cups, with his libido stimulated by his day with Vera but no hope of release there, he did not know how he would resist the lady's advances, or if he wanted to. In fact the nearer she got to his corner of the ballroom, the more beautiful she looked in her blue beaded gown that clung so delicately to her curves, which drove away all thought of Lord Delamere's warning about Lucy.

He smiled broadly at her and made a halfhearted stab at rising to greet her when she reached his side. "Sorry, my lady," he said, not too drunk to feel his grin to be lopsided.

"I'm a little wobbly on my feet just now, but I would love to have you join me in my little corner of the world. Won't you have a seat?"

He watched her blue-beaded backside as she took the chair to his right. There were other things he was supposed to be thinking about, but he could not quite remember what they were. "What can I do for you?" he asked, though he was sure he knew the answer and was growing ever more enthusiastic about the prospect.

Tolliver was nearly too drunk to see the truth when it came to him. "Fetching as you look with the whiskey stars in your eyes, oh hero of the polo field," Lucy said with a laugh, "I have not come to you for that purpose."

Tolliver thought to answer her, but he was sure he would slur his words if he tried.

Lucy went on. "I want you to invite me for breakfast tomorrow morning."

He shrugged, which she had the sense to interpret as a negative response.

"Don't worry, it needn't be early. Why don't we say at ten?" She stood. "Don't get up. I wouldn't want you to hurt yourself." She giggled. "I do think it's time for you to find your pillow."

She looked quite wonderful from behind as she walked away, a fact Tolliver had quite forgotten by the time she approached him the following morning in the dining room at the club. His head hurt too much for sexual fantasies. Though quite debilitated, he had enough brainpower left to wonder at this, especially given his prolonged state of celibacy. He wondered if he was getting old. He'd have his twenty-fourth birthday this year. That could not possibly be too old. The randiest men he knew were quite a bit older than that. The thought made his head hurt more.

When Ndege had wakened him at nine, he had only the vaguest recollection of having seen Lucy in the ballroom the night before, and none at all of having agreed to have breakfast with her. But a note from the lady had arrived that morning to remind him, and Tolliver had arrived at the club with but a few minutes to spare. He had barely taken his seat when she came toward him with her graceful strides and said, sotto voce, "I could see the headache pain in your eyes from halfway across the room. I'll whisper, not to make it worse."

Tolliver had risen when she approached and wished she would hurry and sit down. "Please join me. What will you have?"

"Just a coffee. I had breakfast ages ago." She looked around the dining room, which was, happily, empty except for the two of them and the waiter. The Monday morning business breakfast meetings had ended, and the important and self-important of Nairobi had gone off to their respective desks. It suddenly occurred to Tolliver that if Cranford saw him and Lucy together in the morning he might think they had spent the night together. That thought intensified the pain splitting his forehead. He reached for his coffee cup.

"First of all," Lucy said. "I want to apologize for my unladylike behavior toward you over the past several days. I was very drunk, and you are just too damned attractive."

Tolliver did not know where to look, much less what to say. "You need not have come here to apologize," he said. "I think you were grieving, and it got the better of you."

She looked at him for longer than was comfortable for him before she spoke again. "When I agreed to marry Kirk he was every bit as gorgeous as you are now," she said at last. "I could not have imagined that in fifteen years he would have turned into the slug he now is. I was twenty and he was thirty. If I had let myself go as he has . . ." She did not complete the thought. She did not need to.

"As I said, Mrs.—um—Lucy, you need not apologize to me. Let us forget it ever happened. I have to go on with my investigation, and it would be best if you and I did not see anything of each other until that is over. To tell you the truth, I am late getting to work now. As you undoubtedly saw, I overdid the celebrating last evening."

The waiter approached, and Lucy Buxton ordered a coffee. She turned to Tolliver with an almost motherly concern in her eyes. "I can see you are not at your bright-eyed best. I will get to the point. I did not come just to apologize. I said all that first because I want you to understand the seriousness of what I say next. It is about your investigating my husband in the death of Josiah Pennyman."

Tolliver had barely opened his mouth, when she waved away his objection. "No. No. Don't be shocked at how much I know. You must learn that everyone knows everything here. It is almost totally impossible for a person to have a conversation with anyone in a public place without it becoming common knowledge within a few hours."

He squared his shoulders and made an attempt at dignified speech. "As I have just tried to tell you, Mrs. Buxton, I am not at all sure that I should discuss my investigation with you. There are rules that govern my work."

She was spooning sugar and pouring cream into the coffee the waiter had placed at her elbow. "I have information that will have a profound effect on your thinking about why Josiah Pennyman was killed and who might have done it," she said. "I know that you have established where Kirk was at the time of Josiah's death, that he could not have done it with his own hands. Have you considered that he may have paid someone to do the deed for him?"

She might have hit Tolliver with a thunderbolt. "Why would you imagine such a thing?" he managed to ask once he had recovered his thoughts.

She put down her cup and sighed. "I imagine, though I have never heard you say it, that you think Kirk might have killed Josiah to defend his honor against the man who seduced his wife. Believe me, Captain Tolliver, that would not be anything that would motivate old Kirk. It was Kirk's true love, money, that was at stake."

Tolliver saw where she was going with her line of talk and imagined that she was about to reveal what he already knew from Lord Delamere about Pennyman's loan, but she surprised him. "If Kirk killed Josiah, it would have been to shut him up." She studied him to see if she had engaged his interest.

She had. "Go on, please."

She leaned forward and lowered her voice though the waiter had left and they were alone. "Kirk has been dabbling in land speculation in secret, something that is strictly against the rules, actions that could ruin his reputation as a banker. Such as it is."

Tolliver wanted to know more about that reputation. His mother always tried to stifle his natural curiosity by warning him not to pry. Now it was his duty. "What would you say people think of Mr. Buxton?"

She looked surprised, as if he were the mere boy she sometimes assumed him to be. "He is working for the Standard Bank of India, Mr. Tolliver. It is owned by colonials in the Raj. It does have a London office, but it is not as if he is employed by a venerable old English institution. And he is the branch manager, not a managing director. Kirk Buxton has neither the bloodlines nor the brainpower to aspire to anything that one would actually call prestigious."

Justin Tolliver's headache was getting worse. "Just what has this got to do with the death of Josiah Pennyman?" His tone was harsher than he intended, but the words were spoken, and there was nothing he could do about them now.

She did not seem to mind. "Josiah found out about Kirk's underhanded dealings. Given that Josiah was extremely upset when Kirk rescinded the loan for his improvements on his farm, he threatened my husband, said that if Kirk did not change his mind and give him the money, he would publicly accuse Kirk of using the bank's deposits for his own speculative land deals. Certainly, then, Kirk would have lost his position with the bank. He might very well go to jail. You're a policeman. You must know the law on such matters."

"And this makes you think that Mr. Buxton paid someone to kill Dr. Pennyman?" He was incredulous, and it showed.

Lucy rolled her eyes to the ceiling. "I told you that my husband does not think about anything but money. It is everything to him. It's a short step from understanding that fact to knowing he is capable of using money as a murder weapon." She stood.

Tolliver started to rise, but she held up her lovely hands to stop him. "Don't bother to get up. Just think about what I have said." She picked up her handbag from beside her chair and marched away, showing Tolliver his now favorite view of her, for more reasons than one.

He sank back in his chair. He had to report to D.C. Cranford at eleven. Lucy Buxton had just turned everything he thought he would say upside down.

He looked into his empty coffee cup and around at the deserted dining room. He reached across the table and took the half-cup Lucy had left behind and drank it. He was certain that putting on his pith helmet when he went outside would make his head explode.

Kwai Libazo was happy to take up his post at the wall behind A.D.S. Tolliver in the district commissioner's office. Listening to these men talk had taught him more about them than any of the books by Englishmen that Libazo had read at his mission school in Kibwezi. The window beside him was open, bringing in the sounds of the crews installing the electric light poles. Electricity was a wonder, everyone said. When the whites came to the country with lanterns that could burn and give light in the night, the tribespeople had thought them a form of magic. This new thing, that required all these black wires—they said it would make the night in the town like the day. Kwai Libazo wished they would work faster because he was very keen to see them banish the darkness forever.

Unlike Tolliver's usual posture of standing before his superior's desk, today he had taken a chair. Libazo was happy that his ears were good because the sounds from outside would otherwise drown out Tolliver's voice.

Cranford and Tolliver had begun, as the white men always did, by not speaking about what they had come together to say.

"Very well done, on the polo field yesterday, my boy. Very well, indeed." The district commissioner's voice, as usual, boomed. He always seemed to be speaking to a whole village, even when there was only one person in the room with him. Cranford, of course, would not count Kwai Libazo. British people did not care what he thought, or even if he thought. At first, Libazo had found it insulting when they paid him so little mind, though he knew he could never complain about it. But now, he found it convenient. His insignificance meant they also did not care what he heard. More than once since he joined the police force, he had overheard very helpful information. His missionary teacher had often instructed the boys in his class about the two sides of the coin. With white people there was always the coin, and it always had two sides.

"Thank you, sir," Tolliver was saying, "Thistle is a great pony."

"Capital. Capital. Now let us get this business of the witch doctor over and done with, shall we?"

"Well, sir, I believe you saw in my written report, about Kirk Buxton's whereabouts, etc."

"Damn fine job of work, too." Cranford slammed his hand on a sheaf of papers to his right on the desk. Behind him, the punkah toto, pulling the cord for the overhead fan, gave a shudder of shock. The district commissioner went right on. "I sent a copy of it to London in the dispatch box on this morning's train." He fingered the pages. "This will keep those interfering homebodies in the colonial office in London out of our hair." He ran his hand over his head and what there was left of hair on it.

Captain Tolliver leaned forward and put his forearm on the desk. He pinched the bridge of his nose, which meant that the headache he had complained of coming here was getting worse. "Just this morning, I have found there is something more to add, I am afraid, District Commissioner, sir."

Libazo's attention perked up. When the captain had come to get him and take him along to this meeting, he had said that he needed an extra pair of ears with him, that he had to drop a bombshell, and that he was hung over. These were the kind of terms that Libazo now understood. The captain did not mean to cause an actual explosion, but to say something that would upset his superior very much. Many times in speaking, British people said things in this descriptive way; similar to the way the Kikuyu named white people for things they wore or said. The captain was about to explode his bomb.

"Lucy Buxton suggested to me this morning, sir—"

D.C. Cranford looked very sour and waved his hands in front of him, as if he were trying to stop a wagon. "Let us not bring your pillow talk into this, Mr. Tolliver. I've told you—"

Tolliver leapt to his feet. Now his voice was almost as loud as Cranford's. "If you please, District Commissioner. Your assumptions about Mrs. Buxton and me are entirely wrong. There is no pillow talk. In fact, there is no pillow any-thing between Mrs. Buxton and me. I resent . . ." His voice trailed off. He took several breaths and sat back down. "I apologize, sir. Last week, in her grief over Pennyman's death, and in her cups, Mrs. Buxton lost control and tried to . . . Whatever she thought, I was not her man. I am not her man. Please let me tell you what she suggests."

"Very well, but I don't see how it could possibly change my mind."

Tolliver went on to say something that seemed not to impress Cranford at all, but impressed Libazo very much—that Mr. Buxton might have paid someone to kill the Scot-tish doctor. This was an idea entirely new to Kwai Libazo. Would anyone accept money to kill a person? Certainly he knew that people had killed others to rob their money. The first case he had worked on with Tolliver, six months ago, when Inspector Tolliver had been new to the force, had in-volved such a thing. Also, the Kikuyu and Maasai killed each other in wars to steal cattle. And tribesmen had been known to kill members of their own tribes in rages. But would some-one do it to be paid?

"I'm not having any of it." The district commissioner sounded like a roaring lion.

"But, sir—"

"No, Captain. The entire idea is preposterous. I've known

Kirk Buxton for years. He is a banker, not a member of some secret Chinese killing society. Besides, except for a talent for bridge, the man is practically an idiot. He doesn't have the capacity to organize such an endeavor."

"Now, sir, really. He is the manager of one of the largest banks in Nairobi. Surely if he can run a bank—"

"No. No. First of all, he is only the branch manager. That doesn't take the intelligence of a flea. Banking is the easiest game in the world. It's run on the principle of if you have an orchard we will be happy to lend you an apple. They lend money only to people who don't really need it, charge them for the privilege, and almost always get recompensed no matter what happens. You don't need to be a strategist to be a banker."

"So, what do you think I ought to do about Mrs. Buxton's suggestion, then?"

"Nothing. Absolutely nothing. Waste of time. Can't see how you could ever prove such a thing anyway. You have your man. Get him up before the magistrate immediately, give the court the facts of the case, and put Mbura before a firing squad."

"A firing squad, sir? Not a hanging?"

Libazo had thought they were through with firing squads.

"What's the difference? The disgusting barbarian will be dead at the end of it."

Tolliver stood up, at attention. Libazo knew from his determined posture that he was about to say something dangerous to himself. "I must tell you, sir, that I am absolutely set upon seeing justice is served. I intend to file a report to the colonial office of Mrs. Buxton's accusation. And for the rest of it, if you are set on a premature trial and the execution of Gichinga Mbura before we have exhausted the other possibilities of who might have killed Josiah Pennyman, you will have to find someone else to do it. I will not carry out your order until I have decent evidence that Mbura committed the crime. He may very well be the murderer, sir, but if we are here to bring to this continent all that is best of England and English law and justice, then we must do it properly."

Only with a great effort was Kwai Libazo able to keep his statuelike posture. He had not yet told Tolliver what he had found out on Sunday at Richard Newland's farm. He wanted to blurt it out now, to support Tolliver's contention, but he knew he would lose his position on the police force if he said a word.

His work had become more important to him than anything else in his life. In fact, it was the first thing he had come across that drew all of him, that made him feel like a man. He had been denied warrior status in both his mother's and his father's tribes. He belonged nowhere in his native land. And he knew very well that he could never be seen as a true member of the white people's tribe, though he now served them. But when Justin Tolliver spoke to him of their mission to instill the rule of law and justice, he wanted to serve that. The rule of law and justice was his tribe.

A very red D.C. Cranford was sputtering. "Stop with that immediately, Mr. Tolliver. You risk your position entirely if you continue with this nonsense. Sit back down, man. You are forgetting yourself."

Libazo's heart trembled when he saw Justin Tolliver retake his seat. If Tolliver gave in to Cranford's demands,

Kwai's loyalty to Tolliver would be destroyed, and Kwai's purpose in serving him would be lost.

"That's better," the district commissioner was saying. "I think you are letting your feelings for Lucy Buxton get the better of your good judgment."

Kwai Libazo saw Tolliver's neck and back turn to the stone he himself was trying to imitate. Tolliver gripped the sides of his chair.

"Ah, I seemed to have hit the mark. I have told you that you must not—"

"Begging your pardon, sir, I have already told you, you are mistaken. I do not have the feelings for Mrs. Buxton you imagine."

Cranford patted the air in front of him and laughed. "Ever the gentleman," he said. "You needn't deny it to save the lady's reputation, my boy. I saw it with my own eyes. And quite understandable it was, though I must say—"

Tolliver started to get up again.

"Oh, sit back down. I was a young buck once myself. I understand the temptations of virility, it's just that—"

"Really, Mr. District Commissioner, sir, you must allow me to explain."

The missionaries who taught Kwai Libazo to speak English had made a great point that it was forbidden to interrupt a person who was speaking. Yet, British people seemed to do it to one another all the time.

"I am all ears," the district commissioner said, which almost made Libazo laugh out loud, since the district commissioner did have extremely large ears that stuck out from his head. That and the grayness of his habitual clothing, his hair, his eyes, and even his skin was why the Kikuyu nick-named him Elephant-man.

"Please, let me put aside this notion of my having an . . . of anything serious going on between Mrs. Buxton and my-self. You must believe me. What you saw that night was Mrs. Buxton, having had too much to drink, looking to me for . . . It was not my intention to . . ." The back of Tolliver's neck had changed nearly to the color of Kwai Libazo's uni-form fez.

Tolliver's hands gripped the edge of his chair again. "Sir, I am acting as an investigator here. That is all, and I do think we must deal with Mrs. Buxton's accusation. We are here to serve justice, are we not?"

"Dear boy, what is to stop us imaging that Lucy Buxton is accusing her husband of doing what she herself might have done: hired someone to kill the doctor. She is far clev-erer than her husband, I dare say. If we are going to let our imaginations run wild, suppose Pennyman was throwing her over and she could not stand to lose him. I would not put it past him to be two-timing the lady—given the reputation he arrived with about not being able to control his pudding."

Again Tolliver was struck as silent as Kwai Libazo had been trained to keep himself. It took him a moment and then he said, "With great reluctance, sir, I am going to re-veal that Mrs. Buxton told me that Pennyman had informa-tion about Kirk that could ruin him. Information Pennyman had threatened to reveal."

"What information?"

"Sir, it is an act that could be a crime. I will not accuse Mr. Buxton of it until I have corroboration of his wife's word."

Libazo did not understand the word "corroboration," but it seemed to quell the D.C.'s curiosity.

"Given your confounded idealism, I will not press you for it now, but whatever it is, you had better get to the bottom of it and quickly." Now the district commissioner rose from his chair. "I am in a mood to be a bit lenient about this, my boy, but not for much longer. Let the witch doctor rot in jail a few more days. Give it one last stab to put your conscience to rest on this subject. But I will not stand for any threats of making trouble for me by writing reports to London. I will give you one more chance, but this is the last. And if I hear another word about your writing reports, I will write one that will destroy your career, about your making love to a suspect in the case."

Tolliver opened his mouth as if to object, but Cranford signaled him to hold his words. "It may be stuff and non-sense, but I do not have to take your word on that. If you are going to go about acting like a jumped-up little shit and threatening to go over my head, I shall have to put you in your place. I give you one week to answer for all of this. If you refuse after that to follow my orders and get the witch doctor before the magistrate, I'll have you on a boat back to Portsmouth before you can say Jack Robinson." He then put his left hand on Tolliver's shoulder, like a father would do giving advice to his son. "Get on with it then and give it your best if you must. Youthful idealism will have its day. Then, once you have seen the folly of trying to make a watertight case of this, take the evidence to court. You know very well that when you finally follow my orders, the mumbo-jumbo man will be found guilty and that will be an end on it, and we'll have the barbarian's head." He extended his hand to the captain.

Tolliver shook the district commissioner's hand, an Englishman's sign of having reached an agreement, but Kwai Libazo could not tell exactly what it was they had decided to do. It seemed to have something to do with stopping before the truth was known and taking off Gichinga Mbura's head, something Kwai knew from reading the missionary's English books that the British actually used to do to their criminals. But Kwai Libazo believed Mbura was not the murderer. The god of justice, that he had lately learned to worship, demanded that he save the medicine man's head, even if he despised the man himself.

Libazo marched smartly behind Captain Tolliver out to the lobby of Government House and into the street. "Where can we go from here?" Tolliver said under his breath more to himself than to his companion.

"Sir?" Kwai Libazo was not sure what Tolliver wanted him to say, but he had a very good idea about where they should go.

"Nothing. I was just thinking aloud," Tolliver said. He looked distracted and confused.

"I think, B'wana, that we should go to Richard Newland's farm."

"Why, in God's name?"

"I still do not understand exactly the meaning of proof," Libazo said, "but I often hear you talk of things that might have happened, and if these things actually did happen they would mean it is not proved that Gichinga Mbura killed the mission doctor."

"Yes?" Tolliver did not seem to have understood what Libazo was trying to say, but he had started to walk in the direction of the stable.

"Sir. I thought of such a possibility. Yesterday, I went to Richard Newland's farm to find out if this thing I imagined really did happen. I think it did, sir."

"Well, out with it then. What did you find out?"

"The missionary's son, sir, did not leave two days before the doctor died. His family say that he did, but he did not. The workers at the farm told me this. The hunting party did not leave until the morning of the death, sir."

Tolliver stopped and looked at Libazo. They were so much the same height that they were eye to eye. "You went to the Newland farm to ask that question?"

"Yes, B'wana."

"How did you get there?"

"By the train, sir. And I walked from the station."

For a moment, it seemed as if Tolliver was going to say that he didn't believe Kwai. He was shaking his head as if to say no. "You can't mean you think Otis McIntosh had something to do with his uncle's death. He is just a boy."

"I believe he has fourteen years, sir. If he was a Maasai he would be ready for *emorata*. For circumcision."

Like all white men, Tolliver grimaced at the word. "Still."

"I was only thinking of what might be possible, sir. I understand that you want to make very sure that the only man who could have killed the doctor is Gichinga Mbura."

For the first time, but not for the last, Justin Tolliver realized that he trusted Kwai Libazo's instincts more than he trusted those of any white man he knew.

"You are right, then, Libazo, we must find out why there is a difference between what people are telling us about Otis McIntosh and the truth."

Kwai Libazo was happy with this decision, but when they collected Tolliver's stallion and Kwai's pony at the Afghan, Ali Khan's stable, Tolliver turned not toward the road toward Chania Bridge and Richard Newland's farm, but toward the Parklands section of the town. "There is a question I need to ask of Mrs. Buxton before we leave town," he said.

From time to time, he had taken to doing this, to explaining his actions to Kwai Libazo. A very surprising thing for a British man to do.

For the second time in the past week, Denys Finch Hatton was sitting on Vera McIntosh's veranda, sipping tea. Vera's mother had greeted the young man, but quickly excused herself, citing mission work to be done and leaving only the houseboy Njui to attend on her daughter. It did not escape Vera's notice that her mother was willing to let her take a picnic alone with Justin Tolliver, but she was unwilling to leave her with Denys Finch Hatton here on the veranda.

As usual, Finch Hatton's conversation centered on the local peoples and their habits and any changes Vera had seen since the founding of the Protectorate and the recent influx of settlers. It was a subject that greatly interested Vera as well and that she discussed with relish, especially with one who seemed as sensitive to the problems the British were causing as Vera was. It would all have been quite delightful but for the fact that Finch Hatton's presence made Vera so jumpy and unsure of herself.

For one thing, her caller always seemed to be around when Tolliver arrived and his presence seemed to displease Tolliver very much. Not that Vera was expecting Captain Tolliver to call on an ordinary Monday, but she always hoped to see him. And when the rider appeared at the top of the ridge overlooking the mission an hour ago, she had thought from a distance that he might be Justin. Ever since Saturday, she had had this fantasy that he had come back and that he would kiss her on the back of her neck.

But the rider turned out to be Finch Hatton, with his amazingly shiny eyes and bodily grace, and the fact that he focused so totally on her when she was speaking. He treated her as if she were some African wise woman, when she was nothing more than a girl who had been born here a few months after her missionary parents arrived, had been educated by her parents, and had none of his sophistication or verve. He had listened to her telling him about the camping places along the Uaso Nyiro River that she had visited last year, on safari, with her father and her brother. She had just told Finch Hatton how well she remembered the details of each place. When one was out in the wild, every detail remained forever vivid.

He was gazing out over the fields of fading coffee blossoms, across the river to the hills in the distance. "It's strange," he said. "From far away it looks all of a piece, but then when you are in it, especially if you see one of the rare animals, a leopard or a cheetah particularly, it becomes so distinct in your memory." His voice was beautiful. His accent perfect, but it carried none of the self-importance that she often heard in the voices of many Englishmen. They made her feel out of place. Instead, he made her important, but somehow feeling important made her even more nervous, a discomfort that redoubled when he brought up Captain Tolliver's name.

"Tolliver has arrested the witch doctor."

"Yes, I know." She was suddenly on her guard. What would she say to him if he asked her a question she did not want to answer, about how her uncle had made an enemy of Gichinga?

"How has your father dealt with the presence of the Kikuyu and their medicine man? Converting the natives must have been hard given their beliefs in their witch doctor's powers."

"My father is a joyful Christian, Mr. Finch Hatton. His favorite quote from the Bible is from the Psalms: 'Make a joyful noise unto the Lord all ye lands. Serve the Lord with gladness.'"

Finch Hatton's bright eyes danced with glee. "Not very Scottish of him." He didn't seem in the least worried that he might have insulted her heritage.

Loving her father as she did, she could not take umbrage. She thought the same of him—that he was not at all like the dour clergymen she had met in Glasgow. "His grandfather on his mother's side was an Anglo-Irish bishop. He was named Berkeley as it happened. I think he might have also been somewhere in Berkeley Cole's family tree. Anyway, the medicine man's most powerful weapon is the fear he can engender with his curses. My father's is to have his flock experience the joy of loving Jesus. He thinks joy can drive out fear."

Finch Hatton's bright blue glance left the sunbathed landscape and looked into her face. He seemed pained when he said, "I wish that were true."

She stood his piercing gaze as long as she could and looked down at her heavy boots, that her father insisted she always wear to ward off snakebite. Her father was not entirely immune to fear himself. "I wish that, too. But my father has made a number of converts. I think it is because he is so kind. I am sure if people love Jesus it's because they have grown to love my father." She knew she loved her father better than she loved the Lord. She was supposed to think that wrong, and she would never say it. Not to her father and not to Finch Hatton.

"Speaking of powerful weapons," Denys said, "I understand that the evidence against the native priest is a spear, and that there is some question of it being a Maasai weapon because of its shape."

That Finch Hatton, who had no connection to the deceased or to the police, knew this startled Vera. She did not know why, but she thought it ought to be a secret. She began to feel resentful that he knew it.

He laughed that rich, liquid laugh of his. His eyes danced. "You must not be so surprised. You were born here; you have to know full well that there are not that many people here and to a man, gossip is almost as important to them as making a profit from what they do."

She was just enough put out by his glee in all of this to snap back. "You speak as if only the Europeans are people.

And maybe only the men. There are actually quite a lot of people here, and the Africans don't all gossip all the time."

He put his hands together and bowed his head and spoke contritely. "Point well taken. I do wonder about that assumption though, about who might have used that weapon and why. Is it true that you can tell what tribe made the spear by looking at it."

"Yes," she said, not entirely mollified. "Actually, the local ironworkers can tell which blacksmith made which implement, in much the same way you can tell a Rembrandt from a Rubens."

"Is there a blacksmith nearby?"

She pointed to their right. "Just beyond those woods. At the edge of the Kikuyu village."

"I'd like to see that." He leapt to his feet. "Take me to see it, please."

She rose slowly. "I will speak to my mother."

"Yes, of course." He remained standing while she left the veranda.

Once inside, she quickly found her mother in her workroom near the rear door, teaching three Kikuyu girls to make European dresses for themselves. Fearful of being roped into that effort, Vera quickly asked permission to take Denys Finch Hatton to visit the Kikuyu village. "Do not worry, Mother. I am not at all interested in him," she quickly added.

Her mother's brown eyes looked disbelieving, as if Vera had said something patently impossible. "You may go. Stick to the path."

"Of course." Vera took her rifle from the rack on the wall

of her father's study and pocketed a few shells. She felt vaguely unfaithful to Justin Tolliver as she walked onto the lawn with Denys Finch Hatton. "Perhaps you should take a rifle, too. At this hour the woods are usually safe, but—"

He was already trotting toward the stable to fetch his weapon from the holster on his horse.

The path was empty. The Kikuyu workers were gathered in the shade of the coffee plants taking their midmorning rest. Denys, to Vera's delight, seemed content to leave off their conversation and walk in silence, listening only to the chirping of the insects and the chattering of little gray monkeys in the trees. The path, which ran between the coffee field and the cow pasture on one side and the woods on the other, was only partly shaded this close to midday. It cooled considerably once it plunged into the forest.

Vera was admiring the flowering creepers hanging from tall trees and glistening here and there in pools of sunlight, when suddenly something more beautiful caught her eye. She put out her left arm to stop Finch Hatton and then moved her index finger to her lips. She pointed up at a rain tree a few yards into the woods.

Finch Hatton took a quick, nearly soundless deep breath. About twenty feet from the ground, on a horizontal limb, a leopard was resting. The skin, bones, and gnawed carcass of a bushbuck hung over the limb between him and the trunk. His eyes were half closed. The handsome animal, which might have been deadly under other circumstances, was obviously sated from his early morning kill and not interested in anything but napping and digesting. Still, after admiring its beauty for a brief while, Vera, never taking her eyes from him, backed along the path. Denys, his rifle at the ready, followed her example.

"How did you notice him?" Finch Hatton asked when they had gotten far enough away. "He was practically invisible with his spots in the dappled light."

"His tail hanging down," Vera said. "You learn. When you have done it often enough, your eyes get used to what they are seeing. They seem to do it on their own, without your trying."

Finch Hatton shouldered his rifle. "I think that some people have a talent for it. You must."

Though his compliment gave her a glow, she said, "In a place like this, a person wouldn't live very long if he completely lacked that skill."

"I hope I have it. I want to stay here." He said that with a passion she sometimes heard from British people who seemed to love Africa as much as she did, even though, or perhaps because they were born and raised up there in the chill north.

"Why did you come here in the first place?"

"I am a second son," he said. "I did not want to give my life over to the pursuit of an heiress." He laughed as if it were a joke. She stopped and looked at him to see if it really was.

His expression was completely jocular. "Not really. Doing that was never anything I seriously considered. I may have been born to it, but the sort of life I'd have had in England did not appeal. I needed something more. I thought I would find what I wanted here."

"And did you?"

His beatific smile dawned on his face. "Yes, I think I have."

If this had been a conversation between two characters in the novels Vera's granny sent her every Christmas, his words might have been the prelude to a proposal of marriage. But Finch Hatton was not looking at her when he talked of what he was looking for. His bright eyes scanned the trees and flowers of the forest and the ribbon of blue sky above them on the path. His arm swept an arc. "I did not know until I arrived here that this is what I wanted—a place where life can be forever new."

"I am glad you can see it for what it is." She turned and pointed to a narrow path that forked off from the main way to the village. "The blacksmith is down this way."

They went quickly through a little corner of the forest, wary on the odd chance that a lion might be out looking for breakfast. Pink-blooming African daphnes surrounded their way, turning the scent of this forest from spice to sweet perfume. They emerged into an open area that smelled only of smoke and hot metal. There stood the smithy next to a hollow dug into the ground, lined with clay, and topped with a cone-shaped furnace. Vera pointed at it. "That is where he smelts his ore."

She drew Denys to the open-sided shed under which Muturi Embu, the blacksmith, stood. He was taking a red glowing lump of iron out of the fire with tongs and placing it on a stone before him. He was of short stature, like most of the Kikuyu tribesmen, but very powerful in his upper body. He wore a dark stained cloth tied around his waist that covered him to his ankles and a cowhide apron over his chest. The brown skin of his arms glowed with sweat. Behind him, on the single wall of his shed, hung all manner of spear blades, swords, arrowheads, hoes, knives, axes, and the razors that the Kikuyu, both men and women, used to shave their heads.

Vera greeted him in his language. He bowed to her without letting go of his tongs or saying more than *"Antiriri, wim-wega."*

"Antiriri," Vera answered. "I am well." She asked after his wives and children and told him Finch Hatton's name.

"I suppose," Denys said, "that he works out here away from the village to avoid the danger of the fire."

Vera could not suppress a giggle. "There is fire in or near every single hut in the village. No, he is here because the Kikuyu consider the blacksmith unclean, so he must stay away from the others. Smiths cannot marry except within their group."

"Like the lower castes in India? I didn't know that happened here. Ask him if I can look at the spearheads." It was one of the things Vera liked very much about Finch Hatton. Most white settlers would not have asked permission of a native to do anything. They had not asked permission to move into their country and take it over. They always assumed they had a perfect right to take whatever they wanted. But Finch Hatton was not like that.

When he gained the blacksmith's assent, he carefully took down a spearhead. Vera went to his side and explained to him what about its design made it recognizable as Kikuyu. And how a Maasai spear would be different.

"Ask him if he would make me a Maasai spearhead."

Vera did not like the question but she asked it, and Muturi Embu responded exactly as she expected him to and more respectfully than Finch Hatton deserved. "He says that he will be happy to make a spearhead for you in his design, but if the B'wana wants a Maasai spear, he must go to the Maasai blacksmith to get it. Given the traditional enmity between the Kikuyu and the Maasai, I think he finds the question a bit—" She didn't have the nerve to say "disrespectful."

"I asked," Finch Hatton said, "because I wondered if the Kikuyu witch doctor could have easily gotten his hands on a Kikuyu spear that looked Maasai."

Vera wondered at this. Was Finch Hatton trying to solve the crime? The way Justin Tolliver frowned whenever he saw Denys, he was sure to see such an attempt as meddling. But then she did a little meddling of her own and asked Muturi Embu if and how a Kikuyu might come into possession of a Maasai spear.

"We have taken their spears in battles in the past," the blacksmith told her, "but never as many as they take of ours. But we blacksmiths melt them down and remake them into other things. We would never ever fight with one another's spears or swords. The sword of one's enemy kills one's brother."

"So there are no Maasai spears among the Kikuyu?" She had thought this was the case, but she wanted to hear the blacksmith say it.

"There are traders, who travel all around from the Lake Nam Lolwe—which you call Victoria—all the way to the coast that trade in what the blacksmiths of all the tribes make. There have always been these people. My grandfather spoke of his grandfather trading with them. If a person wants to get a Maasai spear, he can find one."

"Could Gichinga Mbura have gotten one from a trader?"

Muturi Embu put down his work. "Mbura is too proud a man to have killed the Scottish doctor that way. If he had killed him with a spear, any spear, all would have seen that he was afraid of the white doctor's magic."

Once Vera explained what he had said to Finch Hatton, they both saw that this was a much more plausible reason to consider the witch doctor innocent than was the rigmarole about the Maasai spear. She thought she had better tell this to Captain Tolliver. Then, Muturi Embu said something that overrode all that.

"I myself have had Maasai swords and spears from the traders. Since the white man came, I have always been able to trade unusual iron things for goods that please my wives. There are white men who always want to trade for Maasai spears, especially old ones. I think because the Maasai are such fierce warriors that these men think their spears will make them strong, too. I had one during the long rains this year. I have never seen one like it—it had a design on the blade like this." He drew a line in the air with his forefinger.

Vera's skin went cold. The design he traced was that strange Egyptian-like one that was on the spear that had killed her uncle.

Embu smiled with glee. "The trader said that it was very old. I sold it for more rupees than I have ever had from that

white man—Too-many-hats. He always wants to buy all the
Maasai spears. What can he do with so many of them?"

Vera's breath stopped. Too-many-hats was the Kikuyu
name for Richard Newland.

12.

Justin Tolliver left his horse with Kwai Libazo in the shade of a jacaranda tree and approached the Buxton house in Parklands, the toney white residential district of Nairobi. The front door, with glass panels on either side, was far too grand for the size of the building. He pulled the cord for the bell and waited. There was no awning over the doorstep. At this hour, any caller waited in direct sunlight.

In a few seconds, a slender Somali, very grand in a red and blue turban with a brocade vest over a silk robe, opened the door. Tolliver would have expected to see such a creature in the entourage of the Sultan of Zanzibar. Once he had stated his business, the majordomo let him in. The door led through a tiny entryway and directly to a living room decorated with chairs upholstered in embroidered silk and the sort of sandalwood furniture that one found in the London parlors of men who had served in India.

The too-chic Somali left Tolliver standing there holding his pith helmet and disappeared to the back of the house. A few minutes later, Lucy descended the overly wide staircase evidently designed to lend drama to her entrances. She took full advantage of it by pausing halfway down and extending her lithe arms. The gesture might have had the effect she intended if she were wearing the light cotton frock she had sported at breakfast or that blue-beaded evening gown, instead of the rather dowdy usual uniform of European women in the Protectorate, too many layers of khaki twill. "To what do I owe the honor of this call?" She spoke as if she had never tried to drum up his suspicions against her husband.

"I am sorry to disturb you, Mrs. Buxton. I have just one question to ask you about what you told me this morning. I should have thought of it then, but as you know, my head was not right." He did not blush. Not even when she responded with, "Your presence does disturb me, Mr. Tolliver, but you already know that. Can I give you something to drink?"

"No, thank you. I want only this one piece of information. How did Josiah Pennyman find out about Mr. Buxton's dealings, that you say could ruin your husband if the word got out." She frowned so deeply he thought he must reassure her. "By the way, I want you to know that I have not reported the details of what you said to anyone yet. I thought I had better not until—"

She put her fingers on his arm. At closer range, Tolliver could smell gin on her. "Don't you understand?" she said earnestly. "I do not care if Kirk's crimes become known."

"Surely his being accused will make a great deal of difference in your life. It must matter to you."

"He does not matter to me."

Tolliver could not respond in any way—not as a policeman

and certainly not as a well-bred man. In the silent moment that followed, he saw her motivation. She wanted her husband disgraced so she could divorce him. He ignored that suspicion. "It will matter," he said. "If he loses his position, you will lose yours, too." He looked down at the hat in his hand. "You must think about that."

Still she said nothing.

"Was it you who—"

She stopped his words with a gesture and a tinkling laugh and completed his sentence for him. "—Who told Josiah. Of course it was. I thought it might get me free of Kirk, if he was punished and disgraced. Free to marry Dr. Pennyman. You see, that has been my downfall. For all his airs and graces and his endless rubbers of bridge with the aristocrats, Kirk is not one of them and never will be. He will never be my ticket into the upper classes. Since my disappointment in him, I have been looking for the real article."

Everything she was saying surprised Tolliver. The women he knew at home might be scheming viragos, but they would never admit to their plotting—no matter how much gin they had drunk. Standing here listening to her made his blood itch. He could barely stand still for it. But he had to hear her out. There was something in what Lucy was telling him, something that could make a difference in solving the case of Josiah Pennyman. So he steeled himself against the intensity of his discomfort and let her prattle on, even smiled to encourage her.

His reputedly adorable boyish grin did not work its magic, though. Lucy must have read his thoughts in his face. Suddenly the stream of her complaints dried up. She clamped her rather prominent front teeth on her bottom lip, thought for a moment, and finally said stiffly, "I think I have answered what you said was your one question, Assistant District Superintendent Tolliver." This was the first time she had ever addressed him by his title. Coming from a woman of her station, such as she was, it was not a compliment.

His only way to escape the silence that then fell was to run away.

As quickly as was seemly, he made for Libazo and the horses and sped on his way to Newland's farm.

Like all settlers, Justin Tolliver and Richard Newland had more than a passing acquaintance. They did not know each other well, but they had met at cricket matches and club dances and dinners. Tolliver did not know much more about the man than one learned at such events and had never been to Newland's farm. He let Kwai Libazo lead the way, which took them by a very hilly forest road on the north side of the rail line, slow going since they had to be careful of their horses on the uneven surface and wary of what might lurk among the trees on either side.

Tolliver began the trek by amusing himself trying to identify the birds that chattered and flew up on either side of them as they cantered along the flat stretches and picked their careful way up and down the gullies. The only creatures he spotted that he could name were a red-headed weaver and paradise fly-catcher, which he was sure were the easiest to tell, with their distinctive beak colors. He knew every bird in the whole of Yorkshire and had since he was in short pants.

Here, so far, he was hopeless at this. He wondered if Vera McIntosh could teach him their names. Once she came into his mind, he wound up entertaining a fantasy about her that felt more like a honeymoon than a birdwatching excursion.

He forced his mind to concentrate on his investigation. Picturing the nearly apoplectic district commissioner during their meeting that morning drove away any pleasant ideas of what it would be like to make love to Vera. Cranford was losing all patience. Justin could not keep on insisting they eliminate anyone else who might have murdered Pennyman. To Tolliver's way of thinking, the whole business was a terrible muddle. He was supposed to be proving exactly what happened. But how could he do so positively. He could not find a reliable witness among the natives to give him facts for or against Mbura. He had taken the route of process of elimination. A foolish choice since there was no way he could eliminate everyone in the Protectorate, black and white. He was traveling—very like this trip on his horse, sometimes fast, most of the time painstakingly slowly, and he feared he was on a dead-end street.

Each new piece of information, rather than driving away doubt, complicated matters. Libazo's theory that it could have been young Otis McIntosh seemed absurd. The gangly ginger-haired boy was an earnest and studious sort. There was no sharp edge on him.

Tolliver had no idea what to make of Lucy Buxton's latest revelation, nor how he might find out any information that would confirm or negate her latest theory that Buxton had paid someone to do it. Given the scarcity of European women, and Lucy's obvious charms, he imagined that half the male population in Nairobi, married or not, would love to see the voluptuous Mrs. Buxton free, which she certainly would be if her husband turned out to be the murderer. Tolliver tried to push his mind away from any thought of his own libido in that regard, but her willingness to throw herself at . . . His picture of Mrs. Buxton's lovely derriere suddenly evaporated. A passing notion from the conversation he had just had with the lady now blazed in his mind. No one would be happier to see Lucy free of Kirk than Lucy herself. Justin was just beginning to see clearly the real reason Lucy would want to point one of her pretty fingers at her husband, when he heard a crashing sound to his right. Libazo simultaneously stopped in the road in front of him, raised his right arm, and then drew his index finger to his lips. He signaled Tolliver to go back and to his left. Without taking their eyes off where the noise was coming from, they moved behind a sausage tree, where they could still see the road.

"Rhino," Libazo whispered long before Tolliver made out its distinctive shape. Kwai held out his arm in front of Justin's chest. "She has her baby with her."

Two huge animals, not all that different in size, emerged onto the road. The larger, the mother according to Libazo, stopped and waited; the smaller one stopped, too. They did not look around them, but just stood completely still for several minutes. Justin gripped the stock of the rifle in the holster attached to his saddle. He doubted he could stop one charging rhinoceros with it, let alone two. Slowly, hoping not to make a sound, he drew the weapon, but before he had it free, the lead rhino nodded twice, just as a person would do to signal that all was clear, and walked a few yards up the road. The smaller beast followed, and they soon disappeared into the woods on the left side.

Libazo did not lower his arm and Tolliver did not return his rifle to its holster until the crunching sound of the animals' passage disappeared.

The rest of their journey passed without incident, if Tolliver did not count the six giraffes they saw walking away from them when they emerged from the woodland road. They did not stop to watch. He smiled to himself. There was a time when seeing one giraffe, even in a zoo, would have been momentous. He wasn't an old Africa hand yet, but he had taken a step closer.

Before long, they saw Richard Newland's house in the distance. Newland grew sisal. His spread looked like no farm Justin Tolliver had ever seen before. Row upon row of tall spikey plants, the leaves of which gave fiber that could be made into rope, twine, mats. It was hard to believe that such an endeavor could make enough profit to sustain an upperclass English family, but it did. Many families in the Protectorate were doing quite well out of sisal.

The farmhouse was a rather plain affair, long and low with a thatched roof, at the crest of gentle slope surrounded by the croplands that stretched almost to the blue gray hills that looked miles away.

Tolliver and Libazo moved carefully through the rows and dismounted on the scraggly lawn. The inevitable native houseboy in white, with a red fez, came down the few steps from a porch that ran the length of the house. "Mr. Richard is away from home, B'wana," he said in excellent English.

"I understand that," Tolliver said. "Is there no one from the family that I can speak to."

"Only Miss Wilson and the little girl, sir. Mrs. Newland has gone to visit the neighbors. We are expecting her home well before tea."

"I would like to speak to Miss Wilson, then," Tolliver said, though he did not know the woman at all. "And may I trouble you for some water."

"Very good, sir."

Once the houseboy had gone, Tolliver turned to Kwai Libazo. "Do you know who this Miss Wilson is?"

"The governess," Libazo answered, but he pronounced it *gun-ver-ness.*

"Do you think you can find the people you spoke to when you came on Sunday, who told you when the shooting party set off?"

"Yes, sir." Libazo seemed to be imitating the clipped tones of the houseboy's English.

"Go and find them, then, so I can ask them my own questions, and take the horses and water them while you are at it."

Tolliver mounted the steps. The porch was pleasant, wide and set with rattan benches covered with cushions in native cloth and lined with ferns on stands. The houseboy returned carrying a glass and a carafe on a silver tray, quickly followed by Miss Wilson—a thin woman who looked about fifty. Behind her was an extraordinarily pretty little girl of about six, with pale skin, sky-blue eyes, and black curls. Two beautifully groomed collies accompanied them. The dogs took no notice of Tolliver.

He introduced himself but did not state his business.

"How do you do?" the governess said. "I am afraid you have come when the family—"

"Are all away," Tolliver said in unison with her.

She smiled, but her eyes held suspicion, which deepened with Tolliver's first question. "I believe Mr. Newland is away on a shooting safari. I wonder if you can tell exactly when he left."

Smoothly as if she had rehearsed the evasion ahead of time, she indicated a chair and said, "I am forgetting myself, Lieutenant. May I offer you some tea?"

"I am an assistant district superintendent of police," he said. "No, thank you." Tolliver would have loved a cup of tea, but he wanted answers even more. When she didn't speak, Tolliver repeated his question. She made a too dramatic pretense of trying to remember and then said, "I am not sure. Excuse me. Wait here, Ella." She let go of the little girl's hand and went indoors.

"My brother and Otis McIntosh have gone with Papa," little Ella said. "They always get to go away, and I never do. Joseph said you are a policeman." She knit her brows. They were as shiny black as her hair.

"Joseph?"

"Our houseboy. His name used to be something else, but the blasted French priests made him a blasted Catholic. Now we have to call him Joseph. That's what Papa says. Are you a policeman?"

"Yes, I am." Tolliver tried as hard as he could to look as if he were taking her seriously.

"Then can you make Papa and Dickey—that's my brother—

can you make them take me with them when they do interesting things and not leave me here with boring Nanny Wilson?" She glanced over her shoulder to make sure her boring nanny hadn't heard. "It isn't fair that Dickey gets to do all the things that are fun and I get to do all the things that are boring." Tolliver thought of Vera, who had the same complaint and had expressed it in the same open and ingenuous way.

"I understand completely," he said. "I have an older brother who gets to do all the interesting things, too."

"Isn't being a policeman interesting? I should think it is ever so interesting."

Her nanny came out carrying a large white hat, which she tied under the little girl's chin with a length of tulle. "Go then and play on the lawn," she said.

Ella stamped her foot and folded her arms across her chest.

Miss Wilson clamped her hands together in front of her as if she were holding herself back from doing more than scolding the girl. "Now, please young lady."

"You see," Ella said to Justin. She marched down the steps stamping her foot on each one. The dogs followed her.

Once Ella was out of earshot, Miss Wilson indicated a chair for Tolliver and took one herself. "I did not want her to hear any of our discussion. She is a very precocious little thing."

Now I am going to get somewhere, Tolliver thought. He realized that all he wanted to hear was that the hunting party had gone off on schedule and that there was no reason to think that Vera McIntosh's family was withholding anything from him.

"I think I know why you are here," Miss Wilson whispered, though the little girl had gone to the bottom of the lawn and was sitting on a swing that hung from a tree at the edge of the sisal fields. Rather than swinging, she was turning, twisting the ropes around and then letting them unwind so that she spun.

"Can you answer my question?"

"I would rather leave that to Mr. and Mrs. Newland," she said, "but I will tell you what they will not."

The conspiratorial tone in her voice hit Tolliver at the base of the back of his neck and ran a pulse down his spine. He sat very still, not tensing, as his body wanted him to. He waited.

Nanny Wilson looked around again and leaned toward him. "No one in the house will ever tell you this but me, but I feel it must be known at least to you. But before I divulge this, you must promise me that if you must use the information, you will never reveal that it came from me."

"I am not sure that I can do that, if it is evidence you are giving."

She gripped her hands together as she had with the child. "Then, I shan't tell you. If it was to get out that I had revealed a family secret, I would be dismissed and I would never find another position in the Protectorate. I must have your word on this before I proceed."

Tolliver was torn, but the knowledge, whatever it was, might be the answer to all the riddles that had been plaguing him. He made his promise very specific. "Very well. You have my word that no one will ever know that I got it from you." He looked into her pale eyes as he said it.

She nodded curtly to show she accepted his assurance. "That doctor, Pennyman?" She paused as if she wanted Tolliver to acknowledge that he knew who Pennyman was.

"Yes?"

"You do know that he was in an awful scrape in Edinburgh before he came out?"

"Yes, I do."

"Well, Mrs. Newland's family has hushed up exactly what happened. They started a rumor that it was some young wife that he went after." She waited again.

"Yes?" he said softly, trying to hide his impatience.

"Well, that was just a smoke screen to protect the reputation of the person who was—er—accosted by Josiah Pennyman."

A woman rode up to the foot of the lawn. Before she was able to dismount, a native boy in khaki drill shorts and a short-sleeved shirt came running from behind the house to take the reins and lead her horse away. "Darling," she shouted to the girl on the swing, and took her up in a piggyback. Followed by the two collies, she jogged around in circles for a minute and sent the child into peals of laughter before she started across the lawn toward the house.

"Finish what you were saying," Tolliver demanded under his breath.

Miss Wilson inclined her head in the direction of the beautiful mother and child on the grass before them. "That girl in Edinburgh was Mrs. Newland's sister," she said, smiling despite the gravity of what she was revealing while she faced her approaching mistress. "She was barely thirteen years old."

Tolliver burned to ask her why she would reveal the family's secret, but Mrs. Newland and Ella were on the porch before he had the chance of it.

Pretending she wanted to go shopping and spend a day visiting with friends, Vera McIntosh took the late morning train into Nairobi and hired a rickshaw to take her directly to the police station across from the Jeevanjee Gardens. She quickly learned that Captain Tolliver was out. Desperate to tell him what she had learned from the blacksmith, she immediately sought him at the Nairobi Club where she hoped he might be at lunch.

The captain was not there, but true to form, the gossip mill of the Protectorate's capital provided its latest information about him—that he was last seen calling on Lucy Buxton in the late morning. The dancing eyebrows on the person who told Vera this juicy tidbit froze the girl's heart. She had heard an inkling of the Tolliver–Lucy Buxton gossip from one of her mother's visitors but had refused to believe it. Now her feelings warred—on the one hand defending Tolliver as interested merely in solving the murder and on the other condemning his blushes and his boyish idealism as the masks of a traitor. She could not banish the thought that he was like half the other residents of the Protectorate. Going about professing all sorts of moral superiority over the natives, while they engaged only in greed and lust. Her higher self insisted that she had no right to judge Tolliver in this way, but another voice said he was breaking her heart. She could not banish her despair.

Having given up on trying to deliver her new information to the captain and not knowing what to do next, she glanced through the Arab and Indian bazaars and then went to tea at the club. In the late afternoon, she called on her father's dearest friend, the Reverend Bennett, rector of St. Phillip's Church, where she was sure of an invitation to stay at the manse until the morning train could take her back home.

13.

In the darkest hours of the following night, from their separate points of view, a great sense of urgency descended on both Vera McIntosh and Justin Tolliver—an anxiety, a need to be swift that was out of harmony with their surroundings.

Ordinarily, time seemed to pass more slowly in Africa than it did in London or Glasgow or even on a great estate in Yorkshire. In British East Africa, the hours and the days stretched out to match the enormous vistas, the pace was deliberate, the rhythms those of ancient tribal life. But each of the sleepless young people felt an inner storm bearing down, and they wanted to run from it, or to quell it before it overwhelmed their hopes and dreams.

Tolliver had eaten an early supper and spent an hour at his cello. He began with the Bach Suite on his music stand, the sort of music that usually helped him organize his thinking, but soon he was playing randomly and furiously whatever came into his disturbed brain until some poor neighbor in the police barracks sent the hall boy to stop the disturbance.

It was past midnight when he finally abandoned his worries to sleep. But he awoke again in the wee hours, on top of his bed, only half undressed, his mind still roiling with theories about the murder of Josiah Pennyman. None of the explanations he preferred to be true was as likely as the latest, detested ones: that the McIntosh family were covering up the real facts of when their son left and therefore were intentionally thwarting his investigation. Or, equally disturbing, that Richard Newland, a kind man with a beautiful family, well-liked by all, might have killed the Scots physician because Pennyman had harmed, in such a dreadful way, his wife's little sister. And Pennyman's only punishment had been to fork over whatever fortune he had had. He should have been prosecuted to the full extent of the law. Tolliver understood why he had not. Newland's in-laws would not want the news to spread. It would only destroy the girl's chances in society if it became known. Still, he understood Newland's outrage. If Newland was indeed the murderer, Tolliver was not at all sure he had the stomach to arrest him.

And where was the connection, if any, between the lies of the McIntoshes and the crime against Newland's sister-in-law?

Tolliver had respected his promise to Nanny Wilson and refrained from questioning Mrs. Newland about the murder. He had asked her only what day the safari party departed. To his surprise, she readily confirmed what Kwai Libazo had discovered, that her husband, her son, and Otis McIntosh, with their entourage of gun bearers and porters, had left just before dawn on the morning Pennyman's body was discovered.

Her willingness to reveal this fact puzzled Tolliver. Perhaps Mrs. Newland did not know that her husband had avenged the attack on her young sister. Surely she could have figured that out when she heard the news of the murder. If she knew, wouldn't she have lied about his departure time to try to provide him with an alibi? Had she perhaps learned about Libazo's Sunday visit and given up hope of any help from that fiction? Was Vera McIntosh's family complicit in all this? Tolliver's only way to find the truth was to follow the safari party. His impatience stemmed from that. Such excursions were usually arranged weeks, if not a month in advance. Then there was the obstacle of D.C. Cranford.

Across the sleeping town, in the snug guest room of the manse of St. Phillip's, Vera McIntosh's mind grappled with the same subject. She, too, was planning to go after the Newland safari party.

In one way, her heart was back to where it had been two nights before her uncle's death—filled with the excitement at the prospect of going out into the wilderness. If her five months in Glasgow with her granny had taught her anything, it was how much she loved her home in Africa. In fact, having been away from it had fed her infatuation with going into the African wilderness, of what seeing it, hearing it, breathing it did to her soul. She refused to be kept out of it, forced to stay at the mission, going to Nairobi for visits, pretending to live the life of a Scottish maiden. What was the point of pioneering in this exotic place if all one did was try to pretend that here life should be as much as possible like life in Glasgow? That would be to waste all that was glorious in this country. Her heart compelled her into the open spaces.

But now Vera's mind dwelt on something far more serious than a happy jaunt into a landscape where her spirit would feast. She needed to go out there, not to seek bliss, but to answer a brutal question about Richard Newland. Did the man who had just recently acquired a very distinctive Maasai spear use it to kill her uncle? And if he was willing to harm a member of her family, could her brother be safe with him? Her whole body tensed at the thought that Otis might be in danger. She could not imagine how or why Newland would do such a thing to her uncle, much less to harm her brother, Newland's boy's dearest friend. But every sinew in her body was telling her that her brother was in danger over this. So she had made up her mind. She would set out to follow him. She would have to do it on her own.

She would not let herself even think of involving Justin Tolliver. If he wanted to make love to Lucy Buxton— No. She pressed her mind away from that subject. She refused to need him. She would go this alone. She was certain she could. She was born here, raised here; she knew things Tolliver did not know, that her parents did not know, about how to manage. The Newland party had planned to stop at Berkeley Cole's farm on the Naro Moru. It was a great distance away, but not impossible to reach. She knew where to find the help she needed. She knew how to get past her parents. All she needed to do was get moving.

She would tell her parents she had met her friend Frances Bowes in town. This was true. They had chatted briefly in the tearoom at the club yesterday. She would then lie and say Frances had invited her to visit at Fort Hall, where her father was the commandant. Vera's mother and father would never know this was not true. In Scotland, they would have been able to send wires to find out things from far away. Here, blessedly, the telegraph ran only along the railroad and the rail line to Fort Hall was not complete. Vera would be long gone before they found out she was lying, if they ever did.

Vera would ask to take Wangari's brother with her and one or two of the boys from the farm. She would set out as if she was going by way of Chania Bridge, but then she would take the train to Naivasha. From there the journey would be quite easy. And she would show Justin Tolliver what a real girl could do. Let him have his Lucy, if that was the sort he wanted. Vera meant to be a heroine, not a hussy.

She finally fell asleep as dawn was breaking with pictures of her plan fading into dreams.

The image of Vera McIntosh that Tolliver took to breakfast with him the following morning was not exactly like the real thing. But not entirely inaccurate either.

While Tolliver grappled with the idea that his lovely Vera might actually be a deceitful vixen helping her family to cover up a crime, Vera herself was carefully planning to mislead her parents and do what they would never allow. As the day began, Tolliver and Vera were moving in opposite directions, she toward the railroad station and home to begin her deception and departure. He toward Government House and an encounter with the district commissioner. He picked up Kwai Libazo and went directly to his superior's office. There his morning report drew exactly the response he expected.

"Bugger all," Cranford shouted. Tolliver worried that the district commissioner's trumpet voice might be heard as far away as Mombasa, perhaps even in the home office in London if things got worse. And Tolliver was about to make them very much worse.

"I understand, sir, that the delay causes you some—"

"You do not understand at all. I am under constant pressure from the settlers about every minuscule thing that goes wrong here. Twelve days have gone by since a British doctor has been slain by a native. I can't walk the three blocks down the bloody street from here to the club without being stopped by eight men who want to know why we didn't shoot the savage sod on the spot."

"Yes, sir. I understand the difficulty that must cause you." Tolliver knew that in this discussion he was the one who cared about the rule of law. Cranford's cares were much more varied.

"I sincerely doubt you understand. Now, tell me about this new information, which you call extenuating evidence. Bloody waste of time is what I call it."

Tolliver explained about the circumstances between Richard Newland's family and Josiah Pennyman. Cranford's thick gray eyebrows raised higher and higher until Kwai

Libazo, in his accustomed place against the mahogany paneling, thought they would leave his head entirely and fly off like little birds.

This was a curious turn of events for Kwai. The Christians, he guessed, were like the Somalis, very careful about their girls. Neither the Kikuyu nor the Maasai would ever imagine that one man would kill another over one's having had sex with a girl. When the young females of the tribes were ready to, they made love with any man they wanted. They were only required to be faithful to their husbands once they were married. The foreign people were not like that. If a Somali father found that his daughter had been with a man, he would kill her. From what the captain and the district commissioner were saying to each other, among Christians, a man would kill, not the girl, but the man who had been with her. It all seemed very strange to Kwai Libazo.

But it was extremely serious to these British. When Tolliver finished telling his tale, Cranford looked as if he had seen a ghost. "Where did you hear this about Pennyman and Mrs. Newland's younger sister?"

"It was told to me in confidence. I cannot tell you who it was, sir, but I have every reason to believe the story is true."

Cranford's shoulders sagged as if the air had gone out of him. "That is ghastly, positively ghastly."

"I cannot agree more," Tolliver said. "If it is true, and I sincerely believe it is, it could very well be the motive for Josiah Pennyman's murder and make Richard Newland the murderer." He steeled himself for a fresh outburst. When it did not come, he went on. "That is why I think that I must mount a party immediately to go after Newland and bring him back to be questioned."

Cranford did not shout. He laughed. "Have you gone mad? Many people do here, you know, from the sun. Of course we are not going to send out any such party."

"But, sir—"

"My dear boy, I am sure you know full well what such an expedition would cost and how much time it would take. How can we justify the expense and delay?"

"Richard Newland had every reason to want to kill Josiah Pennyman."

"That's as may be, but come to your senses, Tolliver. What self-respecting Englishman would stab another man in the back with a spear? An act of total cowardice. And we all know precisely how cowardly the Kikuyu really are, despite all the professorial treatises about the noble savage that might be written to the contrary. No. We all know full well that this is the work of a fuzzy-wuzzy."

"I must—" Tolliver cut himself off. Cranford was right. A true Englishman's code of honor would preclude such an act, and Newland was a true Englishman. But Tolliver had seen enough double-dealing and backstabbing in his short life to know that the code of honor was sometimes an ideal rather than a closely followed practice. Still, it would be a huge insult to drag Newland back to Nairobi on suspicion alone. Tolliver was too torn between his proper English upbringing and the demands of his position to think what to do.

Cranford held up his hand. "I can see that you are having

trouble relinquishing your latest theory." He sat up straight and squared his shoulders. "Assistant District Superintendent Tolliver, I will chalk your recent flirting with insubordination up to your—ahem—illness last week. But you must prove to me that you are fit for duty or I will have to remove you from your post. You have your man. The witch doctor is the culprit. Let that be an end on it." Tolliver heard the words "or else" even though the district commissioner did not speak them.

Kwai Libazo saw Tolliver do what he never expected. He stood and saluted. "Very good, sir."

Libazo's neck went cold. His new god of justice was slipping away from him again. He marched smartly as he followed his captain out to the room, but his heart was not in it.

Tolliver did not speak until they were out of the building. He turned toward the police station. Libazo feared he was going to see the execution immediately. But then Tolliver said under his breath, "We are going to visit Mbura. I am going to ask you to translate for me, but no matter what I say, you must tell Mbura that his only hope is to fake an illness, to pretend he is dying from being imprisoned. Do you understand what I am trying to accomplish with this?"

Libazo wanted to smile with relief, but he kept his face neutral. "I do."

"You will do it? You will explain this to him, no matter what I say?"

"I will."

Tolliver was relieved. The British settlers universally believed that if the natives were put in jail they would die.

Imprisonment was tantamount to execution. They said that the natives had no concept of the future, that therefore if they were jailed they would think it was permanent, equivalent to being buried alive. Imprisonment would cause them to languish and expire. Tolliver did not believe this was necessarily true. For one thing, he knew that the natives did understand the concept of time. How could they not? Their life was different from an Englishman's, but they lived in time like all human beings. Their babies took nine months to be born. They knew that. They waited for their crops to grow and their fruit to ripen. Tolliver believed that they could therefore look forward to a day when their term of imprisonment would end. If Gichinga Mbura had any sense, however, he would begin to languish and look very sick, very soon. If Mbura would feign illness, Cranford would conclude that he was on the verge of death. That would stay his having to face the noose.

The sergeant of the guard at the jail was a Sikh who Tolliver knew did not speak Kikuyu. When he took him and Libazo past the other snoring prisoners to the cell where Gichinga Mbura was being kept, he asked the guard to remain with them.

Despite Tolliver's intense dislike of the witch doctor, he was relieved to see that he seemed to be surviving his imprisonment quite well, contrary to popular European expectations. In fact, hate gleamed in Mbura's eyes with such intensity that he seemed more than just alive, but to draw increased power from his predicament. Justin tried to inure himself to the fact that the animosity was directed at himself. For the benefit of the Indian jailer, Tolliver asked questions about Mbura's whereabouts at the point the crime was committed. He told Libazo to say that if it were decided that Mbura had killed Pennyman, he would be immediately tried and executed for the crime shortly thereafter. Tolliver trusted that the words Libazo was saying in Kikuyu had nothing to do with such thoughts.

This idea of faked illness had dropped into Tolliver's head while he was with Cranford. He knew he was grasping at straws, looking for any expedient that would delay the witch doctor's execution until Justin could be certain of his guilt or disprove it. Cranford could be difficult but there was no way to try a man too ill to stand up, and not even Cranford would send a man who could not walk to the gallows. Tolliver was not going to see Mbura die if he was not guilty. Everything he had been brought up to believe warred against such an outcome. All his life, like all his family, Tolliver had embraced fervently the need for Britain to wipe out slavery. Right here in East Africa, many of his countrymen had come with that as a primary goal. They were, to this day, trying to stamp out its embers along the coast where, against English law, the Arabs still surreptitiously sold men and shipped them off to work in the plantations on Zanzibar. If British men stood for protecting Africans from slavery, must they not protect them from other injustices as well? Even if the native in question was as arrogant and nasty as Gichinga Mbura seemed to be at this moment, with evil dancing in his eyes.

At that second, another thought occurred to Tolliver. The Indian jailer was watching these proceedings with great interest. It was not every day, thank goodness, that the man heard a discussion of an execution. "Libazo," Tolliver said, choosing his words very carefully, "tell Gichinga Mbura that what you have been telling him about must happen very soon."

Libazo's eyes communicated complete understanding. When they left the jail, the Sikh had taken the bait. He said he would begin to prepare the paperwork for the court case and begin the preliminary work to arrange for the hanging afterward.

Tolliver pretended insensitivity. "I'll go to the club for a meal and then I will come back and sign the court forms," he said.

When Tolliver had finished luncheon, he did not go to the police station but sent Libazo to check on the prisoner. Libazo returned looking properly dismayed. Gichinga Mbura, it seemed, had taken ill, could not or would not eat any of the food that was brought to him for his noon meal and lay on his pallet barely moving.

Tolliver marched quickly to the district commissioner's office and told his superior of the turn of events and managed to convince Cranford that there would probably be no need to arrange Gichinga Mbura's death. All the government of the Protectorate now needed to do was wait. Mbura was in the process of arranging his own demise, by dying of imprisonment, as all understood that African savages certainly would. The district commissioner smiled broadly and allowed as how that would be the best of all possible outcomes. "Save us the trouble of having to justify ourselves to those bleeding hearts in the colonial office."

"That was excellent," Tolliver said to Kwai as they left

Government House and started across the street toward the stables. "And now for the next step in my plan."

"What will that be, sir," Kwai asked, but before the captain had a chance to answer, he collapsed in the middle of the street.

At that very moment, having taken the train back to Athi River and returned home, Vera McIntosh was in the throes of discussing Captain Justin Tolliver with her mother. She had decided to engage her mother's sympathy by revealing that her heart had been broken by Justin Tolliver. When she started the conversation, it was a ruse. Had she known that he was collapsing in the street for the second time in less than ten days, she might have thought better of accusing him to her mother. As it was, she revealed what she had heard about him while she was in town. In the course of her lifetime, Vera had never spoken to her mother in such intimate terms.

"I have thought he wanted— That he was— Oh, Mother, how could I have been so wrong about his feelings for me. I have seen so many signs that he—" In planning this talk, Vera thought she would have to hide her face and fake tears. To her surprise real ones flowed. She never wept in front of her mother. She always went to her father or to Wangari for solace. But today, she knew it was her mother's sympathy she would need if she was to get permission to go away. Otherwise, her plan to be gone would never work at all. What Vera did not expect was that what had started out as playacting would bring her to such a state.

Her mother put aside her sewing and further surprised

Vera by taking her daughter's hand. "This business with Lucy Buxton may just be a fling, darling. Men do that sort of thing, even if their real feelings lie elsewhere."

Vera lost control and sobbed in earnest. "That is an idea I cannot accept. That he could be falling in love with me and still—" Nothing that Vera was saying at this point was purely for effect. She was so overcome with sadness she could not go on. She could not let herself think of what Tolliver was doing with Mrs. Buxton. Proper unmarried Scottish girls, even those of nineteen like her, were not meant to know what men and women did together. But Vera had not grown up in some chilly, cavernous great house in Glasgow. She grew up here, and the Kikuyu girls who were her playmates at three and four were making sex with boys before they were fully grown. All of them were married now and had babies of their own, some as old as four. They had told her everything. She was not supposed to listen to their giggly conversation. The ordinarily stern woman beside her would have been appalled if she knew how detailed were the descriptions of the love act her daughter had heard. But Vera knew about sex. And until yesterday, it was what she wanted to do with Justin Tolliver. But not anymore. The thought of taking the place that that odious Lucy Buxton had occupied in his arms disgusted her. Her dream of him was completely lost. She took out her handkerchief and dried her eyes. "You see, Mother, why I want to get away for a little while to visit Frances?"

"Yes, I see that very well, my dear."

Vera looked at her mother. She seemed a different person in these past weeks. Her grief over her brother's death had softened her more than Vera thought possible. She moved to clinch her mother's approval. "Denys Finch Hatton has been calling very often, too, and he is wonderfully charming, but I do not find him—"

Her mother smiled sadly. "I wondered about that. I think half the women in the Protectorate are in love with him, married or not. And he is lovely and extremely well connected. Perhaps, if you get away for a while, as you suggest, you will learn to think about both of those men in a different way. I would like you to have a choice in the matter of marriage." Her voice had a wistful note Vera had never heard in it before.

"I wish Captain Tolliver had been the hero I wanted him to be."

"Perhaps he will in the end," her mother said, but her tone said she doubted it. "Men like to feel like heroes. That may be particularly true of a man like him who had the possibility of a much easier life but chose to be a policeman."

"I'll go soon if you don't mind, Mama. I was thinking I would take Wangari's brother."

"Yes. Good, and take one of Wangari's girls and three or four of the plantation boys as bearers."

The affection Vera felt when she kissed her mother was sincere, but she felt like a traitor. She wished she could have told the truth, but she comforted herself with the thought that it would be worse for her mother to learn about Newland's buying the murder weapon. How her mother would suffer knowing that their precious Otis had been given into the care of the man who had murdered Uncle Josiah. There was no point in communicating her fears for Otis. Better to let her mother go along in ignorance for the time being.

"Shall I go then and talk to Wangari, Mama, and pack?"

"Fine," her mother said.

Vera sped to her nanny's hut. If luck was with her, she would be off first thing in the morning.

14.

Early the next day, while Vera was bidding her parents goodbye, Justin Tolliver was an hour away in Nairobi dealing with the doctor and Cranford, who stood at the foot of his bed. "Yes, doctor," he said, "but I insist on being taken to the Scottish Hospital. Nurse Freemantle is the one who cured me the last time, and I feel she is the best person to help me now."

At first, both the doctor and the district commissioner looked quite doubtful, but after half an hour of tedious conversation, Tolliver succeeded in convincing them that he could make the journey by train to Athi River, where Kwai Libazo would meet him and take him the rest of the way in a horse trap.

"Have you any news about the condition of Gichinga Mbura?" Tolliver asked Cranford, once the other matter had been settled and the doctor had left.

"Bad off," Cranford said. "Evidently, being told he will be properly punished has done for him." He spoke as a man completely satisfied with himself. "I must say again, this is

the best of all possible outcomes. No need to make an air-
tight case against the savage. No worries about inquires from
London, no excuses to give. We can say with perfect conviction that we justly detained the mumbo-jumbo man and he
upped and died on us."

"I couldn't agree more." Tolliver tried to look appropriately sad and sick.

"I'll be off then." D.C. Cranford took his hat from the chair
in the corner.

"On your way out, sir, I wonder if you would mind having
Kwai Libazo sent here so I can give him his orders."

"Certainly, my boy."

"And I wonder, sir, if I might take a bit of time to recover.
I think I returned to duty too quickly last week."

Cranford looked doubtful.

"That new chap, Oliver Lovett, is coming along quite
well, and he speaks Urdu, so he can communicate much better with the Indian clerks. Since the laws are Indian colonial, the Indian deputy inspectors run things on a day-to-day
basis, really. And as they write everything in Urdu, Lovett
will soon be completely up to snuff."

The D.C.'s caterpillar eyebrows knit.

Tolliver shot his last salvo. "He served in the Indian Army,
in Queen Victoria's own corps." This fact placed the new policeman in India's most elite unit. Tolliver hoped it would be
the icing on Lovett's cake.

Cranford breathed a sigh. "I suppose, if you must. When
is District Superintendent Jodrell returning?"

"He is due back in just over two weeks."

"Very well, then." Cranford picked up his sun helmet and

squared his shoulders. "Now, buck up. I am sure everything will be shipshape and Bristol fashion before very long." And he was gone.

Kwai Libazo arrived within seconds.

"How did you get here so fast?"

"I was waiting in the hall for news of you, sir? I was so afraid of Mbura's curse."

Tolliver laughed. "No such thing. I made it look as if I was ill on purpose."

The flabbergasted look on Libazo's face was the most emotional expression Tolliver had ever seen there. "You are not sick, B'wana?"

"No. It suddenly occurred to me that if Mbura could fake illness, so could I."

"Why, sir?"

"So that we can go after Newland without the district commissioner knowing what we are doing."

"How?"

Tolliver explained his plan for getting them to the Scottish Mission and setting off from there.

"Sir, how will we take enough men without the district commissioner missing them?"

"I doubt the D.C. knows the details of anything that happens here, nor cares when Jodrell is on duty. It's only because the district superintendent is away that he is putting his nose in so deep."

Libazo liked the way the English said things like that, drawing a funny picture of what people were doing. But he did not let himself smile. Tolliver's deception worried him.

Tolliver got out of bed. He was wearing his uniform

trousers with his nightshirt. "You will lead a squad out to the Scottish Mission. Take the same men who went with us to the Masonic Hotel two weeks ago. The new man, Inspector Lovett, will hold the fort here. He's had as much training as I ever did when they left me to my own devices. And I daresay the D.C. will not be over here counting heads in the next little bit."

"Will we hire a tracker?"

Tolliver was taken aback. He knew very well that the Nairobi station's best tracker was out with District Superintendent Patterson from the Kiambu Station, hunting a man-eating lion at Tsavo.

"You will have to be our tracker." Tolliver heard the doubt that had crept into his own voice.

Libazo now looked frightened. "Sir, I cannot. I have no idea how to do that."

"You grew up here. You must know this area like the back of your hand," Tolliver insisted.

"No, sir. I do not. I have never gone toward Mount Kenya in my life."

"Bugger all. Well, whom can we get? You must know someone who would be able to show us the way. We need a first-class tracker."

"I know Kinuthia, sir. He is like me, half Maasai, half Kikuyu. He knows all about traveling through the bush."

"Perfect. Get him. He will be our guide."

"I am not sure I can. He serves an Englishman."

"Which one?"

"The one called Finch Hatton, that the Kikuyu call Bird-with-a-hat-on."

"Good God!" Tolliver had been trying until that moment to keep his voice low, so that anyone passing in the hall would imagine he was too weak to go about his duties. He had to bite his lip to keep from continuing to shout. "There must be someone else."

"There are only the men who work for the safari outfitting companies," Libazo said. "The ones who work for Hilton's or Tarlton's. If we wanted one of them we would have to hire him from the outfitters and pay their price."

Tolliver could not hide his annoyance. And it only got worse when Libazo revealed the gossip the natives were passing about him and Finch Hatton.

"Kinuthia says that you and B'wana Finch Hatton were enemies in your country, sir."

"What nonsense is that?"

"He said that your schools had a contest every year and that you and B'wana Finch Hatton were in the same contest."

Tolliver shook his head. It was absurd that anyone this far away should have heard of something that happened that long ago. It was a cricket match at Lord's nearly ten years ago—Finch Hatton had played for Eton, Tolliver for Harrow. The spectators on both sides had been taken with Finch Hatton's grace and style, though he had not been the top scorer. There was another chap who had claimed that honor. "Yes, well my school won," Tolliver said. The more he thought about Denys Finch Hatton—the hero of one and all wherever he went—the more annoying he found him. He told himself that this was separate from his upset over Finch Hatton's attentions to Vera, though he knew full well he would not care a fig for any of the other differences, if it hadn't been for Vera.

"Kwai," he said. "I have to stay in bed or my ruse will be found out. I need you to take a message to Finch Hatton for me. He is in town, is he not?"

"I saw Kinuthia yesterday. B'wana Finch Hatton does not go about without him."

Tolliver took a paper and pen and scribbled a quick note. "Take this to Finch Hatton right away. I want to see him here in town before I go to the Scottish Mission." Tolliver would not be an excuse for Finch Hatton going anywhere near Vera McIntosh.

It would have been hard for either Justin Tolliver or Vera McIntosh to imagine how they might have reacted to the events of those days had they known what the other was doing and thinking at that moment. Many days later, Clement McIntosh said, in retrospect, that it was not in the Creator's plan for those two young people to know. Sometimes it was very difficult for the missionary to accept what he thought to be his God's will.

As it was, by the time Tolliver sent for Finch Hatton, Vera had already set off with a retinue: five bearers, including Wangari's brother and also Wangari's youngest daughter, Muiri, for female company.

Neither the Reverend nor Mrs. McIntosh had the slightest inkling that their daughter was heading northwest, not east as they had given her permission to do. She traveled with money enough to cover what they thought she was going to do. Vera had estimated what her real costs would be and prayed she had enough.

As soon as she had traveled a few kilometers from her parents' house, she told her Kikuyu companions of her plan. The way toward Fort Hall would have taken her in approximately the same direction as the Athi River Station. If her parents had followed her progress they would have seen no deviation until she detoured to the railroad, bought a second-class ticket for herself and third class for her followers, and space for the bundles the bearers carried.

The 10:21 up train, with a long layover at the Nairobi Station, would take until nearly five in the afternoon to reach Naivasha Station. There she would find Wangari's uncle, the legendary tracker Ngethe Meru, who had gone with the American president Theodore Roosevelt on his journey into the interior.

15.

When Denys Finch Hatton entered Justin Tolliver's room, he looked sincerely dismayed. "Good God, man. What are you doing out of bed? Cranford seems to think you are at death's door."

Tolliver, knowing he needed Finch Hatton, had prepared to ingratiate himself to the man he could think of only as a rival, and a rival with too many advantages. "A bit of overacting on my part I am afraid."

Tolliver offered Denys a chair and explained to him what he wanted, giving only as many of the details as he needed to be convincing. He did not reveal his suspicions about Richard Newland, only emphasized that he needed to find young Otis McIntosh. "I wonder then, if your man Kinuthia can guide us and help us track the Newland party."

Finch Hatton's famously expressive eyes took on a calculating cast. "I take it Ms. McIntosh has told you about our visit to the Kikuyu blacksmith."

Tolliver bit back rising anger over any such traipsing around the countryside Vera might have done in the company of Finch Hatton. *Concentrate on the task at hand*, he told himself. "No. What has that got to do with my request?"

"The blacksmith described a very unusual Maasai spear that he had gotten from an Arab trader. A very old one. He said he sold it Richard Newland not long ago. Miss McIntosh thought it was the very one used to kill Josiah Pennyman. Miss McIntosh said she was going to get word to you of this."

Tolliver's skin turned hot, as if he were running the fever he had been feigning. "I know nothing of this." This was his investigation. It galled him that Finch Hatton had a critical piece of evidence that he did not know. How could Vera not have reported it to him?

"I am sure Miss McIntosh had intended to tell you about it. She did not?" Finch Hatton's words made Tolliver feel worse.

"I have not seen her for days."

"Well," Denys said, "you can ask her. We can stop at the Scottish Mission, on our way to track Newland. We better find out everything the Reverend and Mrs. McIntosh know about exactly where Newland planned to hunt."

Tolliver stood up. "I don't think you need to involve yourself in this. If we can have Kinuthia to show us the way, I will handle the trip."

"Not at all." Finch Hatton's charming smile was going full force and entirely lost on Tolliver. "I will organize Kinuthia, some supplies, and porters. You go down to Athi River looking ill. We will pick you up at the mission and set off. I imagine you will not want Vera and her family to know what we are doing."

Tolliver barely held his temper. An outburst might put Finch Hatton entirely off. If Tolliver alienated him, he was perfectly capable of taking off after Newland on his own and upstaging Tolliver completely. "Very well. I must set off at once for the hospital. When will you meet me there?"

"In the morning."

Tolliver shook Finch Hatton's hand, satisfied that he would, at the very least, be able to speak with Vera alone before she saw Finch Hatton again.

"Tomorrow then," Denys said with a hearty handshake.

While her up train was stopped for the normal long layover at Nairobi Station, Vera McIntosh, fearing being seen and having her ruse discovered, remained onboard, away from the windows that faced the platform, with her head bowed over a book. Had she gotten off the train, she would very likely have encountered Justin Tolliver being dramatically carried on a stretcher through the inelegant corrugated iron station. He was arranging to travel on the down train toward Athi River and Vera's home.

As it was, in that quarter hour they passed very near each other completely unnoticed.

When Tolliver descended at Athi Station in midafternoon, Kwai Libazo was there with a wagon to take him over the bumpy roads to the hospital. Nurse Freemantle, having been forewarned, had a bed ready for him when he arrived. It took her only moments of examination to spot the deceit. Tolliver did not even bother to try to persuade her that he was ill. He needed her as an ally. He told her his plan to track the possible murderer of Josiah Pennyman without regard to his superior officer's orders, and he asked for her help. He counted on two things to motivate her: his supposition, from the way she had cared for Pennyman's corpse, that she had had a tender attachment to the doctor, and in addition his assumption that, like many women who nursed the casualties of the Boer War, she had little respect for officers and the officials of the realm. He must have been right because she immediately agreed to let him stay in hospital overnight in the cause of justice.

"I would like to speak to Miss McIntosh this evening if at all possible," he said. He did not add that Vera knew something about the murder weapon that he wanted to hear about, and he did not reveal that Richard Newland was his quarry. "Would you mind asking her to come visit me here? And would you leave us alone together for a few minutes when she does."

He had been afraid she would be shocked at the very idea of leaving the missionary's daughter alone with him.

But she shocked him instead. "Miss McIntosh is away. She went off this morning with a party of natives to go to Fort Hall for a stay with Frances Bowes, the colonel's daughter." The nurse marched away.

Fear and admiration warred for dominance in Tolliver's heart. He knew in three blinks of his eyes that Vera had gone on the quest he himself was planning. If ever a girl had the pluck to do such a thing on her own it was Vera. *Find her, protect her*, his heart shouted at him. He wanted to leap out of bed and speed after her, but he knew that was impossible on his own. He must wait for Finch Hatton and his tracker and their guns and ammunition. But then, when he found Vera, when he could be sure nothing dreadful had happened to her, Denys would be there, too. He could not imagine anything that could rankle him more.

As Tolliver lay in bed, pretending to the hospital helpers to be weak, inactivity got the better of him. Soon every drop of his blood was alive with anxiety and confusion. His feelings were already at fever pitch, both his admiration for Vera's courage and his concern for her danger. But soon, a pesky voice joined in, one that came into his head sounding like his father's. It warned him about his deepening regard for Vera and asked, in the pater's gruff tones, what kind of girl she was who would lie to her parents and go off on her own on an ill-advised journey into the wilderness. Before long, he could not tell if he should idolize or abhor her. His parents would certainly say this was not the behavior of any girl he should consider as a wife. And a vexing thought kept coming back to him that she had betrayed him by not coming to him with the information she had about the murder weapon. Evidently she had taken Finch Hatton to see the blacksmith. Why had she not taken him? He was, after all, the person in charge of the investigation.

Until he had heard about Richard Newland's relationship to the girl Pennyman had assaulted, he had no reason at all to suspect Newland. Had Vera known all this from the beginning? Did perhaps also her parents know of the Pennyman-Newland connection? Had they all been hiding evidence from him? If so, then why would her discovery that Newland had owned the murder weapon precipitate her trip? He could not imagine that her father would have approved of her going off after Newland on her own. He tried to convince himself that she really did go to Fort Hall to visit Frances Bowes.

The more he lay inert in his bed, the more his mind raced from one possibility to another, and the more muddled he became. When Libazo showed up to tell him that the porters were secreted a mile or so off in the Kikuyu village, Tolliver sent him to talk to the mission natives to confirm what he had concluded about where Vera had gone. After less than half an hour, Kwai returned to say that Wangari, Vera's nanny, readily told him the truth, on the absolute promise that he would reveal it only to Captain Tolliver. And that Captain Tolliver would not inform her parents.

Once the fact that Vera was in danger had been confirmed, Tolliver could not concentrate on anything else. He tried to imagine playing Bach on his cello to quiet his thoughts, but imagining the music did not help. He needed to feel it in his body. And now he could not.

By the time Nurse Freemantle came back to see him, accompanied by a native girl carrying a tray of food, he was in such a state of confusion he could barely formulate a coherent sentence.

"I have not told the reverend that you are here," the nurse said. "I was about to, but then I thought, given your true reason, perhaps you would not want him to know." Her small, piercing dark eyes stared at him expectantly, as if she would read far too much into any answer he gave.

"To be truthful, I do want to speak to him, but I am a bit tired. I wonder if you would tell him that I am here. Please do not reveal my real reason. And ask him to come to see me after he has had his dinner? Would that be alright?"

She agreed readily. Tolliver tucked into the roasted meat and native pumpkin with honey dressing. Without being asked, Nurse Freemantle had taken pity on him and sent the girl back with a bottle of dark ale. He wished he had paper and pen to make some notes. Before talking to McIntosh, he needed to sort things through, put the questions that plagued him in proper order and perspective. He continued to wish for his cello and went over the entire chain of events in his mind.

There were now three men who had very strong motives to have killed Josiah Pennyman. He thought about those motives. He moved the saltcellar to the near left-hand corner of the tray in his lap. Richard Newland was the salt of the earth.

Tolliver fingered the saltcellar and put the pepper shaker beside it. Kirk Buxton: He had the weakest reason as far as Tolliver could think. Jealousy over Lucy's liaison with Penny-man? Some men might kill to avenge their honor. But Kirk Buxton did not seem at all the type. Besides, what honor was there in stabbing a man in the back? Or worse yet, as Lucy suggested, hiring someone else to do it? From all Tolliver had heard, Lucy's affairs were well known and documented before Pennyman even arrived in the Protectorate. Buxton might be peeved about it, but if the banker had ever cared about his wife's adulteries, he did not seem to anymore.

Lucy seemed convinced the murderer was her husband, but if Tolliver thought about it, she seemed all too anxious to come up with ways and means and motivations. It niggled at Tolliver that Lucy showed so much determination in the matter. When Tolliver didn't swallow the hired assassin theory, she came up with that story about Buxton wanting to stop Pennyman revealing his underhanded financial dealings. That might have been less far-fetched, except that it was the lovely Lucy's third try at getting Tolliver to suspect Kirk. If she had had all that information from the beginning, she should have revealed it all at once. Justin hated to think of any woman so coldhearted as to falsely accuse her own husband of murder, especially to slander him with the cowardly act of hiring an assassin.

Even for a woman whose brain was as addled by drink as Lucy's, it was a stretch for Tolliver to believe she was giving him anything useful. He wondered for a moment whether all of her attempts at seduction weren't part of the whole picture, but he remembered full well seeing her down all that drink that day they had had luncheon with the Lord and Lady Delamere. Lucy was a desperate woman. And a pathetic one. Instinct and logic both pointed Tolliver to the conclusion that Buxton was not the killer.

The crime, the fact that Pennyman was stabbed in the back with a spear, seemed to be one of extreme anger. Not a way of avenging honor or silencing a man about to reveal a secret—as would be the case with Buxton. It was more the kind of thing a man would do to blot out evil.

Tolliver moved his fork beside the salt and pepper. The simplest explanation, of course, was that Gichinga Mbura actually did kill Pennyman and that D.C. Cranford was

right, that all Justin's insisting on dotting the "i" and crossing the "t" in "justice" was a bloody waste of time.

Tolliver shook off that doubt. He still believed that the
letter of British law must be applied. In a sense it was more
important in the case of a native accused of a heinous crime.
It was the only way to accomplish the realm's prime objec-
tive. The English were here to bring the Pax Britannica and
civilization to the savages. His mind stopped at the word
"savages."

Having considered the behaviors of Pennyman, Buxton,
and Lucy, what right did he have to call the natives "savages"?
True, they went about practically naked, but it seemed to him
that, while their skin was dark, their souls were lighter than
many of his countrymen's.

He picked up the fork and reversed its direction. The
spear in question had belonged to Richard Newland. Newland had precisely the right kind of motive to make an out-
raged person thrust a weapon into a man, wherever he could
stick it. If he was the murderer, Vera was heading toward him
now. There was a vast open area between here and Berkeley
Cole's farm. She could be anywhere out there. And when
people went on safari they could easily be gone a month or
six weeks. They carried with them the wherewithal to live in
the wilderness. A needle in a haystack in Yorkshire would be
easier to find than even a large party of human beings who
could be anywhere between the Scottish Mission and the
slopes of Mount Kenya.

Tolliver was toying with the idea of betraying Vera to
her father when the native girl arrived to take his tray. "The

reverend has asked me to say he is here to see you," she said. She spoke her English with a native lilt and a touch of Scottish burr that was perfectly charming. "Tell him to please come in straightaway."

She took away the tray with the symbols of Tolliver's suspects that had helped his thinking but also increased his fears for Vera. His conversation with the Reverend McIntosh revealed nothing new. He told Tolliver that Vera had gone to Fort Hall, and for all the world he acted as if he believed it. Tolliver did not disabuse him of the fact.

16.

Vera's journey was delayed for an hour when it was discovered that the tracks had been undermined by digging animals for reasons no one could fathom. The crew onboard had had to make repairs before they could continue on their way toward Lake Victoria. By the time Vera and her motley group descended at Naivasha, it was dark.

As they stood on the platform, the two engines pulled the train away into the primeval darkness, throwing up red sparks like a miniature fireworks display. Once the train's headlight and lanterns had gone, the station and its surroundings were barely visible. Naivasha consisted of a sad collection of grass and wattle shacks and the *boma* of the local tax collector, which included some huts inhabited by his crew of ragtag Indian and native guards. No one had alighted other than Vera and her Kikuyu companions.

The Indian stationmaster lit their way with a single oil lamp. Ngethe Meru's village was three miles away, too far to travel by night. The collector, a Welshman in his cups, staggered out and offered Vera a place in his dwelling. Vera did not think it merited the name "house." As politely as she could, she declined his hospitality. She went instead with her Kikuyu into the one-room station. The Indian asked again if she would not feel more comfortable with the B'wana Collector, but she assured him she preferred to stay in the station.

He brought her and the others some roasted pumpkin, some lovely, chewy Indian bread, and for her alone a crockery bottle of lemonade and quinine water. He left her the oil lamp and went off to his own supper. She had Muiri unpack a camp bed for her and lay down fully dressed to wait for dawn.

The next morning while Vera was making her way to the nearby native village and the hut of Ngethe Meru, Justin Tolliver was sixty-five miles away, as the crow flies. In this case it would have been a pied crow of the horn of Africa, whose black-and-white markings nearly resembled the formal dinner dress favored by the British around well-set tables in Nairobi and Mombasa—as if the diners were in London or Bombay.

Having passed a largely sleepless night, Tolliver was barely awake when Denys Finch Hatton arrived with his tracker and a miraculously well-equipped entourage of porters and gunbearers. Tolliver's good luck in having such a crew would have overjoyed him if he had not immediately contrasted it with the paucity of comfort and safety that Vera was likely to be experiencing. He had to get to her as quickly as possible and still look as if he was pursuing Newland. If his luck held, it would all be one and the same thing.

He tried his best to rush Finch Hatton away before the interloper learned anything of Vera's whereabouts, but he failed at that, too. Blanche McIntosh greeted Denys warmly and told him immediately how sorry Vera would have been to miss him, but that she was away visiting a friend at Fort Hall.

And as soon as Mrs. McIntosh left them, Denys immediately guessed the truth of where Vera had actually gone.

"What, if anything, do we know of the Newland party's direction?" Finch Hatton asked.

"They left from Nyeri," Tolliver said, trying his best to sound as cooperative about it as he knew he had to be under the circumstances.

Finch Hatton discussed the matter with Kinuthia in Maasai. Libazo whispered to Tolliver that the tracker was saying that if they trekked twelve hours a day, they would reach Nyeri in three days. Vera was a day ahead of them, so they would have to make at least eighteen hours a day if they were going to catch her up before she got anywhere near the Newland party.

As it happened, at the same time, Vera was assessing her own possible speed and reaching a far less optimistic conclusion. Her guide, once she arrived in his village, turned out to be a disappointment. Ngethe Meru was still a legend, but he was now a man well past his prime. Vera worried that she would burst into tears when she saw that he was no longer the vital, powerful person she remembered. She had last seen him when she was fourteen. In the five years while she was blossoming into full womanhood, he had sunk all too quickly into old age.

Africans revered the elderly for their wisdom and experience. She prayed those qualities would make up for the stamina he certainly would lack. Enthusiasm he had aplenty. He immediately agreed to go with her. He longed for an opportunity to return to his former life trekking through the wilderness, but he had few chances of it anymore because what safari parties there were looked for fitter men with keener eyes.

Worst of all, Vera was astonished to find that the terrain around Naivasha was mountainous. All she knew of the route of the Newland party was that they had gone first to Nyeri and that they intended to end up at Berkeley Cole's farm. But to get from where she was to Nyeri in a straight line would take them over some very high hills and rough areas. Ngethe said they would have to skirt the highest peaks, which would mean a longer distance than Vera had anticipated from the map she had consulted. Ngethe estimated two or three days, which seemed an eternity to her. But Ngethe made ready very quickly and took with him seven stalwart warriors armed with swords and spears, and that made Vera feel a bit better.

Their party proceeded. Their route took them through forested areas, largely in the shade, making it easier for them to keep moving through midday. But by around two in the afternoon, Ngethe was so tired that Vera wished she had a wagon for him to ride on. But that would have needed oxen. Impossible under the circumstances.

With a sigh, she slowed her pace, walking along beside him. All she could do was pin her hopes on the fact that the Newland party was out to hunt, and therefore they would stop sometimes for days in the same place. In the meanwhile, she vowed to do her best and take in the scene around her. After all, travel through the wilderness was one of her greatest pleasures. The marvels here—the birds, the monkeys, even the ill-tempered baboons—would ordinarily be entertainment enough. She hung her binoculars around her neck and tried to welcome the stops where Ngethe had to nap in the shade for a while before he could go on. They gave her the chance to look about her at the scenery while she rested her own legs.

As it happened, Tolliver marched his party until night fell completely and darkness made movement inadvisable. The crescent moon was waxing, but it gave them insufficient light. Torches would not suffice. The starlight was beautiful, but with nothing else to light their way, the territory was treacherous.

Tolliver was up at first light and pushing them to make tracks. Under these conditions, thirteen or fourteen hours would be their maximum. The loveliness of his surroundings warred with the turmoil of his thoughts. He comforted himself by imagining that one day he and Vera would enjoy peace and harmony in these places. But even those thoughts led to more and bitter imaginings. Was she rushing ahead of him to warn Newland that his guilt had been discovered? What he longed for was to take her in his arms and love her.

But was he going to be forced to arrest her as an accessory to murder? That phantom kiss she had bestowed on him lingered in his thoughts and made him wish he could fly and find her.

Vera and Ngethe Meru and their group arrived at Nyeri at midday and continued on after only a brief respite. They were making good time despite Ngethe's slow pace and her blistered feet. She would push their pace as fast as she could without harming Ngethe, not rest until she had found her brother safe and was nearby to keep him so.

The old tracker proved his mettle in picking up signs of the Newland group only a few leagues out of town. He knew the habits of the safari men and how to find good spots for shooting game. He guessed Newland's tracker and gunbearers also knew the best way to take, and he was right.

Passing through Nyeri the next morning, Tolliver learned from the local people that Vera had left the town not twenty-four hours before. The trail that Kinuthia picked up just after noon was not that of the Newland party but Vera's. As they followed, the tracker confirmed that Vera was on the right trail. Older indications showed that an even larger party had come the same way two weeks or more ago.

Tolliver was relieved. Whoever was guiding Vera had the right skills. Then he wondered if she herself were capable of reading the earth like a tracker. He did not like the idea that she might have such a manly talent that he did not possess.

While Tolliver was wondering what it would be like to be in love with a woman who knew more than he, Ngethe was convincing Vera that they should take a brief detour. Ngethe reckoned that the Newland party would have lingered on the plain that surrounded them, since game was so plentiful here and the little river would give them an ample source of water. There was a high outcropping across the river. Though the Newland party had not crossed here, he proposed that they do so. He wanted to climb the tor. The view from the top would allow them to look out a long, long distance. At dusk, they would very likely be able to see the bonfire Newland's guides would use to signal the position of their camp. Then all they would have to do was to make straight for the camp. If they did not see a fire, then they could easily come back, recross the river, and pick up the Newlands' trail again. Vera welcomed any shortcut that had a chance of getting her to Otis faster.

So they crossed the river.

17.

Kwai Libazo knew immediately that Justin Tolliver was faking a calm exterior and that Denys Finch Hatton was also trying to hide his agitation. Kinuthia had discovered that the two parties he was tracking had gone in different directions. And Kwai rightly guessed that Tolliver was now torn as to which of the groups they should follow.

"Do we think her tracker made a mistake and thought Newland crossed the river here?" Tolliver asked of Finch Hatton.

Libazo waited until Finch Hatton began to interrogate Kinuthia on the subject. "Sir," he said quietly to Tolliver, "Kinuthia already told me that the signs of which way the Newland party went are plain here. I have been trying to learn how to track, watching what Kinuthia looks for. Even I can see very well that the Newland group went that way." He pointed along the course of the river. "The lady's tracker must have been able to see that, too. Yet they crossed." He pointed across the stream.

"But why?"

"I cannot say."

Tolliver disliked the situation. He had hoped to catch Vera up by dusk this evening. Now the light was fading, and he was stuck in a cleft stick. Duty drew him to follow Newland to apprehend the man who very likely had killed Josiah Pennyman. But his blood, his skin, and also his heart, if he admitted it, told him that he must protect Vera from harm.

"Listen, old chap," Finch Hatton was saying, before Tolliver had expressed even the slightest doubt as to how to proceed. "There are two of us. You have your mission to apprehend Newland. You take Kinuthia and follow that way." He pointed in the direction the Newlands had taken. "Miss McIntosh's trail is fresh. I'll take Libazo here and follow her. We will leave ourselves plenty of markings to make it easy for us to get back to this spot. As you go along, drop a line of obvious clues—bread crumbs for us to follow so that we can come along after you."

It was the very last thing Tolliver wanted to do. Not only would he have to leave Vera's safety to Finch Hatton; worse yet, the dreaded Denys would be the hero who rescued her, what Tolliver himself desired with all his heart to be.

She must be quite near. He looked out across the river. If only he could get up high enough to see, he might be able to spot her in the distance. But there was no place nearby. Not even a tall tree he could climb. Three feet off the ground was as high as he could get, and the only trees were along the river bank where they were below the level of the ground that rose slightly across the water. There was a high outcropping on the other side. It would give him the vantage point he needed to see her. It stood about five miles away and was easily a hundred, a hundred and thirty feet high, if his guess was correct given the deceptive distances and sizes of landmarks in the African bush.

But the dark was coming fast. There was practically no dusk here so near the equator. Finch Hatton had begun to tap his foot, like a man about to start a foot race.

"No," Tolliver said. "We should not split our group. We will make camp here tonight and at first light we will make straight for that outcropping in the distance." He pointed to it. "If Newland or Miss McIntosh is anywhere in the area, we will be able to see them from up there."

Finch Hatton looked disappointed and doubtful, but Kinuthia nodded approvingly and Libazo saluted. For the first time in his life, but not the last, Tolliver preferred the approval of the Africans to that of his own race.

Eight miles off, Vera's camp was in turmoil.

Ngethe Meru had climbed the rocky outcropping just before sunset to see if he could spot the fires of the Newland party in the distance. He had, and he pointed out the camp to his three companions. It was no more than three hours' walk to their northeast.

Then, as he turned to descend, something that looked like the movement of people back near the river distracted him. He was about to ask his men to look that way with their younger eyes. He did not watch where he stepped. The snake was sequestered in among the scrub bushes and boulders. It struck.

Down at the foot of the outcropping, organizing the

cooking of their dinner, Vera heard the old man's scream and knew. She dropped what she was doing and ran. *Oh. No. No. No. NO!* Her inner voice was shouting as loud as the three warrior boys who had climbed up with Ngethe.

The old tracker was moaning and crying, being carried down by two of the younger men. The third carried the now-dead snake impaled on his spear.

Vera sank to the ground. The worst. The worst possible. A puff adder.

Ngethe was writhing. Blood was dripping from the wound just above his right ankle. His bearers laid him on the ground before her. The others behind her hopped and shouted, cried out their panic and dread.

Vera covered her face with her hands. Darkness was descending like a pall. She did not make a sound. *Unspeakable. Unspeakable. Unspeakable.* The only word she could think drummed in her brain.

Muiri came and sat beside her. The girl was only fourteen but she was considered a woman by Kikuyu standards. She put a hand on Vera's arm. Vera took Muiri's hand in hers. "We will be alright," she whispered, though she knew that such would not be the case.

Vera rose.

They all knew the consequences of this, as they all knew that death could strike at any time here in this loveliest of all lands. Vera could easily predict what would happen. Ngethe would be dead within a day, in two at the most, in horrible pain the whole while. What Vera did not know was what if anything she could do. She had grown up next to a hospital. At home there were always people who knew what to do with illness or injury. But in this situation she was supposed to take charge. At least that was the way of things here and now.

She went and sat by the fire, and called everyone together around her. One of the men who had carried Ngethe stayed with him, out of earshot. She hardly knew what she was doing, but whatever happened, they were in this together. She needed to be one of them. But she also needed to make sure she did the right thing. As an African. For this was an African problem. And the best way to decide was this way, together—all of them, the African way.

Around their circle, the grave brown faces reflected the red of the fire's flames. "We must do what is best," she said. "We must decide together what that is."

They began to speak their minds. They did not look at one another when they spoke but stared into the flames. They did not have to talk for long about what would happen to Ngethe. None of them saw much point in stating the obvious. Leaving him alone while he died was not an option anyone mentioned. Here, alone, he would have hyenas on him while he still lived. That would be the worst of all choices. The possible ways to deal with his suffering narrowed down within minutes to two: stay with him while he suffered or put him out of his misery.

Vera listened as they argued for the latter. They spoke of kindness, of ending their revered father figure's suffering. She said they could wait, stay with him until the end. It was what she as a Christian had been taught was right. They all grimaced when she suggested Ngethe should be allowed to die in agony. Their dark eyes were tearful when they talked of saying good-bye to him, but they were determined to save him from further suffering. She heard them. And her own father's voice spoke to her in her mind. The priest of the Church of Scotland would say that there was no mercy in killing another person before the Lord took him in His own time.

Vera felt as if a fist were squeezing her heart. "How would we help him to die?" she asked. "Who would do it?" She did not want to think about it. She wanted to run away. She wanted to go to sleep and wake up at home with the sound of the workers spreading out in the coffee fields and the cup rattling on the tray as Njui brought her mother her breakfast. She wanted her uncle to be alive so he could learn to be a better man. And she wanted to silence Ngethe's moans that came through the night as soon as the voices around the fire were still. No one answered her questions.

She put her hand on Muiri's shoulder and leaned on her while she rose on stiff legs. "I will speak to Ngethe," she said. She signaled his men to come with her.

They squatted around the old man as he lay on the ground. "Baba," she said, addressing him as if he were her father, "what do you want us to do for you?"

He looked to his companions, not to her. He said a phrase she did not know, but it contained the word "*muti*," which she understood. It meant "tree." It was from the bark of a tree that they obtained the poison they used on the tips of their arrows and spears when they hunted. Poison that would mean instant death. Her father's voice would not be quiet in her heart.

His men stood. "Leave this to us, little sister," they told her.

She could not stop her tears. She took Ngethe Meru's hand and kissed it. "Good-bye, Baba," she said.

"Yes" was all he answered.

She did not go to the camp bed in her tent, but took her blanket and lay on the ground near the fire with the others. Looking up at the starry sky she loved so well, she tried to believe what her playmates of old had told her, that each star was the soul of a person who had died. That soon Ngethe would be up there shining down upon them.

A sob escaped her when it occurred to her that he would not be dying if she had not brought him here.

18.

Both Tolliver and Vera were awake before first light the next morning, impatient to be away.

After only an hour or so of fitful sleep, she wanted to run as fast as her legs would carry her from the scene of Ngethe's demise.

Two hours' march away, back near the river, Tolliver knew that only action would keep at bay the torrent of worrisome pictures falling into his head of her attacked by lions, gored by buffalo. To keep from beating his head on the ground to halt his imaginings, he was up and moving with the merest lightening of the sky.

"March," he called as his raggedy column formed up. With him at its head they forded the river and moved off, following the trail of Vera's party that led straight to the high tor in the distance.

With fewer people to organize and all of her group determined to be away from the place where they knew Ngethe's remains lay exposed to the carrion eaters, Vera had less trouble getting underway with speed. By the time the sunlight was strong enough to throw a shadow, she and her Kikuyu were several miles gone, making straight for the camp Ngethe had seen before the snake bit him.

But Tolliver had halted. There, over a spot near the high outcropping, buzzards were circling. In three beats of his heart, his hand was in the air. "Doubletime, lads," he shouted. Now Tolliver's target was whatever the scavenger birds had their eyes on. With every step he tried to convince himself that many things having nothing to do with Vera could be dying out there. The area was replete with game. That was the whole point of people coming here to hunt. But those reassuring thoughts were soon overwhelmed by fear: there were other predators out here besides men—lions . . . and there were subtler dangers—deadly things that hid among the rocks. Good God, snakes. The striking cobra was the last thing he wished to imagine.

At the front of his jogging column, he picked up his pace. Suppose, he asked himself, that Newland saw her coming and realized that she had found him out. Then she would become the target of the worst predator of all: a man bent on murder. He ordered himself to stop such imaginings. He tried to laugh at his overly dramatic terrors. But he could not manage it. He just ran faster.

Finch Hatton was keeping pace, of course. He seemed to be treating the whole effort as if it were some sort of sporting event. The boys carrying the heaviest loads were falling quite a bit behind.

The birds were still circling, which could mean that whatever it was had not yet died. Or there could be animals gnawing on whatever the vultures were waiting to get at. Tolliver did not pause when he saw the jackals. He took the rifle slung over his shoulder and held it at the ready, but the beasts ran off without a second glance as the runners approached. The carcass, whatever it was, was still hidden in the grass.

Tolliver held up his hand to signal a stop, but the boys behind him had already done so. He approached, and his stomach turned. It was recognizable as a person, but not easily. The Kikuyu boys exclaimed loudest.

Kwai Libazo came up behind him. "He was a Kikuyu. Do you see the iron necklace? The rings around his ankle? The enlarged earlobes. These are Kikuyu emblems."

"He must have been with Miss McIntosh's party," Finch Hatton said. "But his hair is gray. He must have been quite an old man. Why would she have taken a man so old on such a mission?"

"He must have been her tracker," Tolliver and Kinuthia said in unison.

"Then she is now without a tracker," Libazo said, speaking out of turn, as had become his wont.

It was not Libazo's insolence but what he had said that Tolliver found upsetting. "She has gone off without a tracker then," he said. "It can't have been that long ago." He was already making for the outcropping that loomed above them. "Kinuthia, come with me. Libazo, tell the men to drink and catch their breath," he called over his shoulder.

As they climbed, Tolliver made for the side of the outcropping that faced in the direction where Vera's party must have gone. Before they were more than thirty feet up, Kinuthia touched Tolliver's shoulder and pointed. The emerald green plain that surrounded them stretched for miles in every direction. It was dotted here and there with clumps of thorn trees and herds of antelope. The river they had crossed this morning curved sharply to the right, glistening in the distance. The carrion birds were still circling, but a little farther off from the corpse.

In the middistance, where Kinuthia's finger indicated, Tolliver made out a party of about twenty, trekking away from them. They looked few and very vulnerable in the middle of this vast area. At least sixty Cape buffalo were grazing about a hundred yards off to their right. Tolliver jumped down a level and made to descend and get after them. Kinuthia grabbed his shoulder and pointed again: farther into the distance, off next to the river, at the foot of some low hills, was a large camp; smoke rose from its fires. The Newland camp. Vera and her boys were making directly for it.

And if Tolliver knew anything, there was a murderer there.

Every step Vera took pained her. Blisters on her toes, cramps in her calves. The remorse over Ngethe tortured her soul. Only her fear for Otis could have driven her to go on.

A whiff of smoke in the air told her she was close, though she could not see the Newland camp in the undulating plain. The boys with her chanted as they ran, and suddenly there were eight or ten porters approaching them. They were dressed in the brown and navy uniforms of Tarlton and Company, the leading safari outfitters, which she found odd. Ordinarily, settlers traveled on safari less expensively than one did with Tarlton's.

"Are you with Richard Newland's party?" she asked in Swahili.

"Yes, Miss," the lead boy answered in English. "You look done in, may we help you?" They had a pallet with them, on which she gladly lay herself down.

Richard Newland and his son came out to meet her before she arrived at their campsite. "Where is Otis?" she demanded to know.

"In a minute," Richard said. "Let us get you settled. You've had a difficult time." His aquiline face was careworn, as if he were the one who had spent the last several days tramping through the wilderness as fast as he could move. He led his porters to a camp bed under an acacia tree, where they placed her, pallet and all.

She started to get up, but Newland put out his hand. "Please rest a minute. The boys will bring you some tea. I will be back in a moment." He turned and walked away, pushing his son ahead of him.

Tea was what she longed for, but she did not lie back. "Where is my brother? I want to see him immediately."

Newland waved his right hand over his head, without turning around. "Just a minute." They went into a tent across the clearing. The flap of it closed behind them.

"I will not be put off," she shouted after him. Muiri came and sat beside the camp bed and took Vera's hand. It was entirely unclear whether she wanted to give comfort or get it. Vera herself wanted neither.

Why had her brother not greeted her? Was he in that tent? Was he ill? She jumped up and ran to find out. As she crossed the campground, she saw a flash of red hair to her right. Her heart lifted and then sank. It was Berkeley Cole. Not Otis. She continued toward Newland's tent. He came out just as she arrived and handed her an envelope.

Her name was written on it—"Miss Vera McIntosh"—in her brother's neat and gentlemanly script.

She tore it open. The paper inside said, "Dear Vera, By the time you read this, I will be very far away. I fear we will never see one another again. Uncle Josiah's death is my fault and mine alone. I had to save Mother. Please be very kind to her. Do not blame her. Do not let her confess." In the final sentence, the word "not" was underlined four times. The letter was signed, "Your loving brother, Otis."

She stared at the paper in astonishment, several times opening her mouth to speak, but not able to force out any words.

Richard Newland stood next to her, looking expectantly into her face.

She folded the paper and held it and the envelope to her heart. She looked right into Newland's sad eyes. "Have you read this letter?" Her voice was sharp.

"No," he said, "but I think I know what it says."

"What? You tell me what you think this abominable message says."

He, too, was having difficulty getting his words to flow. "Otis talked to me at length and he—"

A great noise was rising up at the edge of the camp, shouting and clattering. Berkeley Cole came running. "I've seen them. It's Denys, with a large party. They are at doubletime. I think Justin Tolliver is with them."

Vera ran to the noise. With no thought of anything. Just moved to him.

As soon as he saw her, he ran to her. He was sweating and panting.

She threw herself into his arms.

He tried to hold her off. He must smell disgusting.

She held on to him with her arms around his neck. She was weeping.

He embraced her, kissed the top of her head. After a minute or two, he managed gently to peel her arms from him. "I'm a stinking mess," he whispered in her ear. It seemed entirely the wrong thing to say.

"Life is a stinking mess," she said and sank to the ground.

Once the tumult of their arrival had subsided, he took Vera aside and spoke to her first and alone, she sitting on the camp bed under the tree and he cross-legged on the ground beside it. She had a teacup in her hands. His was on the grass next to his foot.

"I came to arrest Richard Newland for your uncle's murder," he said. "As you already know, the murder weapon belonged to him. Finch Hatton told me."

"I came to the police station to tell you," she said, "but you were visiting Mrs. Buxton at the time." The sadness in her brown eyes took on an offended glint.

He could not tell her anything but the truth. "She means nothing to me," he said. "You are the only woman who interests me."

She stopped breathing. Tears came to her eyes. She reached out and touched his face. He took her hand and kissed it.

"When I realized it was Newland," she said after a moment, "I became afraid for my brother, so I came to protect him."

Tolliver realized he had not seen the boy in the helter-skelter of his arrival. "Where is he?"

She reached into her pocket and handed him a paper.

He scanned it quickly. "This shocks me," he said.

"No more than it does me." A tear escaped her eye. He had to force himself not to kiss it as it ran down her cheek.

"Do you believe this?" He held up the note between his index and middle fingers.

"I don't want to, but it is in Otis's hand, and it was sealed in an envelope addressed by him to me." She dug the envelope out of her pocket.

He took it. "I will have to keep these for now."

She snatched them back. "*No!*" She said it so loudly that it caused the boys tending the cook fire several yards away to look over at them. She had suddenly realized that it implicated her mother. He, the policeman, would have to arrest her mother.

"Suppose it isn't true. Suppose the killer really was Richard Newland." She knew her statements were useless.

He shook his head and pointed to the paper in her hand. "How can that be?"

She bit on her bottom lip. "Suppose— Suppose . . . that . . . Richard forced him to write this and then killed him. Suppose he wants to save himself by casting the blame on my poor brother."

"Dearest Vera," he said gently. "That does not seem at all likely. And if it were true, why would your brother have said anything about your mother?"

Defiance won out over the fear in her eyes. "It's absurd. My mother would not have killed her brother. I cannot imagine what my brother meant by saying such a thing."

"Was Otis very fond of your mother? And she of him?"

"Extraordinarily so." Vera did not say what she always thought of her mother—that she did not love her daughter half as much as she loved her son.

"Well, then," Justin said, "it is all very easy to explain. Your brother feared your mother would try to take the blame, to save your brother from being accused. She would not be the first parent to want to make such a sacrifice for a child."

"Do you think it could be true? That Otis did it. That he is afraid my mother will try to shield him by confessing to the crime?"

He nodded an emphatic yes.

She folded up the envelope and the note and pressed them deep into the pocket of her skirt.

"I feel so dirty and sweaty," she said. "I wish I could bathe in the river."

"Can't we?" he asked, before he realized that he might have been talking about them bathing together. He blushed, but he could not banish the thought.

"It doesn't seem so. There could be crocodiles."

"Ah," he said. "Pity."

While the safari boys roasted a haunch of antelope meat and some of the sweet potatoes they had dragged with them all those miles from the Chania Bridge, Tolliver told Newland that he had been a suspect in the killing of Josiah Penny-man. But that he no longer was. That he and Vera would have to go back to Nairobi directly to make the proper depositions and close the case.

Finch Hatton and Cole had come upon them while they spoke. Tolliver's resentment of his rival had all but completely evaporated the moment Vera McIntosh ran toward both of them and threw herself into Tolliver's arms. He had embraced her, his heart singing because she was safe. But also because she had felt to him at that moment like a hard-won prize. She was off in a tent now, bathing, Newland had said.

"What about young Otis?" Denys asked, helping himself to a drink from a tray table between Richard Newland and his glum son. "A fourteen-year-old boy cannot simply vanish. There has to be a way to track him." He looked at Newland as if challenging him to go and find the boy.

"I advised him to go to Lake Victoria and take the steamer into Uganda," Richard Newland said. "I want him to get away. I told him who would help him, gave him the means, and I promised I would never betray him." He poked the fire in front of him, which was dying. One of the porters put more wood on it. "And I never will. Whatever happened, he did my family a favor. We cannot give Antonia's sister her innocence back, but at least the blackguard who took it from her got his just desserts."

"Who would have imagined it?" Cole said. "A spotty youth like Otis McIntosh."

Newland took off his hat and passed his hand through his damp black hair. "He said he did and I believe him. Not only believe him, I applaud him. I wish I had had the courage to do it myself."

Tolliver let them think what they wanted. It would be better if they thought the matter completely settled. But he knew it was not, that there was still a piece of this puzzle missing. The answer to why. Why would Otis McIntosh have killed his uncle? His note to his sister said he did it to save his mother. But to save her from what? There was still at least one question an assistant district supervisor of police needed to answer before he could close the file on this sordid affair. If he clung to the letter of the law, by rights he ought to arrest Newland for helping a murderer escape. He would not. He was happy that he would not have to arrest Vera on that same charge. Vera who was in a tent, bathing now in that huge tin bathtub that Newland had caused his porters to lug through the wilderness along with the crystal and the china from which the party were about to dine.

Vera picked at her supper, though it was the best meal she had had since she left home. She had taken a place next to Justin Tolliver at the table. He put his hand over hers when they were side by side, and left it there while they breathed two breaths. When he took his hand away she looked into his eyes and smiled, rather wanly she imagined.

The gentlemen at the table were assiduously avoiding any mention of her brother or anything at all disturbing, for that matter. Cole and Newland talked of farming, and Dicky Newland quizzed Tolliver about the upcoming cricket match between the Railway Society squad and the Nairobi Club's team. All very civilized and proper, when her heart was broken and all she wanted to do was scream at them that she wanted her Otis back.

When she placed her perfectly pressed white damask napkin next to her plate and said she wanted rest, Tolliver rose and took her gently by the elbow and helped her up. They all made appropriately understanding, murmuring noises.

Muiri helped her disrobe and on with her muslin nightdress. Once Vera lay on her cot, the girl made off. Vera imagined she was finding company among the boys of her village who had come along on this journey. Vera envied her the freedom, envied her the love, if one could call it that, that she would receive. *Yes*, Vera thought, *she did call it love*. Though she had no experience of it herself, from what the girls she had known from babyhood had told her, it was wonderful. The kind of thing that would make one giggle. Vera wept instead, about her own loss. Her own loneliness. She was so tired of weeping.

She was still awake when the camp went completely silent except for the singing of the cicadas and the gurgling of the river. When she heard a movement outside her tent, her first thought was that it was a hippo, but she had not noticed any in the river. Then she heard Tolliver whisper her name. "Vera?" Softly. It was the first time she had ever heard him say it. Not "Miss McIntosh," as would have been proper. "Vera?" he said again, still softly. "I've come to see if you are alright."

She threw off the mosquito netting, drew a shawl around her, and went to the flap of the tent. "Yes," she said.

"You don't need anything?" He was just on the other side of the canvas, his voice barely audible.

She reached out, parted the opening. She moved toward him. He smelled of soap. He was silhouetted against the pale light of the crescent moon. She dropped her shawl and put her hands on his upper arms.

"I need—" She swallowed. "I need you."

It took only one small step for him to be inside the tent with her. The flap closed behind him, and she was in his arms, kissing him. Then there was no separate him deciding what to do, no separate her. Just the two of them entwined, with no way to stop all they wanted to be to each other. Her skin. And his. Her arms. And his lifting her to the cot. His lips. Her breasts. His hands. And hers. The sweet smell of her hair. The quickness of his breath.

When the moment came for him to enter her, he hesitated. But she did not. "Love me. Please just love me," she whispered.

And he did.

19.

Before the sky turned light, Tolliver kissed her once more and left her.

By the time Vera was fully awake, the camp was bustling, and Muiri had folded her shawl and put her few things in her rucksack.

Standing near the fire, Tolliver bid her a proper good morning and went to fetch her a mug of tea.

She let their hands touch momentarily as he handed it to her. She was careful not to look in his eyes. The skin of her arms drank in his nearness. He stayed close. That was enough for her.

Richard Newland and Denys Finch Hatton were splitting off with Cole toward his farm on the Naro Moru River. Kinuthia would go with them. Vera's and Tolliver's party would follow the plain trail back to Nyeri.

"We had best then cross the hills from Nyeri back to Naivasha," Vera said. "I must visit Ngethe's wives and children and tell them what has befallen him." For a second she allowed herself to glance into Justin's eyes. She found the understanding she was looking for in them.

"Is that the way you came?" Finch Hatton asked.

"Yes," Vera said. She was solemn, but he laughed.

"What a girl, you are," he said.

And Justin thought, *If you only knew.* And it satisfied him deeply that Finch Hatton never would really know her. "We can take the train back to Athi River from Naivasha," he said. "And I'll send a telegram to the district commissioner."

"And to my parents," Vera said.

"We had better get underway, then," Tolliver said, taking charge, as was right under the circumstances.

They bid their good-byes, and Tolliver took his group south along the river, while Newland and Cole took their party east.

Vera and Tolliver camped twice more before they reached Nyeri. And each night when all was quiet and Kwai and the other boys were organized on their guard duties, Tolliver found his way to Vera's arms. Their separateness evaporated the minute they embraced. During those nights, Vera learned why the Kikuyu girls giggled when they spoke of sex. With all her sadness still upon her, she could not yet laugh with their lovemaking, but she felt the heaviness in her heart lift when her arms were around Justin and her lips on his.

On the third night, crossing the hills between Nyeri and Naivasha, before darkness fell they stopped in a forest clearing. The boys needed to keep a bonfire going all night to repel any prowling predators. Its light and that of the half moon made their camp brighter than on the previous nights. Justin should not have cared what the askaris and porters thought of him, but he still felt he had to protect Vera from their knowing he was with her in the night. Nonetheless, after barely an hour's hesitation, he gave in to his need for her and made his way to her tent.

When he opened the flap, enough light entered with him to reveal her—beautiful in her white nightdress, sitting cross-legged on her cot.

She leapt up and into his arms with that incredible grace of hers. And the power of his love for her held all his misgivings at bay.

Afterward, as they lay on her little narrow cot, with her body on his, her head on his shoulder, the scent of her enveloping him, he had to talk about the coming days, about how he would shield her from the world's knowledge of their love.

"Tomorrow," he whispered, "we will arrive in Naivasha and we will have to— We cannot let anyone see— We cannot continue to—"

She jumped up, jamming her knee into his hip in the process. "Continue to what? See what? That I am a hussy? That you are not a gentleman? What do we have to hide from the world? Our sin?"

He sat up and reached for her. She was talking much too loudly. He did not want her to hurt. He just wanted to protect her. "Vera, please. Don't—"

"Don't what?" She beat off his hands and stepped back, upsetting the folding washstand in the corner. The metal basin clattered to the ground in the darkness. "Just get out of here, Mr. Proper English Gentleman."

"Oh, Vera, you mustn't interpret what I said that way? What has happened is my fault." As soon as the words were out of his mouth, he knew they were entirely the wrong ones.

"Please, just go." Her voice was quiet now, and cold.

"I do not want the world to think—"

"I know exactly what you don't want the world to think. You don't want anyone to know that you have behaved in an ungentlemanlike fashion. And that I have done what no proper lady would do. Very well. We will tell no one. Now, just go."

"Vera, please, I said it badly. I think—" He tried to take her in his arms, but she pushed him off.

"I know what you think I am."

"I think you are the most wonderful of girls. I love you."

"Very nice," she said completely without warmth. "Now, just go. I have a difficult day tomorrow."

They did not speak to one another at all during the three-hour trek to Naivasha the next morning. Only in silence, in their own minds, which were far from quiet, did they formulate the words to express their remorse, their fear, their longing. They both looked back on those four days and nights as idyllic: walking side by side through the vast wilderness, the colors, the scents, the birds whose names she had told him, the shadows of the clouds on the sea of grass that stretched out for miles, the chants of the porters as they tramped along, the English songs the two of them had sung to keep themselves going. The grazing antelope. The long line of elephants silhouetted against sunset. And then, after dark, the brilliance of the stars as they sat together and dined by lamplight. The delicious nights in one another's arms, the fun of working out who should be where on her impossibly small camp bed. The ecstasy they learned to produce in one another. They both wanted it all back, and they both feared they would never again have it.

His guilt had spoiled it for her. But she held her head high as she walked along those final miles. She refused to see herself as a sinner. If God had made her body, He must have wanted girls to long for love the way she did. The Commandments said she must not commit adultery, but that was only if they were already married and she wanted to lay with someone other than him. But she wanted no one else. She refused to accept what he probably thought. That somehow, by accepting his love, she had condemned herself to his rejection. She wished she could hate him for what he had said. Wished her anger were strong enough to make her stop wanting to have him the way she'd had, in her arms, inside her body in the night.

He hated himself as much as she wished she could hate him. He had said all the wrong things. All he had wanted was to let her know how sorry he was that it would have to stop. That once they reached the railroad, the freedom given to them in the wilderness would be forbidden until they were man and wife. He had imagined a straight line from where they were to their wedding and a lifetime of loving. But he had not said that. He had not remembered that he should say it. It seemed the only possible outcome. He had focused instead on the pain of having to give her up even for a few weeks or months, and he had vowed to himself that not one person would ever think the least wrong thought about her for having given herself to him. He had blundered. Instead of asking her to marry him, he had spoken of what they had to give up. How could he have been so dense? He did not care a fig for all he had been taught of how a girl must defend her virginity to the death. She had given him hers. He did feel like a rotter for letting himself take it. But his intentions were honorable, whatever else anyone would say. And what now could he ever say to erase the insult and the anger his words had created? Having no answer, sometimes despairing that there was an answer, he said nothing.

They arrived in Naivasha at midday. At the station they found out that the down train would leave at 3:38 in the morning. Vera announced to Kwai Libazo, but in Tolliver's presence, that she and Muiri would return in time to take the train. Then she marched off, her back straight and her step determined, to tell her dreadful news to Ngethe Meru's family—that their husband and father would never return. Tolliver loved her as much for her courage as he did for the softness and warmth of her skin and the sparkle of life in her eyes.

He went to the telegrapher and sent a message to D.C. Cranford telling him that he had discovered who had killed Josiah Pennyman and that he should release Gichinga Mbura. Vera had said that she wanted to telegraph her parents, but she had not stopped to do so. He sent a separate cable to Clement McIntosh, from himself, telling him that he had Vera under his protection, that she would arrive at the Athi River Station at 12:25 the next day.

There was no police *boma* in Naivasha, so he went to the local collector and begged a second breakfast and a bath. By the time he returned to the station, he had two telegrams. The first, from Cranford, sank his heart: RETURN AT ONCE STOP YOU ARE IN VIOLATION OF ALL RULES STOP YOUR POSITION IN JEOPARDY STOP WITCH DOCTOR EXECUTED TWO DAYS AGO STOP.

The second, from the Reverend McIntosh, crushed his soul: VERA'S MOTHER DEAD STOP WILL MEET TRAIN STOP TELL HER NOTHING STOP.

20.

During the night hours when they were alone as the train rattled over a long series of trestles, Vera relented and spoke to Tolliver. The carriage had no corridor; the compartments opened only to the outside when the train was in a station. They had only weak light from oil lamps that hung from the ceiling. He could just see her stir, her hand going to her mouth. He could feel she was holding her breath. Then suddenly words were pouring out of her, thoughts that seemed to belong in the middle of a conversation. "I never wept for my uncle. I could not. He was a presence, but never a person to me. Does that sound strange?"

"No," he said.

"He was not a good person."

Tolliver did not think it right to agree so he said nothing.

She made a disapproving groan. "I suppose you think me awful for saying so."

He did not move. He did not speak of his love for her because he feared if he did, he would not be able to control his desire. In the half darkness, with only a few feet of space between them Tolliver wished he could let himself take her in his arms. With the knowledge of her mother's death, he thought he should despise himself for wanting her body so. "I think you are entirely right in your assessment." He was hiding his passion behind a wall of ice, and she was feeling only the cold, he was sure. He felt despicable.

A sob escaped her. "I could not weep for my uncle, but I wept for Ngethe." She sniffled. "I gave his family all the money I had. It seemed a deplorable, patronizing thing to do. As if his life were worth no more than that paltry sum. I thought it would make me feel better, but it made me feel worse. And now I don't think of Ngethe at all. All I think about is Otis. But that is selfish. Otis is alive, but Ngethe is dead."

"I am sure that Ngethe's family knew you were trying to help them."

"They have no death rituals as we do. His safari boys took his life to save him dying in agony. I allowed them to. My father would say that I committed a terrible sin by agreeing to euthanasia, but—" Her emotions overwhelmed her.

"Your father loves you such a great deal, Vera," he said. "I am sure he—"

"Say it again."

"Your father loves you a great deal."

"No. My name."

"Vera."

She was silent.

"Perhaps one day your brother will return to you. I hope he does." Knowing what news awaited her at home, he did not try to touch her. Neither did he want to, aboard this train, because making love to her here would seem sordid, as it had not, could never have out under the stars, surrounded by the earth in its primitive majesty.

At midday the next day, Clement McIntosh was standing on the platform waiting for them. As soon as she saw him through the window, Vera whispered, "You have told him about Otis."

"No," Tolliver said, steeling himself for the pain she would have to bear.

"Then something else is terribly wrong."

The moment the train stopped, Justin opened the door, jumped out, and lifted her down. Her father ran to her and took her by the hands.

"Oh, my lass. Oh, my lass."

"What is it, father?"

"Let me take you home, Vera."

Much as she loved to hear Tolliver call her by her name, when her father said it she knew he was about to tell her something dreadful. But if papa did not know about Otis, what could it be? Nothing could be worse than their losing Otis. "Tell me now. I want to know now."

He led her to the buggy at the end of the platform. Kwai Libazo had loaded her rucksack into it.

"I will walk with the Kikuyus, sir," Kwai whispered to Tolliver, who nodded.

Vera looked over her shoulder at Justin as he helped her into the buggy. He climbed in and took the reins. Her father sat beside her and held her hand, as he would that of a frightened little girl. "Tell me now, Father. Please. It cannot be worse than what I fear."

"Ay, it is, my dearest. I am afraid it is. Your mother—Your mother . . . has taken . . . her own life." He choked on his words.

"*Aiee!*" she screamed. "*Aieeee!*" It was a primal sound. She breathed in raggedy breaths as if taking the shock in from the air. "How? Why?"

Her father supplied no answer.

"Did she know then? About Otis?" She answered her own question. "She knew. She knew he had run away forever." She looked to her father for confirmation.

His sad expression did not change.

"She could not face life without Otis," Vera said.

It was unclear to Tolliver if she believed it or if she needed to believe and was convincing herself of it.

"It is inexplicable, my lass," her father said. "She was my wife for all these years. She told me all her secrets, but . . ." His voice faded.

"Oh, Papa," Vera said. "Oh, Papa . . ."

For the remainder of the half hour it took to drive to the mission, none of them spoke. Once they arrived at the house, Tolliver left her with her father and walked down to the bottom of the lawn. The coffee blossoms were gone. Tiny berries were beginning to form.

Looking back, he watched them sitting on the veranda, facing each other, her lovely hands in her father's. Tolliver's heart ached for them both. He turned away to the view across the Athi Plain, remembering the day he and Vera had looked on this place from their picnicking spot. The simply built stone house behind him had only lately held five of the family. Now, there were only two heartbroken people left. And Tolliver's duty was to get the facts and to do so without regard to the pain the telling would cause to Vera and her father. When he had said yes to becoming a policeman, it had seemed as if it might be another youthful lark. He shook his head and smiled a bitter smile at himself.

Sitting with her father, Vera glanced from time to time at Tolliver's back. Her father had heard the fact of his son's escape with great sadness, but without surprise. Now, he expressed a grim hope that perhaps one day they might get Otis back.

Vera took his hand. "I want to see him, Father. I want to watch him become a man."

Her father gasped and sobbed.

"Oh, Papa, I am sorry. I do not want to make you feel worse."

He kissed her hand. "Never, my lass. Never. You are my solace. My only solace."

Vera's mind was full of questions about why all these ghastly things had happened, but she could not torture her father for more information. Her grief was mixed with remorse. If she had stayed at home both her mother and Ngethe Meru might still be alive. But she kept those thoughts to herself, too. She would not burden her father with her guilt.

As it was, he put his hand over his mouth, closed his pale eyes, and held them tightly shut for a moment.

She leaned forward to put her arm around him and her head on his shoulder.

"We will bury her tomorrow," her father said, once he

had recovered himself. "It comforts me a great deal that you have come home in time. I am so sorry you must be so very sad, my lass."

She reached up and put her hand on his cheek.

He took it and held it tight. "I'd better tell Captain Tolliver what he needs to know." He touched her hair and stood up.

He took his hat from the little table next to the door and walked down to where Tolliver was waiting, near the low hedge that separated the lawn from the plantation.

Tolliver faced away. Vera's heart could not stop hoping he would be hers again one day. If only she could erase all the awful truths he would have to learn about her family.

She went inside. Her mother's coffin was in the parlor. She wanted to speak to her mother in her mind. She wanted to pray for her. But she could not go in there. Not yet. Not alone. She went through to the kitchen yard and off to find Wangari, who would embrace her and not make her talk if she did not want to.

Tolliver turned when he heard Clement McIntosh approaching. The man looked as if he had aged ten years since Justin had last seen him a little over a week ago. The policeman in him needed to know what the missionary could tell him, but Justin the man also knew that he could not interrogate McIntosh as if he were any common witness. He was Vera's father, and Justin still hoped that one day, one day soon, he would be part of this decent, warm-hearted man's family.

As it turned out, he did not have to ask questions.

"Oh, my boy," Clement McIntosh said. "What a dreadful

tale to have to tell." He pulled himself up, straight and tall, as Tolliver imagined he would if he were asked to tell the story in court. Tolliver vowed to himself then and there that the man he wanted for a father would never have to testify. Justice in that regard be damned. The worst injustice that could have happened in this dreadful business happened when they hanged Gichinga Mbura.

Tolliver asked only that they sit down on the nearby bench in the shade of an acacia tree. His legs were done in from all the walking. McIntosh leaned forward and put his forearms on his knees. He spoke evenly and deliberately beginning with his wife's part in her brother's death. "She confessed it to me," he said. "Otis told her that Josiah was on the girls who came to the hospital, black and white. She told the boy she had to put a stop to it. She could not prevent Otis from trying to play his part. He came back from Newland's with Kibene in the night and insisted he would be there with her. He had taken the spear from Newland's collection, which I imagine he thought he could use to defend himself against animals in the darkness. It was the kind of weapon Kibene carried. Blanche had gotten hunting poison from one of the field-workers. She said she wanted her brother's death to be swift. She thought to put the stuff on a kitchen knife. When Otis arrived with the spear, she decided to employ it. She said she thought that there was some kind of justice in Josiah's being killed with such a primitive weapon. She did not think then that some innocent native would be accused." McIntosh stopped and looked up at the branches above them, as if he could force his tears to run the other way. He took out a pocket handkerchief and dried his eyes.

With effort, Tolliver kept himself still.

"Blanche and Otis waited for Josiah to return from wherever he had been," McIntosh went on, still holding the handkerchief. "When she confronted her brother, he laughed at her wanting to defend his victims and stalked off. Otis went after him and tripped him. He fell on his face, and Blanche plunged the spear into his back."

"Do you truly believe her capable of such an act?" Tolliver could not help asking.

"Without remorse," the missionary said. There seemed to be a hint of pride in the way he lifted his head. "My boy, I am sorry to have to tell what a true monster her brother was. She was his victim, too. Perhaps his first, when she was barely ten years old. I cannot begin to tell you how much she despised him for that."

Tolliver put his hand on McIntosh's forearm. "Sir," he said, "perhaps we should leave the rest of this for another day. I do not want to distress you further."

The missionary patted the back of Tolliver's hand. "Thank you, lad, but I am determined to get it all over with now. I will never speak of this unspeakable thing after today."

McIntosh straightened his back again. "I knew what Josiah had done to Blanche when they were children. And that he continued to do it to other young girls. She told me about that long, long ago. She spoke of it again after he died. But I did not learn her role in his death until after she took her own life. She wrote that part of it in a letter. She used the same poison that she had used on her brother. She blamed herself for Gichinga Mbura's execution. She said she should have confessed sooner, but she wanted to make sure that Otis had gotten clean away."

Tolliver could not hold in his curse. "Bloody Cranford. How could he have dragged a sick man to the gallows? And for what?"

"Evidently, Mbura was feigning that illness. He must have thought it would get him released. But he became impatient with his own ruse and came back to life. Once he did, D.C. Cranford . . ." He let his words trail off. He stood up. "I have not told this whole lurid story to Vera. I never want her to know what her mother suffered as a child. I have known for some time that there are more evils, and some worse ones, than those mentioned in the Commandments. What is theft of someone's gold compared to Josiah's theft of his sister's innocence?"

Tolliver tried his best to say something comforting and soon took his leave.

"The funeral will be tomorrow," McIntosh said. "I will bury her here in consecrated ground. I care not what my bishop in Scotland would think about burying a suicide. Whatever sins were committed on it, her body was sacred to me."

21.

The following day, the Reverend McIntosh's friend the Reverend Wilbur Bennett, Rector of St. Phillip's in Nairobi, officiated at the service for Vera's mother. Though Vera was the only organist left at the mission, she was able to stay with her father during the ritual; Tolliver brought his cello to the mission chapel and played the hymns. He stood close to Vera on the lawn as she greeted the mourners. Many attended the ceremony, and as was seemly they left off gossiping about the circumstances of Blanche's death while they were on the mission grounds. On the way back to town, some of them reprised that subject, and nearly all speculated about the possibility of an attachment between Tolliver and the missionary's lovely but somewhat wild daughter. She seemed a very odd choice for a handsome, albeit second son of an earl.

The following day, Kwai Libazo again took up his place against the dark paneling in the office of D.C. Cranford. He was acutely aware of A.D.S. Tolliver's profound anger and disappointment over the execution of Gichinga Mbura. Tolliver had spoken of the need to confront the D.C. about it.

Libazo himself had wondered why it was important to talk of it, since there was no way to bring the medicine man back. When he asked that question on their way here from the stationhouse, Tolliver had given him a look that was halfway between disbelief and admiration. That had become Kwai Libazo's favorite expression to see on Tolliver's face. In the end, Tolliver decided not to confront the D.C.

"District Superintendent Jodrell has already arrived in Mombasa," Cranford was saying. "He informs me that he will take his last week of leave on safari in the Chyulu Hills. You will wait and take up any other questions you have on this matter with him when he returns to duty the first of next month. I will report to London on all I think they need to know."

Tolliver stood up and came to attention, but he did not salute. "In the meanwhile, sir, I would like to recommend Constable Kwai Libazo for an immediate promotion to sergeant."

Libazo could not stop his eyes from opening wider.

"Certainly that can wait until Jodrell returns," the D.C. said. He drew some papers from the side of his desk to the center and turned his complete attention to them.

"Very well," Tolliver said and marched toward the door.

Kwai Libazo was so busy repeating the words "Sergeant Kwai Libazo" in his mind that he almost forgot to follow along.

In the following days, in deference to her father's grief, Vera pressed aside her desire to find out more details of her mother's death and the murder of her uncle. "The least said is the soonest mended," her mother had always advised. Vera doubted her heart would ever mend when it came to this subject, but she could not see how forcing her father to reveal more would stop her grieving.

She lay in bed and longed for Tolliver. The day after her mother's funeral, she wrote to him thanking him for his condolences and complimenting him on his playing at the funeral. A note came back the very next day. "I would like to call on you and your father," he wrote. "Please tell me when I may. I hope it will be soon. Justin Tolliver."

She kissed his signature. Given the state of her father's mourning, she wrote back that midafternoon on the last Sunday of the month would be a good day.

He again responded immediately. "The day cannot come fast enough for me. Please be assured of my undying esteem for you and your father." Vera smiled at how very proper he was being.

On Sunday afternoon two weeks later, Tolliver rode Bosworth out to the Scottish Mission, and as he had hoped, he found Vera and her father on the veranda.

"Dear boy." McIntosh rose when Justin approached. "How very nice of you to come keep us company." He shook Tolliver's hand; some of his usual energy had returned. "We lingered over luncheon, and we are just having a coffee. Would you like one?"

"That would be very lovely, thank you, sir."

Justin looked down at Vera, sitting holding her cup in her lap. The wan, beat-down look that he had seen on her at the funeral had begun to lift. She rang the little silver bell on the table to her left. When Njui appeared, she asked him to bring Captain Tolliver a coffee. It was soon delivered. They sat together for a long time, chatting about the coffee bean crop coming on well and the difficulties of the coming dry season. They said nothing important, nothing disturbing. When, for a few minutes, they ran out of things to say, her father began to nod. She indicated it to Tolliver with her eyes. He signaled her to walk with him out on the lawn.

"I am left alone with my father," she said when they were far enough away to speak without rousing Clement. She was turned away from Tolliver. The lengthening shadows thrown by the setting sun made the plain before them dramatic. Without looking at him, she put her hand on his wrist and squeezed it. "I miss my brother so." She let go of him and bowed her head. "When we were very small children, I was just ten, Otis was just five. We were visiting our grandmother in Glasgow. Otis came to me and told me. He said Uncle Josiah asked him to touch his penis. I didn't know what it meant. I just felt ashamed to hear it. I . . . I . . . let my brother down. I should have told someone. But I was too ashamed to speak of it. I suppose you think me dreadful for saying it now."

"No," he said. "I do not." He could not explain how it made him feel important that she trusted him with her secret—shocking as it was.

"I will never forgive myself." The words came out strangled.

He put his hand on her shoulder. "You were just a child. How could you have known what to do?"

"I should have told my grandmother, but—" She could not say how she disliked and distrusted her mother's mother.

"Sometimes," he said, "I think the worse thing for English people is not being able to say the things we want to, that we ought to."

"Why do you think my mother took her own life? My father agreed with me that it was because she could not live without Otis, but the more I have thought about it, the more I think that I was wrong, that that cannot be all of it."

"Your father told me that he wanted to spare you the details."

She turned to him and looked into his eyes. "I will not stop being troubled by it until I know the truth."

"She felt guilty that Gichinga Mbura was executed wrongly for what she and your brother had done."

She grabbed his forearm with both her hands. "Why did they kill Uncle Josiah?"

Tolliver took her hands in his. "They confronted him with his misdeeds, trying to put a stop to his behavior. He laughed at them. I think they did not mean to take his life, but they lost their tempers."

She stood up tall and straightened her neck. The kind of gesture he had seen on her father. "I would have done the same thing," she said.

He smiled at her, a sad smile but a proud one. "I do not doubt that for a minute."

She turned and looked out over the plain and then glanced back over her shoulder, up into his eyes. Hers shone even in the dim light.

"I love you," he said. "I want you to marry me."

She laughed, making a bitter little sound. "Marry into this family? You would have to be mad."

"I am not asking to marry your family. I am asking to marry you."

She turned back to him. The sun was red over her shoulder. Her eyes were appraising his. "Is it because of what happened in the tent on safari? Because you feel guilty that you made me spoiled goods?"

"It is not about that. It is not out of guilt."

Her heart was beating against her ribs. "That's good, because you needn't feel guilty. You have not spoiled my chances. My father has explained to me that I will inherit quite a lot of money from my grandmother one day. My grandfather may not have been an aristocrat, but he was a very successful man. When my granny dies, I will be quite rich. Plenty of men will want me. Sons of earls even." She knew her tone was wrong, but she could not help it. She was so frightened at this moment—that he wanted to marry her only out of a sense of obligation. That one day he would resent her. "What will you do if Otis ever comes back?" she asked

"If he does, I hope he will be my brother by then."

"Tell me plainly and truly why you want to marry me."

He smiled. "You have not listened to a thing I have said since our last night on safari. I want you to marry me. And yes, it is about what happened in the tent. Not because I feel guilty about it. But because I cannot wait to do it again. I want to spend my life doing that, and every other thing that is important to me, with you."

"I will not go and live in England. I never want to do that." The full moon was rising behind him. It was huge and impossibly beautiful.

He moved closer. The light had turned from red behind

her to silver on her cheeks. "We will visit there certainly," he said, "but I belong here. When I went home two years ago, I thought my infatuation with Africa would fade away, that my love of England would cure it. But I could not stay away. I did not want to give in to Africa. I told myself practical reasons, about money, about adventure, that they were the real reasons I was coming back. That my time here would be only temporary. That I would return to England one day. But I know better than that now. I am here because I cannot resist it. Africa has captured my soul."

She took his hand in hers. "Are you in love with Africa or with me?"

He took her in his arms and held her close. "Once I fell in love with you, it all became one thing. Loving you and being here are all I want now."

She kissed him swiftly on the lips. "Let us go and wake up my father," she said.